PRIME CUT

RAY PEDEN

ISBN: 978-0-9979615-0-8
Cover art & photography – Gene Burch
The image of Patrick Grainger – Mike Barnes

DEDICATION

This novel is for Layne, Tiffany and Hailey.

I've noticed a recurring theme in my stories, namely the unbound love that can flourish between fathers and daughters. Apparently these three ladies inspire me, as daughters, step-daughters, sisters, and mothers. It's the mutual exchange of love between us that sows the seeds for stories where familial ties mean everything.

Enjoy the harvest.

And to think at one time I thought I wanted boys.....

*The most frightening
pages of history
are those which reveal...
a desert of the human spirit.*

-- Haniel Long

*This story is for those with no voice,
in a world too busy, too comfortable to listen.*

Chapter 1

THE NIGHT WAS THICK AS BUTTER with them, swarming the low-country highway, minding their own invertebrate business, captured without warning in the harsh glare of his speeding headlight. With due respect to the victims exploding in a disgusting mosaic of green and yellow against his windshield, Patrick Grainger had more pressing issues. At three in the morning on a Carolina back road he checked his rear-view mirror again.

Still nothing.

So far, so good.

They would assume he'd taken the short sprint east to I-40. Even at this late hour there'd be more traffic, more witnesses, and if he got lucky, maybe a guardian angel Highway Patrol he could fall in behind. With a ten-minute head start that was his best chance to make Raleigh and the safety in numbers there. That's what they would expect.

That's why he turned west, away from the Interstate, and hung a right in Claxton on US 421, a rural two-lane snaking north past musky fields of soybeans and lowland cotton. He could reconnect with I-40 in Greensboro after they'd given up the chase. For now he just needed to put some distance between himself and the Farm.

The throbbing ache at the base of his spine was a sharp reminder there was more to their enterprise than livestock—in this case something worth killing for. His unwelcome visit under the cover of darkness had given them reason to suspect he was a threat. The three bodies he left in his wake removed all doubt. A simple fact-finding mission had turned into a high-stakes game, no limit.

As the needle on his speedometer touched seventy he fought through the pain and drifted away to disturbing images from two days earlier—a parking lot teeming with innocents; an automatic rifle appearing out of nowhere; the panic and chaos that followed. Aimee was out of danger now, lying uncomfortably in a hospital bed in Lexington with bullet holes in her arm and shoulder and a tray full of pain meds. A few inches to the left and there would have been no need. His mounting anger at an unknown adversary, one that nearly cost him his daughter after all they had gone through this past year and a half, forced a hard twist on the throttle of his Harley Davidson.

His left hand crossed over to the right side of his belt and felt for the Colt 45-caliber pistol, an unconscious, reassuring touch borne out of habit. This time it prompted a grimace. In the dark a sharp burn dug into his lower back. He pulled back and swallowed the pain. As silhouettes of trees and silos flew past, he digested his discovery during the last hour: ten warehouses stuck in the middle of nowhere, a virtual housing project of hogs raised for slaughter, packed like live sardines in sweltering bins of mass desperation. And the same unforgettable stench he'd detected on the dead man sprawled in the Kroger parking lot Saturday.

A flicker in the rear-view mirror grabbed his attention, two pin-pricks of light a half mile back that weren't there a minute ago. Someone new was in way too big a hurry. He cranked the throttle again on the handlebar, boosting one more time to eighty but the lights continued to gain ground.

His own headlight spotlighted a flash of deep yellow ahead on the right shoulder. A familiar diamond-shaped sign. With the ache in his back screaming at him he made a decision. He let off the throttle, no brakes, no warning for his uninvited guest a quarter mile back and closing, and leaned into the broad sweep of the curve.

Chapter 2

SIX DAYS EARLIER...

CARTER SWINNEY'S NERVES were unraveling. He'd made it this far, the planning and waiting, the nervous anticipation, and now his hands were shaky and unresponsive. He allowed a long blink to clear his head, then one last check that "video" was still selected. In the uneven light of Building 3 even a dim recording would provide evidence. He drew a breath to steady himself for something he wasn't sure he could stomach and tapped the screen.

The faint blip of the camera phone going live was drowned out by a crescendo of high-pitched squeals, none of them human. Forty feet away a worker in blood-stained coveralls, armed with a steel gate rod, flailed at his victims, two dozen pigs trapped in a last-ditch scramble for survival. Their attacker raved in Spanish, each stroke punctuated with a curse.

They were the throwaways, junk pigs wracked with disease or infections, some simply unable to gain market weight—the fall-behinds. All discarded and deemed unfit for what Sunspring Foods considered profitable slaughter. And now all trying now to avoid the vicious strokes of the rod herding them toward their final moments.

Swinney cringed as each slap of metal landed hard against hide. He fought back the urge to intervene. He couldn't afford to blow his cover, not after weeks setting it up. The victims on his screen were doomed, he'd accepted that. It was their ultimate sacrifice for a greater cause. His video record would give his superiors enough evidence to make life for the next ones more humane.

The bile burned in his throat as each pig fell and a second man placed an electric bolt gun against a squirming forehead. The crack of the trigger and as calmly as selecting another tomato from the salad bar, they would locate another. Swinney panned the camera across the floor of the pit and the growing carcass count.

Once the last victim went still a steady drone of animal fear filled the void, a stream of desperation from nearly seven hundred hogs caged in a windowless 60 x 320-foot prison of suffocating filth. The rod man plodded through the skim of blood and rolled in a motorized four-wheeled metal cart. They piled carcasses as high as space would permit before hauling the first load out the sliding door.

Swinney exhaled and switched off the video. His eyes closed and he wondered again if he really was cut out for this. The big charade, postponing a promising degree, hiring on under the guise of a common laborer. It was a huge sacrifice. He pulled himself together, located Bailey's number on the phone, and attached the video. One touch and it was on its way. When the workers re-entered the building for another load he waited in silence behind a head-high stack of discarded wooden pallets marked for removal with a large "X" in red spray paint. He'd stay out of sight until they were finished before he returned to his job station two buildings away.

While the men labored, the unrelenting squall of animals filled the vast, hollow shell of the building, reverberating off corrugated metal walls, cries for help that would never be answered. The steady din covered the sound of Swinney's rapid breathing. It covered the soft crunch of footsteps approaching from behind. Out of the corner of his eye he saw the shadow too late. A stout grip, arms pinning him, cold metal probes closing on both sides of his head. He never heard the crackle of the electric stun device as the jolt of electricity coursed through his brain.

"*Mierda!* You kill him?"

"No, *idiota*, it knocks him out."

"For pigs maybe, not a man."

A third man, taller than the first two, brushed by them and confirmed a pulse. As he braced to rise, he caught a glint of reflected light and stretched to pick Swinney's phone off the floor. One click and colorful symbols came to life, out of place in the gloom and gray of the warehouse. His finger hovered over a screen splintered with hairline cracks from the fall to the concrete and he touched the green icon.

One sent message . . . two minutes ago . . . one attachment.

He jerked out his own cell phone and made a hurried call.

* * * * *

Carter Swinney stirred. He felt the hard press of the concrete floor against his back. Through a half-conscious haze he tried to focus on three men standing over him. The taller one was agitated as he argued on a cell phone, his words unclear in the fog. Swinney tried to move, straining against the duct tape that bound his wrists behind him. The tall man shot a troubled look at Swinney, a sigh of resignation, and clicked off. In hushed tones he spoke in halting Spanish to the shorter one beside him, the worker who had brandished the steel rod. The Mexican glanced at Swinney and stalked away.

Swinney felt his bearings returning. When he rolled his head to the right he recognized the electric shock tool lying on the floor. A chill ran through him. He struggled but the second worker pinned him down with his boot. When the Mexican returned Swinney's body went rigid.

"No!" He bellowed. His terror exploded through the gloom and foulness of the building, rising over the rooting and squeals of the hogs.

"Please! No! I'll get the video back!" Swinney gaped at the object in the Mexican's hand. His panic had accelerated to wild hysteria. "They're pigs. They're just pigs! It's not worth *that!*" His head was shaking, a desperate plea for mercy. "I'll swear I didn't see anything!"

"It's not the pigs. We deal with that. It's what else you might have found."

"There's nothing else! Nothing," he begged, his face twisted in a tortured prayer.

"Sorry," the tall one said, holding his phone up, "Orders."

Swinney winced, a terrified sense of regret, his promising career in jeopardy. He pictured a brief snapshot of his mother pacing in her kitchen wondering why he hadn't come home for holidays. Then a final, unbelieving stare and his eyes widened as the Mexican checked the batteries and shook his head, not in remorse, more an apology. Nothing else when he stooped to the writhing torso of Carter Swinney, kicking and screaming, and jammed the bolt gun against the young man's forehead.

They loaded the limp body onto the cart and followed the taller man out the door. At Building 9, the leader rolled back the sliding door and led the men down an aisle lined with cages and animals to a far corner. As they approached the open pen, a round of savage snarls came alive behind a heavy-duty rail fence, a raw, primeval chorus of anticipation.

The leader removed the dead man's watch, college ring, belt and metal buckle, and extracted his wallet. From a sheath he pulled out a slender metal device, three feet long, and switched it on. The trigger brought the tip of the cattle prod to life, a sharp, blue sizzle of electricity. He opened the gate and herded the occupants toward the back of the pen while the workers dumped the body in the muddy center. The three men wasted no time backing out while three four-hundred pound boars, ravenous from a minimum feed ration, charged Carter Swinney's body.

"*Huesos?*" one worker asked, unsure of the proper word in English.

The leader watched the ravaging hogs fighting over shares, razor-sharp teeth ripping limbs and flesh. "Bones?" he repeated with a satisfied smirk. "They eat everything."

He pulled out Swinney's phone and checked the name and number displayed there. It took only a few seconds to type a return message and he headed toward the door.

Chapter 3

THE SMALLEST ONE with ears too big for her body was the first to pick up the sound. In the dark the long-haired Chihuahua's tiny head popped up from the flowered comforter and rotated a quarter turn toward the bedroom door. Her low guttural growl was the automatic trigger for the terrier on the other side of the bed. He came to life and broke the night silence with a flurry of high-pitched yaps. It wasn't until the third one, the scruffy shelter refugee, joined in that Bailey Cavanaugh dragged herself from beneath the comforter, a casualty of an interrupted deep sleep.

"Hush." she mumbled, her plea garbled and mixed with half-dreams. She rounded three bedmates in her arms.

As she dragged them back to her she squinted toward the bedside table and the green digital numbers glaring back 3:22. The red butane stick lighter and half-burned joint of Kentucky Blue in the glass ashtray were barely visible in the glow of the night light at the baseboard. She fell back and fluffed her pillow, ready to re-join what had been a strange but satisfying dream when she sensed the restless stirring of her companions still perched on top of the comforter.

She rose on one elbow, annoyed, ready for the battle of wills when she heard the faint scratching. She clamped her hand around the muzzles of the two still making a racket and listened. There it was, weak but steady, a gnawing sound. *Mice? Squirrels in the attic? Damn it!* Half awake, she shushed the pack, rolled the covers back, and slid out of bed, easing barefoot across the floor, listening for the grating noise that continued from the direction of the open bedroom door. As she concentrated, the sound began to register differently in her head, not so much gnawing, more like a steady scratching. Like metal against metal. Then a distinctive click. Through the open bedroom door, forty-two feet away at the far end of her living room, she saw the vertical slice of light when the front door eased open.

An involuntary gasp. She whirled and scanned the bedroom in the near dark, an automatic, wasted search for something, anything, before she issued a silent curse. The lessons from the concealed carry class were useless with her pistol in the kitchen drawer. Yaps from the bed continued. Another terrified glance toward the front door, the opening wider now, the harsh glow from the street light illuminating a man. Then the glint of light on a blade.

She lunged for the flimsy, hollow-core bedroom door and allowed it to touch shut. It wouldn't stop him, locked or not. The two windows weren't an escape option either—both had been painted shut before she moved in. She shushed the dogs and listened, measuring the invader's footsteps crossing the hardwood floor in the living room, a brief silence while he crossed the area rug, picking up again when he neared the bedroom. A creak of hardwood, that annoying spot in the hallway she had no idea how to fix. Her eyes searched the room again. In desperation she grabbed two items in the dark and waited.

The silence lasted longer than she expected. Finally the latent sound of his hand on the knob, a slow turn, and the door opened an inch at a time. A callused hand holding a semi-automatic pistol, not the knife, invaded the bedroom first.

It didn't matter.

Her sudden blast of aerosol spray around the edge of the door caught the intruder full in the face. His sharp curse was followed by a cry of pain as the toxic mix of chemicals from the air freshener—isopropyl alcohol, glycol ethers, tolulene—flooded the man's eyeballs. His hands jerked to his face, fingers digging into eye sockets, swiping at the caustic fluid eating like acid into soft surfaces of his cornea. She held the spray button down, drenching his face and hands with a steady flow of the liquid.

He never heard the click of the butane lighter.

She touched the benign yellow flame to the jet stream and the gush of fire, hissing like a blowtorch, kindled the fluid already awash on the man's face and eyes and the back of his hands. It erupted in a deep-throated flash, spreading instantly to dampened hair, and a roar of flames enveloped his head. His violent rampage erupted into the night.

The biting sting of fire collided with panic and he slung the pistol, freeing hands to slap at the flames. He lurched backward into the hallway, arms thrashing, as he battled the excruciating agony he could find no way to stop. When the gun clattered onto the hardwood he lunged for it, an instant before a volley of six bullets riddled the bedroom door.

Another one!

On the floor her hands grabbed at the gun and she braved her first look up at the invaders on the other side of the door. The lead man was screaming, flailing at the flames that swarmed his head, while the second man dodged helplessly behind him. She managed a clear picture of the second face, his coarse features and leathery skin artfully illuminated by the blaze in a flickering interplay of shadow and light. He was engaged in his own bout of panic, battling not only the momentum of his partner's body and arms wind-milling out of control, but impulsively clawing with his own hands at the blaze in front of him.

She felt a chill the instant his eyes locked onto her there on the floor. Then she watched his cold-blooded bearing turn to fear when his eyes found the pistol in her hands. The crack of four rapid shots from the gun startled her. Two rounds found their mark in the second man's torso, one in his neck. Three was enough. When he dropped to the floor she held her breath, waiting for others.

The lead assailant stumbled, writhing in agony, and fell backward over his fallen partner. The flames on his blackened hands and face were nearly out, but not his hair and he tugged at his shirt, trying to drag it over his head to extinguish what remained. Whether out of sympathy or hatred she didn't care, her self-preservation overruling fear, and the gun echoed three more times.

She crouched, her adrenaline pulsing, and dodged her head into the door opening to check out the living room. Even in the dark, the street light filtering through the bay windows confirmed the room was empty. She staggered backward and stopped in the middle of the bedroom, trembling, short, choppy breaths. Shock took over, legs weakening, losing their ability to hold her upright. It was the acrid stench of burning hair that reminded her she wasn't done. She grabbed a pair of jeans off the floor and smothered the last remaining flickers on the dead man's head. The irony was lost on her when, seconds later, piercing tweets from the smoke alarm in the hall finally kicked in.

Her shelter buddies had abandoned the comforter, cowering under the bed, silent for the first time.

Bailey Cavanaugh's body slid down the edge of the bed to the hardwood floor. She slumped, her legs extending straight out in front of her, trying to comprehend the nightmare that had just stormed into her safe harbor from out of nowhere. The grating beep of the smoke alarm continued unabated.

A cold, wet nose touched her hand, followed by a tongue, then a tentative nudge at her other side. She stirred, craning her neck for one final look into the living room. On unsteady feet she shuffled to her dresser where her charged cell phone was waiting. As her finger hovered over the screen, she stopped at the sight of the new notification: a text message from Carter. Even in the chaotic muddle of her ordeal, it made no sense. She'd already received his incriminating video hours ago and had forwarded it to Fran, and she would have immediately passed it on to the Agency. The message notification looking back at her now was a newer one. Despite two bodies in the hallway, her mental disarray gave her permission to give this new message priority over the call to the police.

"I'm going to take a break, disappear for awhile. Don't worry about me. - Carter."

She settled onto the dresser stool and allowed her hands to fall into her lap as she studied the text. This message wasn't from Carter, she felt certain.

Her head fell back, the harsh, high-pitched tweets of the smoke alarm chirping, refusing to let up. She tried to regroup, pull herself together. *If only someone would walk in and tell her what to do next.* The coppery, metallic stench of burned flesh and the pervasive tang of sulfur from singed hair continued to engage her senses—relentless, penetrating odors that wouldn't go away. In her convoluted reasoning she wondered if the smell might never wash out of her comforter or be covered up by so many coats of fresh paint.

Her disorientation was growing, blurring the boundaries of logic in the orderly world of her bedroom, until it relinquished sensibility altogether to the shock that had finally overtaken her. In her disconcerted state of mind her next decision seemed to make sense. She rose and calmly retrieved the aerosol can that had rolled against the far baseboard. With the smoke alarm's persistent warnings blaring just a few feet away she offered a disapproving stare at the smoke rising from the two bodies in the hallway before spraying a liberal application of Spring Meadows over the offending pile. The familiar, refreshing scent brought a satisfying smile.

She retrieved her phone and with shaky fingers managed to tap out the obligatory three numbers. She sat on the floor, three buddies curled in her lap, and in an unsteady voice, point by halting point, delivered the necessary information to the 911 operator. When the call ended she laid the phone on the floor and pulled her pals close.

Nothing to do but wait for someone to come and tell her what to do next.

Chapter 4

THEY CAME WITH LIMITED EXPECTATIONS other than end-of-week sale prices and clip-out coupons. Except for the observant few who caught the mid-week notice in the paper, the Saturday morning crowd pouring into Regency Centre was unprepared for the protesters gathered near the head of the aisle in front of PetSmart.

Once incoming cars settled for spots at the far ends of rows or drifted into the remote overflow lot, shoppers made the long hike past the rally-goers. A few grumbled at the inconvenience but nearly all took a moment to satisfy their curiosity and examine the colorful, hand-painted signs stabbing the air.

A makeshift stage—two sheets of 3/4" plywood laid on packing crates—was set up in a curbed island. There was room enough for three, all in matching lime-green T-shirts with distinctive logos emblazoned on the front. A woman with a bullhorn worked the crowd while two others handed out flyers and sign-up sheets.

Patrick Grainger took it all in as he leaned back against a wide brick column at the edge of the center's sidewalk. He grinned with some pride at Aimee and Julie walking the line hoisting poster-board signs they'd crafted with colored markers the night before.

NO MORE TORTURE . . . HUMANE TREATMENT OF
ANIMALS . . . ANIMALS HAVE RIGHTS TOO . . .

He understood almost nothing about the movement. Like
the silent majority it was so much easier to look the other way or
simply dismiss it as an over-zealous fringe that meant well. These
things had gone on for years, out of sight, out of mind. But his
daughter's involvement, and Julie's too, over the last couple of
months had at least made him aware of the cause, not that he
could do anything about it. What difference could it make,
passing up a delicious steak or chicken sandwich when it was
already dead and piping hot on the serving line? To no surprise
she had refused to let him off the hook. He had to give them
credit for advocating the principle even though he was still
looking forward to a Quarter Pounder at lunch.

He didn't take his eyes off the busy crowd when Randy
Oliver returned from Starbucks blowing the steam off a Caramel
Macchiato.

"You think our daughters have the makings for hard-core
subversives?" Grainger said. "College isn't far off."

Randy took a sip, debated a snappy comeback, and decided
to play it straight. "I think we're safe." He glanced over at Pat.
"I'd be more concerned about the hard looks *you're* getting."

Pat's brow furrowed, caught off guard momentarily by the
sarcasm. He glanced down, his posture defensive, arms splayed
outward, and gave himself a once-over, then turned back toward
the storefront and checked his reflection in the glass: a navy blue
doo-rag bandana snug around his head, the crusty 5-day beard, a
wrinkled white t-shirt, dusty jeans.

"What?" he said.

"Let's just say you have an image."

"How about we just say I don't give a shit," Pat said, as he
returned to his spot in front of the brick column, leaned back,
and propped one boot sole against the brick.

"What got them into this animal rights crap, anyway," Pat asked.

"Her teacher," Randy said. "Fran Mitchner's been a PETA activist awhile. She's the one passing out flyers. The lady beside her with the bullhorn, that's her partner. Bailey . . . something-or-other."

"Partner?" Grainger had seen the best and the worst on four continents, a lot of it contrary to his own persuasions, and he'd always tried to take things at face value. Some concepts he hadn't reconciled yet, especially when they hit close to home, like now. He took a long, judgmental look at the lady with the bullhorn and fought back a fleeting thought about lifestyle choices and whether they might be contagious. "You OK with that?"

"It's a new world," Randy shrugged. "She's a good teacher, involved with the kids. She throws ideas out there for them to consider—like this," he said, pointing. "Makes them think for themselves."

Pat turned toward the crowd, his concerns for gender bias diverted for the moment, and fell back to the one personal hang-up that seemed to bother him even more. "But Aimee's a *meat* person," he said, tracking her UK blue sweatshirt walking the line. "You know—normal."

"Karen made lasagna last night. Our girls are into the humane treatment angle, not going vegan. At least not so far."

"Maybe if my daughter lived with me I'd know more about her, you think?" Pat said, unable to hide a twinge of regret.

As he watched them, sisters not by blood but as kindred spirits, he wondered how fate had taken such a turn, steering all of them in directions they never anticipated. None of them could have seen any of it coming, this grand experiment and the terrible circumstance that started it. A scene played out with no script. The sights and sounds of the morning crowd melted away as his mind wandered back to that sunny afternoon in Georgia, the rest area filled with road-weary travelers, all oblivious to the evils that would lead him and the others to that barn and one final, life-altering denouement. It seemed like another lifetime ago. But over time his nightmares had been replaced with hope, and hope replaced with promise now that destiny had intervened. So here they were, nearly two years later, the bond between him and Randy and Karen inexplicably, unalterably linked forever by the two revolutionaries walking the picket line for animal rights.

"It's a work in progress," Randy said. "When you're both ready, you'll know." He threw a friendly backhand against Pat's arm. "You'll know."

Pat settled back against the brick column. "You covering this for the State Journal?" he asked.

"I put a reporter and photographer on it. Today I'm just a parent like you."

Passersby came and went, a few accepting flyers or signing up for emails, most sliding past indifferent to the cause. Despite the orderly nature of the assembly Pat's internal compass remained vigilant, instincts hard-wired over the years. Troublemakers were always a possibility, especially during a wacko election year. From his safe distance he absentmindedly evaluated every pedestrian passing the stage, the position of their arms, hands in their pockets, any single, unremarkable behavior that might signal trouble. Over the tops of the mass of vehicles in the lot he followed the path of each car that entered, tracked it to a parking spot, made a brief note of driver and passenger as they got out. But as the morning dragged on, the mood of the day confirmed it was decidedly non-threatening. It was times like this he regretted the curse of his past. Old habits and training imbedded into his subconscious made it difficult to stand back and enjoy simple pleasures.

"You sure you don't want a coffee?" Randy asked. He waited for an answer but none came. He turned and caught Pat staring at a white plumber's service van with the logo of an oversized red pipe wrench on the side. It had come to a stop in the middle of the driving lane two aisles over from the stage, idling in place. By itself it attracted no attention from the crowd. But, like the others, Pat had followed it when it entered the shopping center at the far end. He'd watched it passing up open slots, circling the perimeter of the rear overflow parking once—then twice. Surveillance.

"Pat, did you hear what I . . ."

Pat silenced him with a raised hand. Randy took the cue and turned toward the crowd, searching for the unfamiliar.

"What is it? What . . ."

They both saw it at the same time, the side door to the plumber's van gliding open from the inside. Pat pushed off from the brick column and his hand fell to the Colt in its holster. Then like an all-too-familiar *Breaking-News-at-Six* headline, a calm, uneventful Saturday morning turned unthinkable. The black barrel of an assault rifle inched out from the shadows of the van's interior.

Pat lunged toward the aisle, full sprint, pistol drawn, racking a round into the chamber as he ran. Startled heads turned toward him as he shouted out desperate warnings. Then too late he recognized the indistinct, muffled report from the rifle's sound suppression device—a muted pop lost in the swirling mix of passing cars and slamming doors and the idle chatter of innocents, all of them blissfully unaware. Just a single shot before the driver of the van gunned the engine and the shooter braced himself against a fixed seat in the depths of the van and reached for the door handle.

Pat halted mid stride and raised his weapon. Bystanders and the risk of ricochet made it an impossible choice but he couldn't wait. He fired two high rounds into the hole in the side of the van-on-the-move two aisles away. The shots caught the shooter off guard. In his panic the man released the door handle and staggered inside the moving van, his left hand braced against the door jamb. As he tried to regain his balance to return fire, his right arm swung the rifle upward, triggering a short burst of wild, involuntary rounds into the crowd. From thirty feet Pat's next shot didn't miss. The man recoiled at the impact from the bullet in his chest, frozen in time like a store mannequin, and his lifeless body tumbled onto the pavement, the rifle still gripped in his hands. The van screeched into the drive lane, scattering plumbing tools across the pavement. Pat emptied his magazine at the back door but the van made it to the exit drive, swerved out onto the highway, and disappeared twisting and dodging into the flow of traffic.

Pat rushed to the dead man. When he leaned down to drag the rifle away, he detected the strong, unmistakable odor of ammonia and a crusty residue on the soles of the man's boots.

The shooter's silenced round had gone undetected in the crowd. It was Pat's gunshots that had triggered panic. People were scattering for cover behind cars, some diving to the pavement, one by one coming to grips with the surreal notion of another mass shooting, only here in their own world. Then a woman's high-pitched scream rose above the confusion. She was staring up at the stage, shrieking at the circle of blood spreading from the wound in Bailey Cavanaugh's abdomen, just before the bullhorn dropped to the pavement and the protest leader collapsed on the edge of the stage. Pat twisted back toward the bedlam and recognized the UK blue sweatshirt among the fallen.

He was at his daughter's side in seconds, lifting her head and leaning in. Her eyes were open, her face contorted in pain. Blood oozed from bullet holes in her shoulder and left arm but it wasn't pulsing, so the bullets hadn't hit a major artery.

Randy had dropped in beside him. Pat asked without looking up, "Julie?"

"She's OK."

A few feet away a man was cradling his wife's head in his lap. She wasn't moving. Randy held Aimee's head while Pat scooted over and placed two fingers against the woman's neck. Her husband stared, his silence a desperate plea for good news. When the man recognized the resignation in Pat's eyes his shoulders fell.

Pat scuttled back to his daughter. She was losing too much blood. Waiting for an ambulance was too big a risk. He scooped her up and lumbered toward Randy's SUV with Randy and Julie two steps behind.

Chapter 5

SATURDAY MORNINGS in emergency rooms can sometimes be slow. A car accident, the occasional soccer injury, an uninsured sore throat. By mid-morning late night guests from Friday's bar fights and domestic altercations have usually been released to the police or moved to "in patient" and barring an unusual circumstance, it's often several hours before the predictable Saturday evening crush hits.

On another slow Saturday at Central Baptist Hospital the automatic doors to the ER slid open and an unusual circumstance charged in with a young girl in his arms dripping a trail of blood behind him. Pat Grainger crowded against the chest-high Information Desk and rattled off the status of his patient with the military precision of a medic.

From the other side of the counter the nurse technician took a quick visual of the blood still spreading across Aimee's sweatshirt and issued a command into the intercom mike: "Gunshot wound, Level 2." Seconds later double doors burst open. Pat slipped around the corner and laid Aimee on the gurney. She grimaced when her arm fell into its new position.

"We've got her," the nurse said. She placed a reassuring hand on Pat's shoulder. "You wait out here." She gestured toward the waiting room and three gawking visitors now energized by the sudden burst of activity.

"I'm her father," Pat said as he stepped around her and fell in line behind the gurney.

She moved between him and the double doors. "I don't think you heard me." She touched the palm of her hand against his chest. "Nobody gets into ER until we identify who's who." She glanced down at the pistol on his belt. "I hope you follow me."

Her demeanor caught him off guard, her words not so much a request as they were absolute. He backed up a step and read her name badge.

"Heidi, I lost her once. I can't let that happen again."

"We'll stop the bleeding, give her IVs," she said, expertly maneuvering him back into the waiting room while she talked. "We'll let you know when we get her stabilized." She had a disarmingly pleasant personality for someone who refused to give ground. "Now if you'll give me some ID so I can verify you're her father . . ."

His eyes were still focused on the swinging double doors as he pulled out his driver's license and insurance card. After she made copies he found a seat in an uncomfortable chair across from a TV where a CNN talking head rambled on about the election. He was leaning forward, elbows on his knees, when Randy and Julie joined him.

"She OK?" Julie asked.

"I hope so," Pat said. He managed a comforting glance. "She could move her arm."

He'd already been mentally reconstructing the events at the protest, walking through each frame step by step. When he got to the point where the rifle protruded from the van, a cold fact hit him.

"Beside the woman next to Aimee," he asked, "the one that

didn't make it, was anybody else hurt?"

"You didn't see?"

Pat shook his head.

"Bailey Cavanaugh," Randy said. "Fran Mitchner's . . .uh . . ." He caught himself, a fleeting glance at Julie.

"They were lovers, Dad, OK? Other than the Phys Ed teacher and a couple of jerks, nobody cares."

"How bad?" Pat asked.

"Stomach."

Pat shook his head. Gut shots seldom ended well.

Pat returned to his study in concentration, silent for half a minute before he dropped an empty question into the middle of the room, one that made no sense to the three visitors still straining too hard to eavesdrop.

"What's so important about freakin' animal rights that's worth shooting somebody?"

Any chance for discussion was interrupted by the rumble of an ambulance pulling into the drive thru, the squeal of brakes, doors slamming, indistinct voices on the move. A second ER nurse behind the Information Desk scurried into action and disappeared through the double doors. Obviously victims brought in by ambulance went straight to ER through a separate entrance and bypassed the waiting room altogether.

A minute later the main automatic doors to the waiting room did slide open and Fran Mitchner straggled in by herself. She was distraught, her clothes spattered with blood. She stumbled to the Information Desk, disoriented, and made a scattered attempt to gather information on her partner. She never saw Randy, Pat, and Julie rushing to her.

While Randy and Julie held her upright, Pat filled in the gaps with Heidi.

"The new patient that just came in, is it Bailey Cavanaugh? This is her friend."

Heidi came out from behind the desk. "I can't tell you that, but they're working on the patient now." She made an effort to comfort them, but her grim expression was a giveaway. "That's all I can say." Her eyes offered a silent request for Pat to guide Fran Mitchner back into the waiting room.

They led Fran's trembling body to a chair. She wasn't in full shock but her appearance suggested it couldn't be far behind. Her head was shaking, her mind lost in the reality of the moment.

Pat handed his billfold to Julie. "Find a coke machine."

He stooped in front of Fran's chair and tipped up her head. "It'll be OK," he said, doing his best to hide the lie. Now didn't seem like the right time for honesty. Aimee's wounds weren't pulsing blood, so he was optimistic. Bailey Cavanaugh was in a different boat. Her chances hung precisely on which organs the bullet had torn into.

"She was barely breathing," Fran sobbed.

"I know," Pat said, "but they've got equipment, manpower. Just hold on. Be ready for her when she pulls out of it."

She forced herself to take deep breaths. Julie returned with a Sprite and Pat unscrewed the top. "Take a sip. It'll help."

"I don't want it," she snapped, smacking his hand away, sloshing soda onto the floor. "I've had first aid . . . she's not going to make it."

"You don't know that. Now take this."

He placed the plastic bottle in Fran's hand and held her fingers firmly around it until he was sure she would hold on. She looked down at the bottle, recognizing it for the first time. Once she swallowed, her shoulders sank. She was lost, drifting, words dribbling out, incoherent ramblings with no final destination.

"The last few days . . . the break-in . . . the fire . . . Carter . . . now this . . ." Her voice trailed off.

"Wait a minute . . ." Pat said, as the silent alarms went off in his head. His instincts were systematically processing the string of circumstances too serious and too convenient to be marked down as a random streak of unrelated bad fortune. "What about a break-in? And a fire? And who's Carter?"

"Leave me the hell alone," she said, pulling away.

"No, I want to hear it. Please."

"You're not police," she said, angry and frightened.

"No, but all that *means* something."

"What's it to you?"

"Look," he said, trying for her confidence, "I'm Aimee's father. I stopped the guy that shot Bailey."

"You *shot* him?"

Pat nodded.

She seemed afraid of the next question. "Is he alive?"

"No."

She turned away, looking for some measure of peace in that bit of news. It may have been justice but it wasn't enough. She released a long, trembling sigh and slumped back in her chair, unsure what might come next. Then she leaned forward, her forehead cradled in her hands. After a few seconds of grace she glanced up at him and tried to leak a forced smile, a weak attempt to sidestep the gravity of the moment, anything to distance herself from the present.

"You're Aimee's dad?"

Another nod.

She took a sip of soda. As she stared at his face her memory began to reach back. The more she thought, the more random pieces from conversations in previous days began to fall into place. "You . . . wouldn't be that guy that rescued Julie, would you . . .?"

"It's a long story. Tell me about the break-in, Fran. And all the rest . . . please."

Pat drug a chair around in front of Fran Mitchner and listened as she conceded and shared a halting recount, traumatic highlights of Bailey Cavanaugh's last three days, a convoluted tale that unfolded like a Machiavellian tragedy. When she was finished Pat and Randy looked at each other. Even in their silence they agreed there was no way so many sequential acts of violence and a colleague's disappearance didn't share some connective tissue. It was a link that Fran Mitchner hadn't made yet. With all the implications on the table he still couldn't help returning to one unique point with more than a hint of professional respect.

"She set the guy's face on fire?"

"You got a problem with that?"

Pat shrugged his hands in surrender.

"Look," Pat said, "any chance we could take a look at the video that your friend Carter made? And where exactly is this farm?"

"Claxton, in North Carolina," she said, a little calmer now, as she fished her cell phone out of her back pocket. A search brought up the video. Pat, Randy, and Julie watched for a long minute, grimacing at the most unsettling parts before they shut it off.

Randy laid his hand on her shoulder. "Would you be willing to send me a copy of that? I'm a newspaper editor."

Fran hesitated. "I should probably check with the regional office first."

"I won't use it until they give me permission. I promise."

Randy handed her a pen and two business cards, one with his email and one for Fran to write on the back the name and location of the farm operation where Carter Swinney worked. When she had finished Pat memorized the information and prodded her. "I'd like to talk to Carter. How can I reach him?"

"That's another thing. We don't know where he is. He sent us a text saying he was gonna hide out for awhile, but that's not like him. He knows protocol. We told him not to go to Claxton without a partner."

Their conversation was interrupted when the automatic doors to the waiting room slid open and a quartet of stern faces, three of them in uniform, streamed into the waiting room.

Chapter 6

AS SOON AS THE LEAD MAN flashed his badge Pat knew it was time to become inconspicuous. He moved out of the way and settled into the seat beside Julie while the police detective took charge, analyzing faces, trying to place everyone in his circle of interested parties. The blood on the front of Fran's t-shirt made his decision on where to start a no-brainer.

"Are you related to the shooting victim . . ." He checked his notes. ". . . a Bailey Cavanaugh?"

"No," Fran said. Her voice was shaky, almost apologetic. "But we're . . . a couple."

He settled in the chair in front of her and softened his tone. "Does she have any family, somebody we can call?"

She struggled to recall bits and pieces. "A brother in Ft. Lauderdale—Larry, I think. Her parents live in Fort Scott, Kansas." A notable sigh revealed a labored sadness, apparently on a topic that had been discussed too many times. "They're not close."

"I understand," he said. He nodded to a uniformed officer who jotted down the information and hurried off.

He surveyed the others. "And you folks are . . ."

"My daughter was wounded in the shooting," Pat said. "They've got her back in ER now."

"Yeah, we got that call." He checked his note pad. "Aimee Grainger? How is she?"

"I'm optimistic."

"You got a permit for that?" The question came out of the blue from one of the young officers standing behind the detective. He was staring at Pat's Colt.

Pat's eyes slowly rose to the remark. "Last time I checked, I don't need one." He locked eyes with the young officer.

"Cut the bullshit," the detective said as his hand parted the air between them. He shot a look of rebuke over his shoulder at the young policeman. "We're not here to debate open carry." He turned back to Fran Mitchner and gave her a second to relax.

"You know any reason why someone would want to shoot your friend? I mean, this whole protest today . . . animal rights? That's not exactly something worth killing for."

The detective clicked on his pocket recorder while she repeated her story, laying out the detailed chronology. He was taking notes when the doors from the ER swung open. Pat caught a physician in blood-stained scrubs commenting to Heidi. She motioned for Pat. He was across the room in seconds.

"She's gonna be OK," the doctor said. "She's lost some blood, but the bullet didn't hit any major arteries. Fortunately there's no bone damage. All in all, she got very lucky, if you can consider getting shot lucky. She's stable, getting blood and fluids. There'll be some rehab, but it looks like she'll be OK in time. We probably want to keep her for a couple days."

"Can I see her?"

"We've got her sedated. Maybe in a few hours."

"Did you recover the bullets?"

The question caught the doctor off guard. "Actually, we did."

When the doctor walked away Pat exchanged a thumbs up with Heidi. He glanced back at Randy, a silent tilt of his head, and slipped down the hall toward the restrooms. Randy excused himself while the detective continued his questioning of Fran

Mitchner, and found Pat waiting around the corner.

"What's the deal?" Randy asked.

"Aimee's gonna be OK. They're gonna keep her for a few days, but I've got to get out of here."

"Why? You didn't do anything wrong. That guy you shot was a cold-blooded killer. I saw it all."

"May be, but as soon as they find out I'm the guy who shot him they'll have to hold me, 24 hours, maybe more. That's assuming eyewitnesses verify my story and the Commonwealth's Attorney decides I'm not a risk. Either way, they'll take my gun for ballistics and I'd kinda like to pay a visit to Claxton before the trail gets cold."

"Good Lord Pat, that's why we have cops. Let them do their job."

"Look, this wasn't a simple drive-by. It was planned. And the two guys in the van weren't independent operators. Somebody sent them. I'd be surprised if the driver hasn't already called in by now. By the time the detectives write their reports and bring in the Feds, what do you think will be left to find? They have to follow protocol. I don't."

"This is a bad idea and you know it."

"Probably, but some dead asshole shot my daughter, and an even bigger asshole sent him. When you get that video from Fran, email it to me, will you?"

"I can't be part of this. What do I tell those guys?" He thumbed toward the waiting room. "They could get me for obstruction, interference in an investigation, who knows what. That girl out there? I'd like to see her graduate without having to ask for early parole."

"Just tell 'em you loaned me a dollar for a coke and I went to the bathroom. Look, my bike's parked out at Regency. I'll get a taxi and be on the road before they know what happened. I'll be back in a couple days."

Pat pivoted and headed toward the front entrance, leaving Randy standing in the hall outside the men's restroom.

* * * * *

Randy settled back into the seat beside Julie. The detective was concluding his interview with Fran Mitchner.

"So you have no clue why someone would want to shoot your friend over this protest?" the detective asked.

"No. But Aimee's father thinks the shooting today is connected to the break-in."

"The man that was just sitting here?"

"Yeah, Mr. Grainger. The guy that shot Bailey."

"What makes you think *he* shot him?"

"He told me."

The detective twisted in his seat. "Where is he?"

Blank faces.

He turned to Randy. "You just talked to him. Where is he?"

"Said he was going to the men's room."

The detective barked an order to the two policemen. "Go find him and bring him back here. Peacefully, if possible."

As the uniforms headed off down the hallway, the double doors from the ER swung open again and a second doctor emerged. His hospital green scrubs were also stained with fresh blood. A quick glance at Heidi and she pointed toward the group. When he approached them his expression was impossible to misinterpret. Fran saw it coming and she had no way to stop it.

The doctor shook his head. "I'm sorry. We couldn't save her."

Fran's wail broke the silence of the waiting room. Julie and Randy held her, offering comfort that wouldn't come. While Fran broke down, the two uniforms returned in a brisk jog.

"He's gone."

Chapter 7

HIS VANTAGE POINT was concealed in a grove of box elder and shortleaf pine overlooking a complex of long, narrow metal warehouses, ten of them lined up side by side. From his position on the crest of the hill, the patchwork fields of tobacco and sweet potatoes that extended toward town had been invisible an hour or so earlier, asleep under a gray morning mist. By nine o'clock the fog had burned off and he had a clear, unobstructed view of Fox Hill Farm and the gauzy North Carolina landscape that disappeared at the horizon.

Randy had phoned an update during the trip down. Two people were dead. Aimee was awake and in some pain, but no complications. She had literally dodged a bullet. Pat was no longer second-guessing his decision to pay a visit. It was time to peel back a few layers.

Lying on his stomach, he swept his high-mag binoculars across the property. Using a parked pickup truck as his only available reference, he estimated the structures to be maybe 60 feet wide and five times that long, spaced approximately 30 feet apart. Each had sliding metal barn doors and standard man doors on both ends, and no windows. Ten commercial metal buildings identical in size and shape, poorly maintained based on the grime and streaks of rust that had accumulated on the metal panels. There were no markings, no distinguishing features, and no equipment—with one exception.

On the north wall of Building 8, nestled inside a chain link enclosure the size of a small bedroom, was a bank of generators, pumps, fire-suppression equipment and valves, a few other pieces of machinery he couldn't identify. Unlike the other structures, three vent stacks penetrated the roof, one releasing a steady stream of smoke. Behind it was a small gravel parking lot already occupied by three vehicles when he arrived at 7:00 a.m.

Despite the hard lines of the warehouses and drives, it was impossible not to notice the intimidating irregular shape north of the complex. Larger than a baseball field, the sewage treatment lagoon was crusted over with a stagnant, brown scum. The only indication it contained liquid came from the telltale trickle that fanned the surface at the entry point, an intermittent discharge from an overcrowded city of hogs. The manmade pond of raw sewage stood an imposing watch over a placid grove of natural forest and the clear water stream that ran through it. In the broad flat fields to the west, two giant mechanical arms were already pumping effluent from the pond and spraying it onto the fields.

Shortly after 7:30 Pat had observed two crew-cab pickup trucks navigating the half-mile gravel drive from the state highway. Once they parked, ten men in work clothes spilled out and split up, entering the warehouses in two-man teams. Each crew spent three to four hours before moving to the next. By the time the first crew switched buildings at 11:00, the number of vehicles in the parking lot at Building 8 had increased to seven.

Pat fished a chicken sandwich and soft drink out of a small back pack. The growl in his stomach reminded him he hadn't eaten since last night. After he left Randy at the hospital, he'd made it back to his bike at the shopping center. A quick stop at his apartment in Frankfort for a change of clothes and his laptop, and he set out for Carolina, a hard 8-hour push, heading east along I-64 before breaking south at Charleston.

He allowed himself a fast food burger plus the necessary stops for gas and short breaks. Unlike his more well-padded comrades, his slim framework had never provided enough natural stuffing for saddle-sore relief on long trips. He bypassed Raleigh and a little after midnight he settled into a cheap motel that didn't care who he was and asked few questions. The town of Claxton wouldn't be awake and open to the public until Monday, so Sunday was the day to observe.

Around 4:30 a large box truck pulled off the highway onto the gravel entrance drive to the farm. It was in no hurry. When it neared the complex Pat recognized the familiar orange-and-blue FedEx logo on the side. A Sunday delivery by FedEx sparked his interest. Once the truck turned around in the driveway, the garage door to Building 8 slid open and the truck backed up until the first two feet of the box disappeared inside the opening.

The driver getting out of the truck was expected. The passenger exiting the other side of the cab with an assault rifle was not. That armed guard was joined by another from the building while the driver disappeared inside. Pat squinted for detail but the distance was too great and the gap between the truck box and door frame was too narrow. Whatever packages they were loading or unloading he couldn't tell. A little over an hour later the driver and guard got back in the truck and it rumbled down the drive to the state highway and turned north. Pat swerved his binoculars back to the warehouse in time to catch men milling around inside as the sliding door slammed shut. Within minutes, four of the cars that had been parked all day in the lot also left.

Pat pushed up from his prone position, stretched to energize muscles that had grown stiff during the day's vigil, and began a mile trek back through the woods to his bike parked behind an abandoned service station one highway over. It was time to see what Google had to say about Sunspring Foods. Assuming the internet connection in his motel was working, it was going to be a long night.

* * * * *

Diego was not looking forward to delivering bad news. Perhaps the international lines would be clogged and he could use that as a delay tactic. But he knew it would do no good to postpone it. He opened the laptop and clicked the Skype icon. Allowing the cursor to hover over that first name on the contact list wouldn't make it go away. A long breath and he clicked.

The call picked up in six rings. The female voice belonged to the maid but she knew precisely how things worked. A few words in Spanish to the other room, the heavy sound of footsteps on plank floors, and the Captain sat down in front of his screen.

"So, you have good news, yes?" he said.

Diego's expression gave him away, he knew it. No way to hide fear when they were face to face like this.

"Some good, yes."

"Some?" A mild scowl. "Does this mean there was a problem?"

"Our target . . . the woman? It was a good shot. In the stomach. Guillermo believes she could not survive it."

"This is good. But I am hearing a hesitation in your voice."

"We did have one problem."

"Just get it out, *cabron*. It does not go away because you are afraid to tell it."

Diego took a deep breath. "Of course we made sure there were no police at this shopping center. A peaceful gathering about the animals. But there was this cowboy . . . you know how these Americans are so in love with their guns."

"Go on."

"While they were driving away, the *vaquero* shot Luis."

"He is dead?"

"Yes."

"It is the risk we take," the Captain said.

"They have his body."

"Qué chingados! First your team of so-called professionals is set on fire by the woman, and now this? Are you sure you have your end under control, Diego? Eh?"

"It is a small setback."

"Not so small. You left three men behind. It could lead police to the Farm and that is something we cannot have. As much as you did not want to tell *me* this, can you imagine how much I do not want to tell *him?*"

Diego watched the Captain's arm reach toward the laptop and the screen went blue.

Chapter 8

THE BELL TINKLING over the doorway reduced the chance for an inconspicuous entry into Hoagland's Diner. A few heads offered a passing glance, although the majority ignored the stranger, loyal to their coffee and eggs and whatever conversation and local gossip made the time pass.

One booth in the corner was empty with dirty plates waiting to be bussed. The three empty stools at the counter were better suited to his purpose. Pat Grainger slid onto the one nearest the cash register and clasped his hands on worn Formica. Game on.

He caught the waitress's eye and she raised the coffee pot in her hand, a question that required no words. Pat nodded and as she made a pass down the counter filling half-empty cups, she snared a clean one from the back bar and placed it in front of him. He read Doris' name tag while she poured.

"Any chance a fellow could get a good breakfast here?" he said.

"We serve a few now and then." She slipped a plastic covered menu from under the counter and laid it open in front of him. "Depends on how picky you are."

He couldn't tell if it was a mischievous glint in her eye or that she had already heard the full repertoire of lazy opening lines over time. Regardless, she could be a good candidate. As she walked away he took note of the manner she carried—confident, irreverent, an acquired judge of character carved out over the years, likely wasted on an unappreciative crowd of familiar faces. He also noticed how she'd given him a clear look at her empty ring finger. She was interesting. Now if she could just be a resource.

When she returned she leaned forward, her hands spread on the counter.

"See anything that looks good?" she said.

She was making this way too easy. Her flirtatious energy was infectious. At the same time it seemed to come with a harmless innocence. Regardless, it stirred a welcome note that he hadn't felt in a long while and it caught him off guard.

Fourteen years since Allison's death. Sometimes it seemed like another lifetime. He still hadn't shed the grief, although the healing that came with each passing summer had helped. His miraculous reconnection with Aimee a year and a half ago had helped. Randy and Karen's family and the deepening friendship they had forged from their traumatic encounter had helped.

Even so, his ability to move on had been a struggle. There'd been a few moments, unplanned and limited to meaningless dips in shallow water, always after too much alcohol made promises that couldn't hold up in the light of day. Grace was taking its own sweet time. The fact that Doris had played the first few pleasant notes in a harmless game, waiting for him to respond with a jingle of his own, was oddly satisfying. He hadn't come prepared for that. He blinked and pulled himself together. He was here for a reason.

"I'll go with number one, over easy, bacon, wheat toast, hash browns instead of juice."

"You didn't wait for me to ask choices," she said with a fake pout, as her pen caught up with the details. She laid the back of her hand on her hip. The gleam was there. "Even regulars wait for me to ask. Let me guess." She studied him. "You're . . . an engineer."

"Not even close. Maybe I'm a poet," he said, trying to keep pace with her contagious attitude.

"I doubt it," she said, pointing to his gun.

He caught himself looking. *Touché.*

"Truth is I'm trying to find a place around here, Fox Hill Farm. You know anything about it?"

She squinted, stroking her chin, and looked him over. After a lifetime of ups and downs she was confident in her ability to judge men. "You're no pig farmer, that's for sure. A reporter, maybe?"

"Nope."

"I know. You're one of those PETA nuts. Am I right?"

"What's a peetah?" Pat said, feigning ignorance.

She threw an exaggerated eye-roll. "Gawd, tell me you're kidding."

In truth, after last night's journey through the screen pages of Google he'd learned more than he wanted to know about PETA and ASPCA. Hogs, cattle, chickens, turkeys, all victims of the ruthless corporate machine that feeds billions with no regard for the means and methods. Noble causes for sure, but ones that Bailey Cavanaugh paid too high a price for. And Carter Swinney too, if Pat's suspicions were correct.

"People . . . for the Ethical . . . Treatment . . . of Animals," she said, counting the words on her fingers one by one to make sure it fit the acronym. "They've been fighting with that farm for years. They send in people undercover to take pictures."

"What for?" It was a question he already knew the answer to.

"Look, I like a good pork chop as much as anybody, but there's got to be a more humane way to raise the critters. You don't want to know how they treat the poor things." Her disapproval was obvious. "It's not a nice place."

"Actually, I'm looking for a friend that works for Fox Hill. Fellow named Carter Swinney. I haven't heard from him in awhile."

Her eyes registered. "I know him. From his credit card. Tall guy, looks like a college boy? Came in here a lot." She shook her head in judgment. "He did not belong out there."

"That's what I told him."

"The farm's out on Catnip Hill Road, but other than what I told you I don't know much else." She shook her head. "I'll get your order going."

When she left, Pat pulled out his phone and made a call. After a few pleasantries and excuses with Randy he got right to it.

"I tried the Raleigh News & Observer website last night. All their archives are available to the public back to 1990, but the greedy bastards charge for every article. You think you could have one of your tech raiders dig up some dirt on Fox Hill, say, over the past five years or so. Been a lot of run-ins out there and I'd like to know what happened. Maybe some names?"

"I'll see what I can do. By the way, we're 'greedy bastards' too. So much news online these days, newspapers are dropping like flies. I'll show you how to search when you get back."

"Thanks, but I've got my hands full here."

"You do know the cops are looking for you."

"I'll be back tomorrow. I'll give the Lexington police a heads up."

Pat slid his phone in his pocket and finished his coffee. When Doris refilled it, they played eye tag and traded playful remarks. He didn't give a second thought to the man in the worn straw cowboy hat two seats over pushing back from the counter, leaving a half-eaten breakfast. Outside the diner he made a call.

"I'm at Hoagland's. Some dude's asking questions about Fox Hill. Doris has been running her mouth."

"Another *activista*," Diego said. "No problem. Public record."

"He was asking questions about the Swinney kid. *That's* not public record. And this cat's not working solo. He called somebody about digging through some archives."

"Get his license plate."

* * * * *

Randy ran his finger down the State Journal's office registry and punched in the numbers.

"Tracey, you in the middle of something?"

"Always, boss. My feet never touch the ground. Why?"

"If you've got a minute, come in here."

Tracey turned the corner at Randy's door and took a seat across the desk from him. Randy handed her his legal sheet of notes and gave her the bullet points on Claxton, Fox Hill, and Sunspring Foods.

"Get me up to speed on factory farming and animal treatment," he said. "You'll find a lot of the Fox Hill stuff in the Raleigh News & Observer archives but don't stop there. See what you can gather in a few hours. And save it all. It could make for a tasty series. You remember the mileage we got out of that conspiracy with Pat last year."

"Another award-winning crusade? You think your head will fit through the door this time?"

"I'll try to keep it in check."

* * * * *

The straw hat cowboy leaned against his truck and watched Pat amble across the parking lot to his Harley Davidson. He jotted down the plate number, got in the truck, and made the call while he waited for Pat to mount up. When Pat pulled out of the lot the truck followed at a respectful distance until Pat turned into a gravel parking lot in front of an unremarkable one-story brick building. The cowboy cruised past and hung a right onto a side street a block away.

"Our boy just paid a visit to the Sheriff."

Diego's brow furrowed. "I sent the plate number to my guy at the station. Name is Patrick Grainger, from Kentucky. It's registered in Frankfort. It's the capital but I never heard of it."

"I bet he never heard of Claxton, either, until now. What you want me to do?"

"Go back to the Center. I need to call the Captain."

Chapter 9

PAT SMOOTHED ASIDE some pine needles and scooped out a landing spot for his phone. Same nest, same grove of trees as yesterday. He was hands free on speaker this time catching up with Randy while his binoculars swept the grounds below.

"I had a chat with the Darden County Sheriff yesterday. He's not a fan of Fox Hill. Lot of issues the last few years. Caught them using illegals."

"Anything on Carter Swinney?" Randy asked.

"One person remembered him. That's it."

"I've got a bad feeling about that young man," he sighed. "Anyway, I've got Tracey working up a folder. We'll go over it together when you get back." He paused. "You *are* coming back in the near future, aren't you?"

"Leaving tomorrow morning. Thought I'd give it one more day here at the farm."

"Pat, whatever you're doing, is it serving a purpose?"

"Surveillance is kinda like that box of chocolates, Randy. You never know what you're going to get."

"I saw that movie. It also said 'run, Forrest, run.'"

"I'm being careful. How's Aimee?"

"Karen and Julie visited last night. She's recovering. We're going to smuggle in a chicken burrito tonight."

Pat smiled and switched from personal to business without missing a beat.

"The sheriff was generous with his background information. It's not just the farm that's causing trouble. The farm lobbies are in Sunspring's back pocket." Pat lowered his binoculars to rant. "The bought-and-paid-for jackasses in the legislature passed some freaking bill that makes it a crime to photograph illegal farm activity, no matter how bad. And it's not just about animals. Unsafe working conditions, environmental pollution from animal waste, processing tainted meat, you name it."

"The Ag-gag law," Randy said. "It's being challenged in court. I'm beginning to think our daughters are on to something."

Pat switched horses. "How about *our* investigation? Is the FBI getting involved?"

"Probably, but it's just Monday morning. If the police have already invited in the Feds, Lexington will have to brief their Raleigh counterparts, get a search warrant, set up a site visit. And who knows what their current caseload is. I may give Phil Damron at the State Police a call. He's one of their lead detectives. Maybe he can keep me in the loop."

Pat disconnected and returned to his surveillance. As the day dragged on he picked out no new activity other than the early morning shift of ten workers. Since Pat's first stop had been the diner, he'd missed their arrival, but just before noon they trickled out two at a time and gravitated to a shady spot under a lone ash tree and pulled out lunches.

Pat mulled his online research from last night. Fox Hill's website proclaimed to be nothing more than a legitimate factory farm raising hogs for slaughter at Sunspring's massive processing plant twenty miles away in Bledsoe. It stood to reason the two-man shifts he'd been observing were tasked with the chore of feeding and maintaining hogs in the warehouses below.

An hour after lunch his binoculars picked out a delivery truck coming in from the county highway. It was conspicuous by the refrigeration unit mounted over the cab. He followed it around the back of Building 8 and watched workers from inside unload two dozen boxes, all bearing the familiar shape, markings, and ventilation holes signifying fresh produce.

At the end of the day Pat's questions were outnumbering his answers. Questions that could only be resolved after a proper inspection, and he was fairly certain an invitation would not be coming.

* * * * *

The birthing shed had seen better days, a worn out relic from a smaller operation that had fallen under the weight of competition and time. As Pat's flashlight sliced streaks through the darkened metal interior he picked out no evidence of recent activity, only the rusted steel skeletons of blood-stained cages abandoned to the elements. The shed's only value at 2:00 in the morning was its proximity to Fox Hill, a short quarter-mile jaunt compared to his inconvenient overland hike the day before.

He parked his bike inside near the corrugated metal end wall and covered it with a dusty scrap of tarp. With a quarter-moon simmering in the darkness he set out using trees along the creek as cover. Within a few minutes he approached the complex of warehouses from the rear.

Three pole-mounted halogen lights spaced across the rear of the property were all that illuminated the back ends of ten long, slender structures. Another three lights stood guard along the front. He observed only two vehicles, both parked behind Building 8. The warehouse nearest the state road would be the safest first visit.

His binoculars scanned for motion lights and cameras on eaves and gutter lines and found none. Hugging the undergrowth at the base of the hill, he raced in a running crouch through an open expanse of untended field grass. At the first building he dodged across a scattering of weed-infested gravel to the metal personnel door. A quick twist on the knob confirmed what he already suspected. Less than a minute later his rake pick tripped the last pin in the lock and he felt the tension in the cylinder release.

The instant the door swung open a gust of stomach-churning vapor forced him back—the overpowering fetor of ammonia, a concentrated version of the scent that clung to the dead assassin in the Regency Centre parking lot. He fought his gag reflex and acclimated to the stench before he slipped inside.

In the dim light of six mercury vapor fixtures, he wasn't prepared for the enormity of what spread out in front of him. Other than a narrow walk path for entry, the first ten feet of the building was stacked wall-to-wall and head-high with pallets of feed sacks and plastic jugs of liquid antibiotics. A fork lift stood guard in the corner next to a rack of hand tools and boxes of plastic gloves.

It was ten feet farther in that he encountered the brutal reality of hog factory farming. He stared slack-jawed into the vast chamber of corrugated metal, a housing project of cramped metal cages running the length of the building, the distance great enough he had to squint to see the far end. Six rows of cages, assembled back to back in three bays with narrow aisles between to allow for feed and maintenance. Each cage was barely six feet by two feet, not enough to allow their occupants to turn around.

As he eased his way down one aisle the hogs became aware of him. A few struggled to their feet, cramming anxious snouts through openings in cages; others emitted plaintive squeals of distress, or perhaps cries of lingering pain from the exposed sores dotting their hides. As he passed, many began chewing feverishly on the steel bars of the cage doors. The unnerving comparison to a turn-of-the-century mental institution didn't escape him.

As he crept down the aisle his flashlight flickered through the bars. Beneath shifting bodies, fattened to the point their legs would barely hold them up, Pat identified narrow troughs with slotted grates that also ran the length of the building. He blanched at the harsh reality of pigs living and sleeping in their own waste, all of which was eventually swept by water or their own urine into channels under the slab and piped to the giant treatment pond to the north. A literal skim of solid and liquid fecal matter lathered the concrete floor, infusing the air in the warehouse with a pungent, sickening cloud of hydrogen nitride.

When he reached the front of the building Pat noted a separate inventory of feed and antibiotics lining the front wall, much like the one in the rear, plus one isolated concrete slab, enclosed by a low railing. It was identical to the one in Carter Swinney's video.

The clamor of the inmates had built to an uncomfortable level. He'd seen enough and retreated to his entry point. Once he slipped out the back door he breathed in gulps of clean North Carolina night air and leaned forward with his hands on his knees and pondered what he had just witnessed. He rose and released an audible sigh, checked his surroundings, and moved to the second warehouse.

Inside the second building he encountered an arrangement indistinguishable from the first—a prison of hogs housed in inhumane conditions, their brief life spent waiting for slaughter in cages that permitted no movement, no exposure to sun or fresh air, only forced feeding, excrement, and the workers that passed daily in front of their cage door.

The third building proved to be no different until he made his way to the front of the warehouse. As he neared the isolated concrete slab, virtually identical to the ones he had seen in the first two structures, he recognized the rickety stack of wooden pallets with a large "X" spray painted on the side in red.

He crossed the concrete, careful to avoid the black patches of dried blood, and took a position behind the stack of pallets—the precise location that Carter Swinney had occupied. His imagination engaged and the scene from Swinney's revealing moment began to flicker in his mind in real time, audio and visual highlights of that violent day, the squeals and curses from the dim video playing again, trying to sneak back into the present. He shook his head and forced himself to shake free.

His flashlight scoured the area. As he turned to leave he caught a brief glimpse of color. On his knees he used his handkerchief to fish out a red Swiss army knife from under the bottom pallet. He slipped it in his pocket.

With his camera phone he staged a final few seconds of his own video, a simulation of Swinney's scene without the actors. Once he shut it off, hanging around any longer seemed counterproductive and he retreated to the back door. When he exited, any chance to take in a clean breath of night air was interrupted by the two semi-automatic rifles pointed at his head.

Chapter 10

PAT STUMBLED HEADFIRST through the back door of Building 8, courtesy of a violent shove from the lead guard, and broke his fall, not against a pallet of feed, but a desk. Instead of another rank, dimly lit warehouse crammed with animals awaiting slaughter he found himself in a pristine, windowless paneled room outfitted with an armada of high-tech office equipment, desks bearing personal computers and oversized flat-panel monitors, a trio of scanner/printers, and what appeared to be a dedicated computer server. Storage units and filing cabinets took up one wall. One metal shelf was packed with an inventory of sophisticated electronic equipment not expected for a run-of-the-mill pig farm. A row of wall clocks displaying US and foreign time zones lined the soffit on the far wall.

To the left of the door stood the heart of it all, a state-of-the art surveillance station with a master control panel and a dozen TV monitors. Multiple screens were switching automatically through a changing array of real-time videos transmitted by active infrared cameras, most of them transmitting from inside the hog warehouses. One monitor apparently was devoted to nothing but exterior shots, flipping at regular intervals between cameras mounted to each of the six light poles. He had missed them all.

They'd been watching him as soon as he entered the first warehouse.

The moment Pat stumbled into the room he caught the bottom row of monitors going dark. The technician at the surveillance station had killed the feed on purpose. He was an older Hispanic man with mismatched khaki shirt and pants, an abundant white mustache, and a standard-issue Glock 19 strapped into a leather holster. He was the only other person in the room.

One guard held a pistol on Pat while the second retrieved a roll of duct tape off a shelf and bound Pat's arms behind him. As they worked, the old technician came out from behind his control panel. With a ballpoint pen he lifted the left sleeve of Pat's gray cotton T-shirt. The man had caught the bottom half of Pat's full-color tattoo during his grand entry and now he wanted to see it all: a gold sword and three lightning bolts on a blue shield – *Special Forces, Airborne.* The old Mexican allowed a blank acknowledgement and quietly returned to his seat at the station.

The lead guard didn't hold a similar level of respect for Pat or the technician.

"Quit fucking around, Enrique and call Diego."

They shoved Pat through the aisle of desks into a well-lit room that opened off the back. At the left side of the room were four beds with metal frames, two upper bunks with blankets made and tucked, and two lower bunks with covers thrown back in a hurry, apparently occupied minutes earlier by the two guards. They forced Pat into a chair at a table on the opposite end of the room and stood at a safe distance with rifles aimed.

Twenty minutes later Pat heard the outer door to the office open, followed by a few brisk words in Spanish. A young man appeared at the door to the sleeping room. A crooked smile was plastered on his face. He made a quick evaluation and spit out a question in his native tongue. Pat's Spanish had never been more than elementary. Even though he managed to piece together the gist of the question, he decided playing it dumb might come in handy.

The young man switched to fluent English. "So, a visit in the middle of the night?"

Pat remained silent.

The man took a dominant stance in front of Pat. "And you didn't even ask permission," he said.

He leaned down, his head at Pat's level, close enough to make eye contact. Seconds passed. Without warning he smashed the back of his hand against Pat's jaw, throwing his full weight into the swing. Pat's head took the punch, lurching sideways, and when it returned his stare met the young man.

A voice of authority bellowed from the doorway.

"Detener!"

The room turned to the command.

Deep wrinkles formed in Diego's forehead, a mixture of surprise and confusion when he recognized the young man. "Alejandro?"

The young man slid in behind a self-righteous grin. "It's 'Alex' now. 'Alejandro' was too old fashioned. The ladies at University like 'Alex' better."

Diego ignored the sarcasm. "What are you doing here?"

Alex's ingratiating attitude came easy, partly a product of his privileged youth, partly because of his raw ambition, but even more due to his family's unchallenged sway in a lawless region where violence and power ruled.

"With the setbacks recently my uncle thought another pair of eyes might be . . . let's say, informative."

"The *Capitán* mentioned nothing to me about your coming."

"I'm sure he planned to tell you," he said, his head cocked in smug disrespect. "They flew me in today."

Diego called over his shoulder to the front room. The white mustache appeared at the doorway.

"Enrique, you called him?" he said, pointing.

"Please, Diego, I do only what I am told," Enrique said, a nervous hitch in his voice. "You are my *lider*, but when the *Capitán* calls with a direct order, what am I to do?"

The stage was set and Diego knew it could only be settled between him and the Captain. That would come tomorrow. Tonight he had more important issues. He turned back to Alex.

"Your uncle may have sent you, but unless you have orders to kill me you will do nothing but observe . . . and I am sure, report back like a dutiful *culo beso*. Do you understand?"

Even Alex's nod of acceptance was condescending as he stepped out of the way.

"You want me to leave, Diego?" Enrique asked.

"No, I think you must stay, just to make sure the *Capitán* gets a true picture."

Diego stared a hole in the young man before moving to the side table where he picked up the wallet the guards had extracted from Pat. A quick glance at the driver's license reaffirmed what he already suspected. He pulled a chair up in front of their captive, his demeanor cordial, like old friends chatting over coffee.

"So, Mr. Patrick Grainger, how was your breakfast this morning at Hoagland's? I hope Doris recommended the biscuits and gravy. It is very tasty."

Chapter 11

WHEN TO ANSWER, when to disregard, when to lie. An important lesson from the past—pick and choose. Sometimes the interrogated can gather as much information as the questioner.

"Wheat toast," Pat answered, as he struggled inconspicuously with the bindings on his wrists. "I'm watching my cholesterol."

"I see," Diego said. A warm, fatherly smile spread across his face. "Wheat toast. But you were particularly interested in one of our former employees, a young man, Swinney I think is his name?"

"He owes me money. You seen him?" Pat said. He skipped past his brief disappointment that he may have misjudged Doris.

"Regrettably, the young man resigned a few days ago. Perhaps it was about a woman, no?"

"It usually is."

"So I must ask, what's so important about our *operación* here that you break in at night?"

"You know how us animal lovers are," Pat said. "Passionate about the cause."

"I think it is maybe more than that. You come to us, what you Americans say 'packing heat.'" He glanced over at Pat's Colt lying on the table with the full magazine beside it. "That doesn't fit the image, this lover of animals."

"Your methods here are pretty harsh."

"I understand. Many feel that way, but for the time being we break no laws. And it is more profitable, the way we do it. So you see you have wasted your time. And now what are we to do with you? Obviously you have seen our technology," he said, sweeping his arm back toward the office. "That makes you wonder, yes? And with questions comes attention, and that's something we do not want."

"No problem," Pat said, his attitude dismissive, matter-of-fact. "Charge me with trespassing, breaking and entering. You caught me red-handed."

"How about we kill you instead," Alex interrupted, "like the other animal lovers." He was on his feet, restless, impatient with Diego's methodical questioning.

Diego silenced him with a fierce look and a hand thrust into the air, but not before he picked up on Pat's reaction to Alex's outburst. It was the involuntary flicker of seething hatred in Pat's face that gave him away.

"You know more than you are telling me, I think," Diego said. He fumbled around in his memory, trying to put pieces together. *The animal lovers, Swinney and the lady at the shopping center. Why does this anger him so much?* He pulled his hand to his mouth and reflected. Something seemed familiar, close by, crawling around in the details. He remembered the police report. *Luis was killed by a single armed man. At the shopping center. Three others were also shot . . .* A flicker of recognition. From his breast pocket he pulled out the documents he received that afternoon and scanned through them, finally coming across the one name that had been calling to him.

"Ahh," he said, nodding in satisfaction at his discovery. Without looking back he held the police report out for Alex to see. "It seems that a young lady was wounded in our most unfortunate accident. Her name is also Grainger." He turned back to Pat. "Would you know of this person?"

When to answer, when to disregard, when to lie. Pick and choose.

"Sorry. What was her name again?"

"Very smooth, my friend," Diego said, wagging his finger. "You have learned this trick somewhere, I think." He leaned forward within inches of Pat's face, staring into his eyes, looking for that one involuntary gleam of anger bubbling beneath the surface that would give him away. "A daughter, perhaps?"

"You don't care who dies, do you?"

"I'm sorry, but no. Our product is, as you say, replaceable? For every one we lose, there is always another to take its place. Supply and demand. I think as an *Americano* capitalist you must understand this."

Over Diego's shoulder, Pat could see Enrique struggling with the conversation spilling out before him. The old man was visibly uncomfortable, shifting his weight from one leg to the other, trying to process the cold philosophy of life and death spouting from his *lider's* mouth.

Like flicking a switch, Diego's warm, fatherly disposition disappeared.

"Governments and armies have tried to stop us and failed. You are one, we are many. *El vientre del dragón de Tlaxcala,"* he said proudly, his voice rising in a memorized pledge of solidarity.

"And if it was *your* daughter?" Pat asked, his anger building.

"Another story, of course. She was in the wrong place at the wrong time. I'm sorry, my friend," he said with the cold dispassion of the classic psychopath, "but she was expendable."

Pat snapped. He lunged from the chair toward Diego, out of control, but with his hands taped behind him there was no end game, only an uncontrolled rage. The nearest guard lurched forward to hold him back but Alex had been waiting for his chance and was already there, throwing 170 pounds of muscle hard against Pat and forcing him back toward the bunk beds. With shoulders and arms pushing against Pat's chest Alex shoved him backward over the metal end rail of the bottom bunk and slammed his own body down against him. Pat felt a searing pain as his spine bent over the rail. The legion of muscles surrounding it tried to resist Alex's momentum.

Diego had backed away, willing to let the fight take its course. Just when he thought it was over, as Enrique and the guards were pulling Alex away, Pat's leg levered upward, a vicious thrust, and caught the young man solidly between his legs, forcing him to the ground in a collapsing bundle of muffled agony. It was with some amusement, even professional respect, that Diego watched an opponent with his hands secured behind him delivering some deserved retribution to a self-important young snitch. Alex groaned, his hands held snug against his throbbing groin as he tried unsuccessfully to manage the pain. Pat righted himself and Enrique helped him struggle into a sitting position on the side of the bed.

Once Alex's pain began to subside and his senses returned, a slow cry of revenge swelled, starting low as he pulled up his pants leg and withdrew a knife from a sheath. Both guards saw it coming and as he staggered to his feet they struggled to hold him back. It was when Enrique turned to help them that Pat saw his opportunity: the security strap on Enrique's holster hanging loose, the pistol within reach, daring him.

A person never knows what he is capable of until his options are limited to one. With the sharp throb in his spine Pat sprang from the bed, twisted his body, and with arms still secured behind him, he glanced over his shoulder and grabbed blindly for the Glock. His aim wasn't perfect but it didn't have to be. His hand glanced off the belt onto the pistol's grip and jerked it out of the holster.

In a long career he had never given any thought to how difficult it might be to rack the slide on an automatic pistol and then chamber the first round using nothing but wrist action. Fortunately his subtle efforts over the last few minutes, the straining and stretching of his wrists, had gained enough play in his bindings.

His unexpected movements and the ratcheting click of the gun's slide took the room by surprise. Before the guards could aim their weapons, the Glock in Pat's hand fired twice, upside down by necessity, a single shot into each man. Even with his arms behind his back, accuracy wasn't an issue at such close range.

Out of the corner of his eye he caught Diego rising and unsnapping the leather guard on his pistol.

"I wouldn't."

Diego froze, his hand hovering inches above the pistol grip, and took a long, thoughtful look into the barrel of the Glock. Even behind Pat's back and upside down, it was pointed near enough to center mass of Diego's chest that his options were also limited to one. He wet his lips and slowly raised his hands.

"On your knees, hands on your head."

While Diego kneeled, Pat heard the rage in Alex's voice as the young man charged, knife raised, his judgment blinded by hubris and the foolish bluster that comes with an insufferable surrender. One shot in his upper thigh stopped the advance. The young man dropped to his knees and grabbed at the pain. Pat was almost prepared to offer some unsolicited advice, tell him how it's best to concede defeat and take a conciliatory tone when your adversary has the upper hand. But this was one of those times when conceit and arrogance didn't know when to call it quits. With blood spreading from the bullet hole in his leg and his fury spinning out of control Alex continued to spit out a stream of vile expletives in Spanish, a slobbering torrent of crude remarks.

His disrespect required no translation. More importantly, Pat's halting Spanish was solid enough to catch the one all-important word that made it way too personal: *hija*—daughter. Pat's face was a blank canvas when his second shot into the young man's forehead ended it. The body swayed for a moment when the muscles went slack before it toppled face first against the concrete.

With his foot Pat flipped the body over and dragged the knife out of Alex's hand and swept it over to Enrique.

"Cut me loose, old man. *Comprende?*"

Enrique nodded. He picked up Alex's knife and Pat backed up to him.

"Careful."

Once the old man cut through the duct tape, Pat motioned him to the bed on the other side of the room. Pat massaged his wrists as he approached Diego, still on his knees, his hands on his head.

"What were you saying about 'wrong place at the wrong time'?"

"Please . . . they were just words, *Senor*. We didn't even know your daughter."

He pressed the gun barrel against the man's head. "Cross your heart and hope to die?"

"Please . . . an accident . . . we didn't know she would be there . . ." His eyes closed, waiting.

Diego's apology, even delivered by a begging coward, made it harder to justify another death. Pat pulled the gun away and swung it down across Diego's temple, a vicious stroke calculated to inflict maximum pain when he regained consciousness.

One was left.

Pat pulled up a chair in front of Enrique sitting quietly on the bed, hands clasped together.

"Why?" Pat finally asked.

"What do you mean?"

"Your gun. You practically handed it to me."

Enrique stared at the floor. "I was careless."

"I watched you when Diego was speaking."

The old man was shaking his head, staring at the floor. "It's not right. Treating them like animals. *They* . . ." he said, pointing to the men on the floor, "are the animals."

"What do you mean 'treating them like animals'?"

The old man choked up, then raised his head and looked into Pat's eyes.

"I'm sorry about your daughter, *Senor.*"

"What have they done, Enrique?"

"You cannot help."

"Help who?"

The radio at the surveillance station interrupted them, the agitated voice shouting through the static. "Enrique? What's happening? Enrique? The perimeter guard said he heard shots."

"*Senor*, you have to leave," Enrique said. "They will be here quickly, many men."

"Who are they?"

"You must leave. Please, hit me on the head or they will know."

"I can't do that. Come with me."

"I must stay. Now please . . . hit me and go. Or we will both die."

The voice squawking from the radio sounded again. Enrique slipped off the bed onto his knees and waited.

"*Señor* Grainger. You must."

He had no time to argue. Pat locked his arms around Enrique's neck, found the pressure point on the carotid artery, and within a few seconds the man lost consciousness. With his knife Pat cut a small gash in the old man's temple, enough to draw blood, and lowered him to the concrete slab.

Seconds later Pat was hustling through underbrush on the way back to the birthing shed.

Chapter 12

"Despertarse! Despertarse!"

The guard's frantic urging wasn'tt working. It took a wet rag against the face to stir Diego's senses, first a twitch in his arms followed by a drawn-out groan. The throbbing ache in his skull was his first sensation, as planned. Two men lifted him into a chair and the train wreck of his interrogation minutes earlier started coming back to him. Blurry eyes struggled to focus on the havoc left behind: two guards crumpled on the floor; Alex spread-eagle on his back, the hole in his forehead encircled by a crust of drying blood; Enrique being helped to his feet, blood dripping from his temple. The clock on the wall told Diego it wasn't too late. *He came from Kentucky. He would escape to Kentucky.*

All eyes widened when he barked the orders.

"Mierda, get them out of bed, *inmediatamente,"* he shouted. He staggered to his feet and shoved a guard toward the radio at the surveillance station, rattling off instructions and routes while the guard repeated them to the men barely awake on the other end of the connection.

He slumped into a chair and the haze washed back over him. He took a gulp of water and tried to imagine the fallout when he would have to make the call.

*****

Pat's Harley slowed at the intersection of Catnip Hill Road and Hwy 24. A right turn would have him on I-40 in less than four minutes. But things had taken an unexpected turn for the worse. Fortunately a half hour on Google Maps in the motel last night had given him an alternate route, in case. He turned left.

He made Claxton in nine minutes. Even at this late hour he couldn't afford to be stopped. He eased off to the speed limit and took the deserted bypass. The town was asleep as he cruised by the regular suspects: Walmart, McDonald's, local restaurants and churches, some sitting quietly in the dark, others sparsely illuminated by halogen lights standing guard over empty parking lots. He passed only one sign of life, a 24-hour convenience store with a lone police cruiser parked at the front door.

On the way out of town he left behind the last lingering signs of urban civilization—the city treatment plant, an elementary school, the local Farm Bureau. As the lights and ambient warmth of the township fell away the night air gave way to a brisk chill, and the landscape transitioned from development to groves of forest, broad expanses of cropland, farmhouses and barns comfortable in their isolation lining both sides of the sinuous two-lane highway. He shifted in his seat, searching for any position to ease the stabbing pain in his lower back, and glanced in his rearview mirror, relieved that he had it to himself.

*****

"Who is this *gringo* we are chasing?"

"Don't ask questions," the driver said, "Ramiro just said we must stop him."

"What little we make, it is maybe not worth chasing someone in the middle of the night."

"*Cállate.* Don't forget how you lived before I brought you up here, *cabron.* You eat well for once in your life."

"*Sí*, but the pigs, they are disgusting work. And now we are the posse?"

"Stop complaining. Is your gun loaded?"

The passenger chambered the first round. "Now slow down. You will run off the road in the dark."

"We're almost to Claxton," said the third one in the back seat. "Why does he send us? The *Americano* on his motorcycle will go for the Interstate. The others will be the ones to catch him, not us."

The two-way radio hanging on the dash interrupted the conversation.

"He came your way," Ramiro rambled through the static, "not the Interstate."

The man in the passenger seat reached for the talk button. "How do you know this?"

"Diego called his man with the police. The night shift saw a motorcycle passing the Circle-6 store a few minutes ago."

"Why do the *policía* not pick him up?"

"Because, *idiota*, he does not have the entire police force in his pocket. Now go faster, he is maybe five or six minutes ahead of you. You can catch up before he reaches Spivey."

The driver stepped on the gas and took the fork to the bypass. When they passed the Circle-6 the police cruiser was still parked at the front door. The driver reduced his speed. As soon as he was out of sight he pushed it back to 80, braking only for the curves.

* * * * *

Eleven minutes later they spotted the single tail-light up ahead.

"There!"

The truck engine responded with the familiar diesel rattle when the accelerator pedal went to the floor. The gap between them began to narrow. They had closed to within a quarter mile when the tail-light disappeared left around a sweeping curve.

"You are gaining," said the one in the back seat as he racked the slide on his pistol.

A dozen seconds later the truck slowed and steered into the curve, ready to accelerate and resume the chase when their headlights spotlighted a man in sunglasses standing alone on the centerline of the road two hundred feet ahead.

* * * * *

Pat was waiting for them, his motorcycle parked on the left shoulder, purring at a smooth idle. He stood fast on the center of the night pavement, a stern parent waiting for his wayward children, and watched as the startled driver hit the brakes, an involuntary, automatic response. Then the growl of the engine revving, just as predictable, and the truck took aim and accelerated through the last third of the curve.

Behind his sunglasses the bright glare of the oncoming headlights had little effect on his vision. Pat raised Enrique's Glock and four shots found a home in the driver's side windshield. In the time it took to say 'holy shit' in Spanish, the truck was rudderless. Front wheels that had been steering through the curve under the steady hand of a live driver straightened out and the truck found a new route, thundering in a direct line across the outer shoulder, jumping the roadside ditch, and taking out a woven wire fence on the right-of-way.

As it careened out of control into a broad field of cotton the front wheels slammed into the first plowed row, snapping the front axle. Momentum propelled it forward at 70 miles an hour, forcing the rear wheels up and over and throwing the truck body into an inevitable twist. The once-showroom-quality Crew-Cab flipped, plunging into a relentless series of barrel rolls, too many to count, in a deafening highlight reel of metal and broken glass, wiping out a helpless mechanical irrigation tower on the way. The tumbling death trap began to slow down and as its energy ebbed it gave one last roll signifying the end and the truck's tortured frame submitted with a final grating creak of straining metal. It came to rest upside down in the dark, rocking, the smoke, shattered glass, and scattered clouds of rich Carolina dirt and airborne cotton plants lost in the chaos.

Pat had calmly watched the band of would-be killers self-destruct. Once all flying debris finally hit the ground the scene went quiet, settling into an eerie back-road silence. Nothing but the lonely hiss escaping from the truck's cooling system. He circled through the fresh gap in the fence and crept toward the mechanical carcass waiting patiently for him in the soft pallor of Carolina moonlight. He dodged around the mangled legs of the irrigation tower and with the Glock held forward he approached the truck, its battered roof caved in, front tires blown, its mechanical underbelly exposed like a grease-slicked cockroach. The three men sent to kill him had been tossed inside the cab like a summer salad, their bodies mangled, broken, drenched in blood.

As he turned to leave, the radio in the crushed cab began squawking a round of excited questions. He grimaced from the pain in his back as he bent to check the three dead men one last time and fired one round into the radio, silencing the voice.

On the way back to his motorcycle he retraced the mental map he made the night before. If more were coming, Greensboro would be risky, Raleigh even more so. Better to detour east at Sanford, catch Carthage and pick up I-74 to Knoxville. It would take longer to get home, but the spasms in his back, now firing on all cylinders, convinced him he wasn't up for a fight.

He mounted his bike, broke the night silence with one final curse, an agonizing scream at the pain digging into his spine, and eased back onto the pavement, accelerating through five gears.

Chapter 13

"I KNOW WHY you are calling, Diego, and I am sorry, but only a little. I should have told you I was sending Alejandro, but it was a last minute thing. I think with all that has happened lately you can use some help."

Diego squirmed in his chair. The gash in his temple had been cleaned and bandaged but his headache was still pounding. The pain relievers had not kicked in yet, and he had to deliver some disturbing news. Even with two thousand miles separating them he had no idea how to maneuver the conversation so that their Skype connection would not explode in his face.

"I . . . I was surprised, that's all."

"You are still in command. I told Alejandro that. Just let him help. He is skilled in many electronic methods. He has studied public relations. Even the psychology of the mind, you know? University is useful for something, at least."

Diego's feet were stuttering on the concrete.

The Captain continued. "I know my nephew is quite . . . let's say reckless, to be fair, and he has much to learn about restraint, but that you can teach him. I hope you will be OK with this?"

Diego pushed away from the table, his anxiety running loose and tried to walk it off in a trail of circles but it was getting him nowhere. The Captain watched via the laptop's camera and made no comment until his Farm Manager returned to his seat.

"So, what now? Did we lose another man?"

Diego pulled himself together. This would not go away. Get it out and brace for the aftermath.

"It is much worse, *Capitán*."

The Captain waited.

"It is Alejandro. He . . ."

"Get it out. What has he done this time?"

"He . . . is dead."

Diego waited for the firestorm that never came. The Captain stared empty into the screen, no expression, dispassionate for some time before words finally came.

"What happened to my nephew, Diego?"

Diego gathered himself and spent the next few minutes detailing the break-in and capture, the interrogation that had gone from textbook to disaster, and the final impulsive streak of arrogance that got the Captain's nephew killed. Then he stopped, held his tongue, and waited.

The Captain made a slow turn in his seat, eyes wandering off into space, seemingly unburdened with expected grief. Gradually his head began to nod, slowly as if some answer had come to him, and the corners of his mouth arched downward in acceptance as he reconciled it to himself.

"His father gave him too much, all the finest things, nothing held back. Not enough of the firm hand that teaches a man how to be a man," he said, contemplative. "The fight for power killed my brother. I tried to take his son and show him, but it was too late. You cannot teach a snake to be a turtle and expect it to be."

He looked down at his hands, then cleared his head as if nothing had happened and turned back to the screen.

"So who is this American that killed my nephew?"

"He is from Kentucky, a hillbilly perhaps—Patrick Grainger.

From his license plate. That's all we know."

"A hillbilly? This man that kills three men with his hands tied behind his back and disables two more? You underestimate this 'hillbilly' maybe?"

Diego was silent.

"Send me what you have the minute we hang up. I have better resources. Much better. By tomorrow I will know everything I need to know about Mr. Grainger. I think he will regret taking such an interest in the pigs."

"What do you want me to do for now?"

"Our business does not stop. You take care of that as you always have. I will deal with this Patrick Grainger myself."

When they disconnected, the Captain leaned back in the swivel chair, his hands clasped on his belly and shook his head in regret. With no one in the room he felt free to carry on an open conversation with ghosts of the past.

"Brother, you got greedy for power and it got you killed. Now your son's arrogance did him in. And you say that *I* am the soft one?" He chuckled, not out of humor but of vindication.

He mentally continued his recollection of their tortured history, the early beginnings, the climb to the top, the senseless endings, when the email on his computer chimed. He opened Diego's attachment and committed it to memory before copying it to a file. Then he forwarded it to a frequently-used resource with a note and a high-priority flag:

Complete background check on Subject, inmediatamente. Life history, occupation, family, military service, arrest record, location, everything! Use every available resource. No limit to expense. I want it by tomorrow morning. Confirm receipt of message.

In less than a minute a reply appeared on his screen from an official military email account:

Message received.

* * * * *

The pain woke him before the alarm did. Pat's first attempt to locate the clock was halted mid-reach by the stabbing pain at the base of his spine. He pulled back. After a moment of relief he tried to roll, the move again cut short by what felt like a hot knife gouging a plug out of his spinal cord. His eyes were wide open now and he wondered what the maid in this Motel 6 in Knoxville was going to think when she walked in and found him in bed paralyzed. He had made it this far last night before the grinding ache in his back told him no more.

His left hand finger-walked across the sheet to the base of his spine and tried without success to massage the offending joint. Finally he confronted a hard truth: he was going to have to fight through it. He didn't try to hold back the agonizing bellow as he pushed off the mattress with his left arm while pulling on the edge of the bed with his right. His legs also refused to move under their own power without pain. He used his left arm to shove his legs to the side of the bed and allowed them to slide to the floor, prompting another groan.

His body grudgingly allowed him to push up from the bed and he hobbled to the bathroom for bladder relief and a hot shower that lasted until the water turned lukewarm. Once out, he popped four 200-mg ibuprofen tabs and called Randy. His mention of the body count didn't go well.

"Only six? That's the best you could do?" Randy said. "Your prints are on a gun that killed six people?"

"I've got the gun. And do you really think those bodies are still in that building? The last thing those guys want is for the FBI to go poking around, and I'm sure as hell not going to tell them about it yet. At least not until I can establish that it was self-defense."

"You can't just ignore it. What the hell's going on down there that they'd kill Bailey Cavanaugh for it?"

"Good question. I got no answers. I'm heading home if my

back will hold up."

"They must have done a number on you. You need a doctor."

"Forget it. I'll be fine in a few days."

"Don't be a fool. I know a good chiropractor. A friend. I'll make an appointment for this afternoon."

Chapter 14

DIEGO HELD THE FBI's search warrant up to the screen.

"I couldn't stop them. *Gracias a Dios,* after five buildings, they found no need to check the rest. The smell, it got to them."

"They had questions?" the Captain asked.

"*Sí.* I took them to the business office, showed them our records. Some questions about the animals but they already know we do nothing illegal. Lot of questions about the boy. I told them he quit, no reason, nothing else. And that I will be sending his paycheck to the address he gave us. After seeing the pigs I think these FBI understood why the college boy would not want to work here, even if he was a *revolucionario.*"

"Building 8?"

"They walked right by it to see the lagoon. They found that *repulsivo.* Perhaps it is good that our operation is so disgusting."

"Send me a copy of the warrant."

Without further comment the Captain killed the connection. The events of the last two days were troubling. He pulled up a number on his cell phone.

"We have problems in Claxton. I'm not sure our man in charge can handle it. I may have a job for you."

* * * * *

Angel handed Pat Grainger a clipboard and a pen.

"The first two sheets are contact information, medical history. The third one you color in the exact areas that are bothering you," she said, pointing to frontal and rear diagrams of a human figure. "Explain what movements cause pain, and on that bar scale below, estimate the degree of pain, so we can track your progress."

He waited for her to finish. "I'm not excited about being here."

"Nobody ever is," she said, as she took his insurance card and made copies.

Three patients were reading magazines in the waiting room. When the door opened the fourth time, the nurse got his attention. "Mr. Grainger?"

She pointed him toward the left examination room. Two cushioned treatment benches were the only furniture. The walls were plastered with oversized plastic posters of muscle groups and skeletal diagrams, and a working mock-up of a vertebra/disc/spinal cord was sitting on a low shelf. She nodded toward Pat's holstered gun.

"Make sure that's not loaded and put it on the shelf along with your keys and wallet. Cell phone too. Doc will be right in."

Pat was emptying his pockets when Dr. Jonathan Hall swept into the room with Pat's clipboard information and a firm handshake. Their introductions were brief.

"So, what'd you do to yourself?" Hall finally said as he skimmed through Pat's chart.

"I fell."

Hall squinted. "Randy implied there might have been a little scuffle."

"He exaggerates," Pat said. He was here for pain relief, not counseling.

"Well, then let's take a look."

He checked out Pat's posture and ran him through a few choreographed movements, then positioned him face down on the cushioned table. Pat's groans and his sharp recoil from certain touches made Doc's preliminary diagnosis easy.

"Your 'fall' jammed your vertebrae—imbrication we call it. Damaged the tissue in the joints. The pain is from the muscle spasms, just your body's way of letting you know. We have to loosen that up. Stay where you are, I'm going to send Jackie back in."

A few seconds later Jackie returned with a small rolling stand. The silence was broken by the low hum of the mechanical massage percussor.

"I watched you coming in," she said, as she ran the hand-held device up and down his back. "You were listing starboard pretty bad."

"Are you a chiropractor, too?"

"No, I'm the wife, but it doesn't take a college degree to see you hunched over like an old man."

"Very funny."

"Don't worry, I'm a licensed massage therapist. You're gonna love me before we get through with you."

"The way that vibrating gadget feels on my back, I love you already. No offense."

"None taken."

A minute later Doc Hall re-entered. As he was checking the chart one more time, Pat raised his head off the table.

"I guess you've popped Randy's back a few times?"

"Popped, no," he said. "Randy is a frequent patient but," he said, raising his finger in the air as if he were reciting from a textbook, "we perform 'spinal adjustments for the correction of vertebral dysfunction.'" He shrugged at Pat's blank stare. "Spine, muscles, nervous system, they're all tied together. Most people don't realize."

"To be honest I'm only here because Randy insisted. This would take care of itself in time."

"Well, let's see if we can speed it along."

Doc's hands moved along Pat's back with light pressure, concentrating on joints loosened by the percussor. Pat's body stiffened, an automatic defense, as he braced for whatever might be coming. His movements were imperceptible other than the involuntary groans that came with each gentle push.

Doc shook his head. "You've got one joint here . . ." He continued to roam, guiding sure hands along Pat's spine, analyzing the remaining vertebrae. Then he returned to the original spot.

"I want you to take a deep breath in and then blow it out," Doc said.

The moment Pat expelled the breath was the moment his body relaxed and, as planned, the precise moment Doc chose to exert a firm, practiced force. Doc felt the vertebra give and slide back toward its original position. Pat groaned and allowed the pain to subside.

"That feels better already, Doc."

"You act surprised."

"I wasn't expecting much."

Doc's hands moved along Pat's spine, feeling for other minor joint misalignment and giving selected ones a lesser adjustment when he noticed Pat's pistol.

"Is that a Colt on the shelf?"

"How'd you know?"

"It's a familiar gun. In this day and age we can't have too many," he said as his hands continued to walk up and down Pat's back.

"I'll agree. Except for assault weapons, of course."

"Actually assault weapon is a misleading term," Doc said, his hands still on the move. "The rifles available to the public are semi-automatics. Those aren't assault rifles."

"Semantics," Pat said, "Semi-automatics were designed for the Army—rapid fire, high velocity rounds, maximum penetration. Built for one purpose, to kill as fast and efficiently as possible. They don't belong in the hands of the average citizen."

"Some people would disagree," Doc said. "It's not the gun that kills, it's the person behind it." He released his hands. "You can get up now."

Pat eased his body to the edge of the bench. "Doc, semi's are killing machines. And please don't bring up the bullshit argument about target practice and hunting. If a guy needs an AR-15 to hunt maybe he needs to worry more about his marksmanship than his Second Amendment rights."

"Sorry, but there're too many crazies out there. I don't plan to be caught defenseless."

"You got a good hand gun?"

"One or two."

"Good. Easy to grab and fire in tight quarters. An AR-15 round can penetrate the walls of your house, maybe your neighbor's house? Sorry to rant, Doc, but I've seen good men cut in half with these things. Too many innocent people getting killed by wackos carrying 'non-assault' rifles."

"That's true, but we're not going to stop the wackos with a few laws. It'd be a nightmare to enforce and the crooks ignore them. Then who's going to protect my family."

"Guess we're gonna have to agree to disagree, Doc."

"No problem. I'm a chiropractor, not a politician."

Pat wriggled into a standing position and shook himself out. "This does feel better. Does this session fix me?"

"Afraid not. We helped it, but it's not like slipping a card back in the deck. Have to move it a little at a time. I want to see you back here tomorrow. When did you . . . 'fall'?" he said.

Pat ignored the pointed sarcasm. "Yesterday."

"Your muscles have been working overtime to protect your vertebra so there'll be soreness. Angel will give you some cold packs. Twenty minutes on, twenty off, through the evening. We'll save massage therapy for tomorrow."

"How many trips is this going to take?"

"A few. Don't worry, your insurance covers most of it."

"It's not that," Pat said. "I just need to . . . keep a low profile for a few days."

"Randy told me all about the parking lot. Nice shot, by the way. I'll see you tomorrow."

When Pat left the office and mounted his bike he felt the tension in his back looser than when he came. *The Doc's probably a card-carrying member of the NRA, but he's a chiropractor, not a politician. And my back feels better. Deal with it.*

Chapter 15

"THE FBI PULLED a search warrant on the farm in Claxton." Phil Damron was in his office at Kentucky State Police Headquarters skimming through his notes as he spoke. "That animal rights lady, Mitchner, was right. It's a hell-hole for pigs."

Randy punched the speakerphone button and laid the receiver in the cradle. "Don't guess they found any sign of the Swinney kid." He took another bite of his Subway.

"Not yet. You heard anything from your buddy, Grainger?"

"Why? The Commonwealth's Attorney cleared him. A lot of witnesses saw the whole thing, me included."

"He's clean on the shooting, although I'm not a fan of citizens playing cop. We need to run his gun through ballistics, match it up with the slug in the killer and the ass-end of that ditched plumbing van. I'm actually more interested in another piece of information we just got off the wire from the Sheriff in Darden County in North Carolina. Seems like a pickup truck from Fox Hill was found in a cotton field Monday night with three illegals inside, what was left of them. From the crime scene photo the damn thing looked like last one out in a demolition derby."

"What's that got to do with Pat?"

"Four bullet holes in the driver's face. How many people you know can do that?"

"I wouldn't know."

"The slugs were 9-mil and as I recall, Grainger fires a 45. But c'mon, Randy, even if it's not from his gun, this has his name written all over it. Some illegal nacho from Fox Hill shoots Grainger's daughter at a rally and then two days later this happens. You have any idea where he was Monday?"

"Wasn't my day to watch him. Is he a suspect?"

"Not yet, but we still need his gun. And I'd like to have a man-to-man to remind him that we're the cops. And that we have resources. When he goes off on his own, shit happens. You two have become friends. Thought you might know where he is?"

Randy raised his eyebrows at his lunch guest on the other side of the desk and waited for an answer.

Pat Grainger took a gulp from his Dr. Pepper and leaned over toward the speaker phone. "Sergeant, I've got a chiropractor's appointment in two hours. How about I run out to your office as soon as I finish this Stromboli. I'll bring my weapon."

* * * * *

Marcela knocked on the door to the bathroom. "Your computer, Lambito. The emails you have been waiting for have come."

The Captain took time to wash his hands. The messages weren't going anywhere.

At the desk he clicked the icon—eight emails. A lot of data. He expected that. He opened each email and saved every attached document to a folder before printing it, then settled back in the chair with an iced guava juice.

The first three batches were straightforward military history: Patrick Grainger's DD-214, basic training records, orders for duty assignments and transfers, commendations and medals, and numerous performance reports during two Gulf Wars, in particular his prominent role in a Green Beret Special Forces unit in northern Iraq. Several documents were heavily redacted and three were blanked out altogether marked 'Confidential - Unavailable for Viewing.'

The next two batches were generic white papers available to the public via DoD and other government agency sources. Most of them dealt with a massive financial/logistical conspiracy by a prominent Defense Contractor, Wyndham-Lynch, at Camp Ahmadi in Kuwait in 2002 during the build up to the second Gulf War. A quick read revealed that SSG Patrick Grainger had exposed the conspiracy and had been called to provide testimony but was excused due to 'personal circumstances', the most notable being his six weeks in a coma following an IED explosion and the death of his wife and daughter back home in the States during that same period.

The balance of the reports included dozens of articles, op-ed pieces, police reports, and obituaries from Kentucky newspapers in Campbellsville, Lexington, and Frankfort plus the Macon Telegraph and the Richmond Times-Dispatch in Virginia. The most revealing information came from a notable journalistic series by Randy Oliver, Managing Editor of the Frankfort State Journal, which made the rounds in syndication to major papers across the US. The story, citing actions and information from a confidential source, code named Lachesis, connected the Kuwait conspiracy to officers and enlisted men that served at camp Ahmadi, as well as to Wyndham-Lynch.

After an hour and a half reading, the Captain laid the papers on the desk and pinched the bridge of his nose. His quarry was no gap-toothed hick. "Lachesis"?—it was an intriguing cover name. He would have to look it up later. For now finding the best way to eliminate Patrick Grainger was the order of the day. Under normal circumstances he would mobilize one of their assassins, perhaps a contract operative in the States with a working familiarity of the region. In this case, considering his target's obvious skills, such an obvious choice presented more than an acceptable amount of risk. *El Araña* would insist on a safer option.

Grainger had already penetrated Fox Hill. Even if he hadn't yet discovered its true purpose, the documents on the desk suggested it would only be a matter of time. Patrick Grainger could not be allowed to live. His friend, Randy Oliver, and his syndicated articles had to be silenced as well.

He pulled out his cell phone and dialed. "This is Lambito. Is *he* there?"

"Of course."

When the leader of *Cartel Independiente de Tlaxcala* came to the phone, the Captain wasted no time.

"That threat I told you about in Claxton? I just got the information I requested. There is some risk."

"You said it was merely one man."

"A dangerous man. And now a newspaper. We must not underestimate him like Diego did. Can I meet you at *Los Pelecanos* later this afternoon?"

"I assume you will have something in mind by then."

"I usually do." He ended the call.

The Captain stared out the window at two gazelle grazing on the manicured lawn, and weighed his options. *El Araña* had not clawed and murdered his way to the top of one of the most ruthless trafficking cartels in Mexico by being careless. He would agree to pursue Patrick Grainger only if he believed this man was a legitimate threat to their operation. He would not be swayed by the Captain's personal interest in revenge. Alejandro was an arrogant upstart but he was still family. It was difficult to take that off the table. The *soldados* and *policia* that tracked down and killed the Captain's brother had lived only long enough to regret their actions. Alejandro deserved a similar respect. So far Alejandro's death was still under wraps. It would be better not to share that part of the story with *el Araña* until Grainger was dead.

He picked up the documents and read through them again, searching for an answer, some gap in Grainger's armor. Finally he came to one passage in Randy Oliver's syndicated newspaper series and the solution came to him. Patrick Grainger was a professional but more importantly a man of conscience. This would make his undoing so simple.

Chapter 16

"YOU'RE WALKING more upright today," Jackie said as he passed through the door to the treatment room.

Pat placed his gun and phone on the shelf. "I was able to get out of bed this morning without waking the neighbors."

Without prompting he laid face down on the padded bench and she massaged his spine with the vibrator as Doc wandered in with Pat's updated clipboard chart. Once she finished, Doc ran through an adjustment regimen similar to the previous day. Despite his best efforts to hang tough, Pat responded with the same grunts and groans as discs and vertebrae inched back closer to where they belonged. When Doc finished Pat sat on the edge of the bench and did a couple of mild side stretches.

"Not bad, Doc. You might make it in this business."

"Fortunately you're in pretty good shape, but I'd still recommend not climbing steel anytime soon."

Pat's double-take stopped him mid-stretch. "What makes you think . . .?"

"I read Randy's exposé story in the paper. Interesting stuff. Especially that mystery steelworker . . . the undercover source."

Pat averted his eyes. "Yeah, I read that story too."

"Randy and I've been friends a few years. You did the right thing. By the way, how's your daughter?"

"Better. They sent her home today . . . I mean to Randy's."

He was stumbling over his explanation, one that on the surface he knew made little sense, even to himself, even now, a year and a half later.

"Relax," Doc said. "If you daughter—what's her name, Aimee?—and Julie are close, maybe that's where she needs to be for now."

It was a complicated situation and Pat had still not found any easy answers. So many humbling, dramatic life changes for both of them. Her calm, steady, happy life had been turned upside down, forcing her to abandon the person she thought she was and come to terms with the person she actually was. Knowing that it was a product of the lies manufactured by her adoptive parents only made it a little easier. And even though Pat's long-spiraling hopelessness had been resurrected by that circumstance, he still wasn't certain how he should fit into the scheme of things. He was lost in his thoughts when Doc's voice brought him out of it.

"I have a daughter myself. A good bit older than Aimee. If I were in your shoes, I'd probably be a complete nutcase. We do the best we can."

"Just how much do you know about Aimee and me?" Pat said.

Doc sat down on the adjacent padded bench. "Enough. I know I don't have any answers."

Pat lowered his guard, perhaps because Doc was a healer, or possibly because he was simply another father. "I wonder what she's doing every day. I just want to watch her grow up. I want to be the Dad she and I missed out on for so long." He looked down at his hands folded in his lap. "I'm still not sure I'm her best option."

"I don't know. Randy thinks you are. Or will be when you're both ready. Have you talked about it?"

"A little. She's comfortable at the Oliver's. She's almost like a sister with Julie and Brad. And Karen is the mother figure I can't offer her. It's so easy for her there. Still, she and I see each other a lot, and it's growing on both of us, so we'll see. I'm heading over after I leave here to check up on her rehab."

"She's been through a lot for a teenager. Give it time. Our congregation will be praying for you."

"Thanks, but don't bring this up in church. I prefer inconspicuous."

"It's a small congregation and I'm the pastor."

Pat dropped another double-take. "A gun-loving pastor," he said, shaking his head. "Who woulda guessed?"

Doc laughed. "God makes no judgments on the Second Amendment. I'm going to let Jackie work on you today, loosen up those muscles. Come see me tomorrow afternoon."

* * * * *

"Central Baptist Hospital. Patient Records."

"Yes, I'm checking on the status of a patient."

"What name?"

"Aimee Grainger."

"Just a minute." Pause . . . computer keys clacking . . . pause. "She was dismissed yesterday."

"Could you give me her address, please?"

"I'm sorry, we only release that information to family members."

"This is Michael Botts with Midland Insurance and Fidelity. Miss Grainger was injured in a shooting at Regency Centre this past Saturday. Her family has requested a claim form so they can submit their notarized statement regarding incidental and negligent damages, not that I think there are any, but I just need to know where to mail it."

"Uh, shouldn't that be handled between her primary insurance company and you?"

"Usually, but we're a supplemental carrier for the shopping center and we handle special coverage for Clauses D and M which deal with what's classified as terroristic engagement, which as you know is new to the industry and extremely uncommon, and somehow we've been getting our wires crossed between her insurance company and us as the supplemental carrier. I just need an address to send the forms, that's all. It would help expedite their claim."

"Uh, well, uh . . . the address listed on her sheet is 1950 Sheffield Lane, Frankfort, Kentucky. 40601."

"Thanks so much. You've been a big help."

When the connection ended, the caller dialed another number.

Chapter 17

LOIS LAID HER PURSE on her reception desk and poked her head into his office. "First one in? You must've been here awhile."

Pat Grainger leaned back from the drafting table and dropped his mechanical pencil on the steel erection plans spread out there.

"Why would you think that?"

"Your bike. The pipes were cool."

He nodded approval at her observation. "I've been off a couple of days so I thought I'd get an early start, try to get caught up."

She retreated to the coffee pot and poured a cup before she returned to his office. "We all read about that shoot-out Saturday at Regency. Our hero." She faked a swoon. "How's your daughter?"

"On the mend. She got out of the hospital yesterday. I went by for a couple hours. It shook her up pretty bad. She knew one of the people that died. It's not just another headline."

"Our country is off the rails," Lois said, shaking her head. She blew on her coffee and took a sip. "You were off a couple of days. Been hanging around the hospital? Bored to death reading old copies of Better Homes and Gardens in the waiting room?"

Pat reflected briefly on his visit to Claxton, the hog

warehouses, the capture and escape, the deadly confrontation with the truck on the Carolina back road, and held back a smile. "Yeah, pretty boring."

"You could've taken more time if you needed it, you know." She pointed to the plans on the table. "That job you're estimating doesn't bid for two weeks."

"I know, but Bob Brannon was good enough to let me come in from the field and sit behind this cushy desk for a few years so I could watch my daughter grow up. I don't want to take a chance on getting fired."

"You've made a lot of money for Brannon Steel. I think you're safe." She paused to form her question. "You think you'll ever go back out? You loved that life."

"I love my daughter more."

She started to back out of the doorway, then stopped. Pat caught her looking.

"What?" he said.

She pointed at his belt. "You do realize there's no gun in your holster?"

He grinned, barely. "Yeah, the State Police needed to verify ballistics on the bullet that killed the Regency shooter."

"I've never seen you without it. You feel naked?"

"You wish."

"Pffft." Lois scoffed and turned away. Over her shoulder she said, "By the way, Pike called in yesterday with some questions on the Civic Center in Louisville. Nothing urgent, but he said give him a buzz."

Pat checked his watch. "I'll wait until his morning break."

Pat leaned his elbows on the spread-out plans and allowed himself a couple of minutes second guessing the State Police and FBI on where their investigation was going. He promised Randy and Karen he would back off and let the authorities do their job. At some point he'd have to break down and share what he found in Building 8, but that would require disclosure about the deadly confrontation and he wasn't prepared to wade into that legal minefield yet. For now there was no way to prove it was self-defense, or that it even happened at all. The farm would've cleaned all evidence of the capture and escape, and the bodies were undoubtedly in a place they would never be found. There was only one way to prove his innocence—a single witness—and that man apparently had his own personal reason for being there. The question had been nagging him. In time he'd have to pay another visit.

He picked up his cup and checked the contents. Even under stealth battlefield conditions he'd never been fond of cold coffee. He slid off the stool and headed for the pot.

* * * * *

"This is Bravo. We have the Prize."

The Captain shifted in his chair. "It went without problems?"

"Affirmative. Everyone was gone. We went in through the garage."

"You are clear on where to make the delivery?"

"You're not paying me for mistakes. We're on the road now."

"Your men, they are dependable? We had some setbacks with Diego's crew."

"All three were with me in Afghanistan. They have experience. And they understand the consequences for failure, as do I."

"You will make certain you and your men keep a zero profile. And there is to be no personal contact. *Nada!* Crude men sometimes think they can take liberties. This is not one of those times. The Prize is not our ultimate target, so it must remain unspoiled. If your men lose control, *el Araña* will spare no expense to find them. *Comprende?*"

* * * * *

"I leave you guys on your own for a few days and things fall apart?"

"Look, maybe you've found a soft rocking chair in Brannon's office," Pike said, "but real men have to hang steel, so don't give me any shit."

"I see your people skills haven't improved," Pat chuckled. "What's up?"

The next ten minutes were taken up by a discussion of two connection details that weren't coming together on the second floor, east wing of the Civic Center. Comparison of field and office plans yielded a simple solution, and Pat authorized the field welds from his office. Once the details were settled, Pike dropped back to a personal conversation.

"How's your daughter?"

"Better. She's hurting but she'll be OK. I'm going to call her after lunch and check up."

"Patrick, the mangy bastards that shot her have got something coming, you know that don't you?"

"Yeah, but I promised Randy I'd let the Feds handle it."

"That's fine but if you need me to round up a posse, Granny, Mongo, and Axle haven't forgotten how much fun we had in Lexington. We're ready."

"I hope our vigilante days are over, Pike. But thanks, Buddy. Miss me yet?"

"Good riddance, I say. But we manage. We've picked up some new guys that can carry their weight. We even found a crew of Mexicans, believe it or not, that are damn good hands."

"I may run down and visit next week. We'll hit your favorite spot."

When the call ended, Pat checked his watch again. Mid morning, she should be up. He dialed Aimee's number and the call went to voice mail.

Chapter 18

THE RECEPTIONIST dropped a UPS cardboard envelope on Randy's desk. *No return address. Curious.* He opened the package and pulled out a single sheet. On it was a list of website addresses for different newspapers or TV news outlets. The coded text in most of the URLs had one common word sprinkled through the string of characters and symbols: *massacre.*

He typed in the first link, a news story with a CNN byline. When it opened he recognized the old headline:

Remains could be those of missing Mexican students

The 43 Mexican students who disappeared in southern Mexico on September 26, 2014 were abducted by police on order of a local mayor, and are believed to have been turned over to members of the Guerreros Unidos gang. The gang killed them and burned their bodies before throwing their remains in a river, the nation's Attorney General said Friday. The victims were young men mostly in their 20s studying to become teachers at Ayotzinapa Rural Teachers' College in Iguala, Guerrero, Mexico.

Randy didn't need to read the whole story. Like anyone that kept up with world news he was familiar with it. He backed out and typed in the second URL address, a press article from the Dallas Morning News:

> Ciudad Juarez, May 13, 2012. - Mexican authorities found at least 49 decapitated and dismembered bodies along a highway in the northern border city of Nuevo Leon, 80 miles southwest of the US border. Identified as members of Los Zetas Cartel, nine were left hanging from a bridge to the entrance to the town. The rest were decapitated with their heads stuffed in ice coolers in a Chrysler Voyager. The area has become a battleground for a brutal conflict between the Zetas and the Gulf Cartels, and reports of forced disappearances have become increasingly common in recent years.

It was another story that Randy had read in various news publications back when the event had occurred. The photograph leading into the story showed the nine hanging bodies. Despite his presumption that all of the links would lead to similar articles, he continued. The third was not a regular AP news outlet but a website, Borderland Beat, which kept tabs on the continuing violence in Mexico:

> Boca del Rio Massacre
> The bodies of 23 male and 12 female murder victims were found abandoned, bound, and gagged in front of the Plaza Americas commercial area this afternoon in Boca del Rio, a suburb of Veracruz. The bodies were scattered behind two abandoned flatbed trucks on Manuel Avila Camacho Boulevard that were left at the scene during rush hour traffic.

Then a fourth, another CNN byline:

> Agents of the Jalisco Prosecutor General's
> Office exhumed 67 bodies in a field near the
> town of La Barca, between Jalisco and
> Michoacan states. The killings are believed to be
> connected to an ongoing turf war between the
> Jalisco New Generation Cartel and the Knights
> Templar. Most of the bodies are believed to be
> members of the Knights Templar Cartel. The
> mass graves were discovered after 20 people,
> including local police, were detained as part of a
> kidnapping ring.

Randy glanced at the entire list. It contained 12 URL
addresses. Reluctantly he decided to type in one more, this time
another story from Borderland Beat:

> Saturday night, an armed group of men forced
> their way into a disco in Uruapan, Michoacan
> and rolled five human heads onto the dance
> floor. La Familia, one of the most powerful and
> vicious cartels in Mexico, claimed credit in a
> newspaper advertisement the following week,
> stating their goal was to butcher all rival gangs
> and exercise complete control of the trafficking
> market in Michoacan.

The full color photograph of five decapitated heads on the
floor of the disco was enough to make him click off and push
away from the computer. He took a deep breath, partly to clear
his head from the gruesome details, and partly to question why
would someone anonymously send him links to real-life stories of
the Mexican drug wars from old news sources? He dialed an

interoffice number:

"Ginny, when you signed for that UPS package, was it our regular driver?"

"No, it was a new guy. Wasn't wearing his brown. Come to think of it, he didn't ask me to sign for it."

* * * * *

Randy dodged in and out of busy four-lane traffic on East Main hill. He knew it was senseless getting worked up over nothing, but the gnawing feeling in his gut wouldn't let him drop it. After Julie's grinding ordeal last year he took nothing for granted. His call to Aimee's cell phone had gone to voice mail. He tried his home land line and got no answer there either. Foolish or not, he'd wait with her until Karen got home to talk him down, preferably with a Mark on the rocks to take the sting out of what was bound to be a well-deserved lecture on over-reacting.

When he pulled in the driveway he made a conscious decision to slow down. Better to not broadcast his free-wheeling paranoia to Aimee or the neighbors. He opened the front door in what felt like slow motion, his mind racing, and he heard himself calling to her.

When he turned the corner in the kitchen he saw the sheet of paper on the counter, weighed down by her cell phone.

"Aimee?" he called out. "Aimee!"

Nothing.

He slid the note out from under the phone. The block letters were enlarged to 18-point Verdana, all caps. As he read, he felt his legs give way, an empty, debilitating, bone-chilling terror. When he finished an overwhelming helplessness took him over, refusing to let him get a full breath. He let the page flutter to the counter and stormed up the stairs to her bedroom, calling frantically, shouts that he knew wouldn't be answered. He opened her door to a room in shambles, the comforter on her bed shredded in angry slits, clothes from her closet scattered, the contents of her dresser spilled out in piles.

Panic drove him back down stairs and he read the message a second time. Then he remembered the phone. He picked it up and played the video of Aimee, held securely by two men, their faces silent behind black masks. Her mouth was bound with a cotton rag. The fear in her eyes was inescapable as they patiently led her toward the garage. The camera went dark.

His fingers shook as he fumbled and fished his own phone out of his pocket. His mind was short circuiting, his thoughts scattered, unable to bring focus, before he finally gathered himself and pulled up Pat's number and dialed. He paced as the phone finally went to voice mail.

"Shit! Pick up!"

He dialed again, same result. Then he remembered Pat's appointment at the chiropractor. He checked his watch and dashed for the car.

Chapter 19

JACKIE WAS MAKING her first pass with the percussor when Pat's phone jittered on the wooden shelf. It came to a stop. Seconds later it rang again.

"You need to answer that?" Jackie asked.

"Whatever it is can wait until after you guys work your magic."

She finished her prep work. "Doc's running behind. Don't go anywhere."

Three minutes later Doc entered the room. "Sorry, one patient can back up appointments the rest of the afternoon. But then after you I've got a half-hour gap. Go figure."

They spent a few minutes reviewing the steady improvements in Pat's back. With some time to kill the conversation drifted cautiously into the unexpected journey Pat and his daughter had taken during the last year. Like most of Franklin County Doc had followed the story in the paper. It was a candid conversation with Randy during lunch at Two Sisters Cafe that filled in some gaps and gave it new meaning. That personal insight was making his growing connection with Pat more comfortable. Finally he stood up.

"Let's see if we can finish you up today," he said, extending his arm toward the bench. "Face down."

Doc worked in silence, his hands making practiced moves, manipulating joints and discs with precision. Following the spinal adjustment he directed Pat face up and moved around to the head of the bench. With a firm grip on Pat's head, he paused, an obvious delay while he waited for his patient to relax, than an abrupt twist to the right, and Pat heard the crack when the vertebra slipped into place. A second maneuver, another pause, and a firm twist to the left, and C-1 centered itself. Doc was positioning Pat on his side for a lateral adjustment when they both heard loud voices in the waiting room. A moment later Randy Oliver barged into the exam room with a handful of pages and a vaporous expression.

Several seconds of awkward silence hung in the air. Doc was speechless, caught off guard by the intrusion, but Pat read Randy's face and righted himself.

"What's wrong?"

Randy hesitated, unsure how to deliver an impossible message. "Aimee," he finally said.

Pat's eyes widened. "What? Did her wound open up?"

Randy shook his head. "No . . . no . . . somebody . . ." He swallowed hard and held out the note.

Pat snatched it and read.

PATRICK GRAINGER
YOU SHOULD NOT HAVE INTERFERED. WE HAVE YOUR DAUGHTER.

WE ARE CIVILIZED PEOPLE. WE HAVE FAMILIES OF OUR OWN.

WE DO NOT WISH TO HURT HER BUT DO NOT DOUBT WHAT WE ARE CAPABLE OF.

ASK YOUR FRIEND OLIVER TO SHOW YOU THE NEWS STORIES.

DO NOT THINK YOU CAN FIND US. YOU ARE ONE, WE ARE MANY. ONE DIES, THREE MORE ARE BORN. THE BELLY OF THE DRAGON WILL NEVER BE FILLED.

ONCE WE HAVE HER IN A SECURE PLACE WE WILL CONTACT YOU. IF YOU SHARE THIS WITH POLICE – WE WILL SEND YOU HER HEAD.

Randy waited for the eruption—or the total collapse—he had no idea which, but neither came. Instead, an intractable expression carved out of granite as Patrick Grainger's head rose slowly from the note.

"You found this at home . . . just now?"

Randy nodded.

Pat glanced off to the side, looking at nothing in particular, the gears turning. "This could be some screwed up prank. How could you be positive?"

"Her room was tossed," Randy said. He reluctantly handed Aimee's cell phone to Pat, gingerly as if it might disintegrate, and the three men watched the video in stony silence.

When it ended Pat's eyes closed. The firestorm started before he even saw it coming, building momentum, unbidden, climbing without conscious thought from the dregs of an abandoned past. One by one, lessons learned and perfected during the brash, ruthless, long-forgotten history of his young manhood re-appeared, an unexpected return to worn out pages from a life of violence. He had been forced to revisit these lessons nearly two years earlier. In the final analysis they may have saved Aimee. The whole sordid affair had brought them together, father and daughter, when neither could have ever imagined an inkling of their real story. But when the smoke had cleared he promised to leave it all behind for good. Until now.

Randy's voice echoed off in the distance. "We have to call the police."

"No!" Pat said, his eyes blazing.

"But—"

"You saw what it said!"

He read it again, his finger following each line, the wheels turning, looking for answers anywhere, even in the most subtle of places—a sentence; a phrase; a word.

"What news stories are they talking about?" he asked.

Randy handed him the copies he made at the office of the five press articles he had opened and read. The lead paragraphs told Pat all he needed to know.

"Cartels," he said under his breath. "The farm's a fucking cover for a goddamned drug trafficking cartel." He whirled, his hands pressed against his head as he analyzed. "This is how these assholes think. 'You are one, we are many. One dies, three more are born.' You see? Every time the Mexican police crush one kingpin, three more spring up to fill the void. They're right. It's a battle we'll never win."

"Dammit, Pat, I told you to stay out of it," Randy said.

"But why would a drug cartel kidnap Aimee? She's an innocent girl," Doc said.

The question hung in the air. Only Pat knew the answer. He stared blankly into the wall when he answered.

"Because I killed one of theirs."

Randy and Doc looked at each other.

"A nephew to some big shot—*el Capitán*, they called him," Pat continued. He was connecting the dots now. "This is his vengeance." He scanned the note a third time. A speck flickered in his memory and his finger fell to the telltale line—*the belly of the dragon*— and Diego's cryptic boast during the interrogation came rushing back: '*El vientre del dragón de Tlaxcala.*' He filtered the words into the violent montage of the past few days: *the assassination at Regency . . . the armed guards at the farm . . . the high-tech control room. A Cartel.* It all made sense now.

He pulled out the Glock he had saved from the encounter at the farm and checked the half-empty magazine. "Where's the nearest gun store?"

"Are you crazy?" Randy's voice was rising. "Haven't you learned anything? You've got to call the FBI."

"The police go in, they could kill Aimee. One man might have a chance."

"Christ, Pat, you can't go after a drug cartel," Randy said. "You heard them: one against many."

Pat turned sharply to Randy. "I think I know where they took her."

"And if you're wrong?"

Pat glanced down at Enrique's Glock. "Then I know someone who can help."

"Don't be a fool, man."

"I don't have a choice, Randy. This is on me. I just wish I had a little more firepower."

Doc laid his hand on Pat's shoulder and swung him around until they were face to face.

"What do you need?"

Chapter 20

THE SIMPLE WOODEN DESK in Dr. Jonathan Hall's nondescript office was buried under a layer of insurance forms, professional papers, clipboards and binders, computer printouts, handwritten notes on lined pages, all weighed down with trade and medical books in unstable piles. Personal memorabilia and a half-empty Diet Coke rested in the few clear areas of desktop. Off to the side an oversized exercise ball had been rolled under the edge of a self-contained computer console that housed a MacBook Pro and monitor. The main wing of the desk had its own MacBook Pro laptop with scanner and wireless printer. Above that storage slots were crammed with CD-R discs, cables, thumb drives, and the usual inventory of computer accessories.

The wall on one side of the room was covered with a half-dozen professional certificates and awards in the traditional thin black frames, plus a proud collection of framed family photos, a

Kentucky Colonel certificate, and a signed team picture of the University of Kentucky 1998 NCAA basketball champs. The opposite wall was dominated by a large shelving unit stocked with rows of books, periodicals, magazines, DVDs, and instructional seminars. One section had been devoted to a collection of bibles in multiple editions, lexicons, biblical commentaries, and an assortment of books related to bible studies, all standing watch over their secular cousins. Nothing seemed out of the ordinary until Doc made a deliberate bee-line around his desk toward a locked door and pulled out a key.

A flick of a switch and the darkened interior of a walk-in closet came alive under the cool florescent glow revealing a compact arsenal of handguns, semi-automatic rifles, and shotguns.

"Holy shit," Randy said.

Doc took the Glock 19 from Pat's hand, opened a smooth-gliding drawer beneath the wall of pistols, and pulled out a handful of loaded magazines plus a 50-round box of 9-millimeter ammunition, and stuffed all of it into a backpack he picked up from the floor. He backed out of the way and waved them in. "Don't just stand there, browse."

Pat was uncharacteristically distracted as he scanned the inventory, all weapons he was intimately familiar with.

"Doc, other than two semi-automatics, I count, what, three M16s?" He tentatively rolled open the drawer below them and withdrew a fully-charged 30-round magazine. "Where did you get all this shit?"

"Doesn't matter," Doc said. "Some people collect stamps. Me . . ." He simply shrugged. "Pick what you want and enough ammo to go with it. I'd recommend a couple more pistols. I've been accused of being partial to Glocks." He pointed to the brass-and-walnut plaque at the end of the closet they had not yet noticed.

With grateful appreciation to

Jonathan P. Hall

(AKA – "Johnny Glock")
CEO – Integrated Intelligence Devices
Ft. Lauderdale, Florida

*for twenty years of devoted service to his country and for
his imagination and innovative developments in the field
of electronic technology and intelligence systems.*

General Michael T. Lennon, Assistant Director
Central Intelligence Agency

Beneath that was a second one, a brushed-chrome sheet of aluminum engraved and mounted on a half-inch thick slab of Plexiglas:

*On this 17th day of March, 1989
The U. S. Marshals Service presents this*

America's Star Award

to

Jonathan P. Hall

Integrated Intelligence Devices

For meritorious service in the development and
innovation in advanced electronic intelligence
technology for the U.S. Witness Security Program.

"Doc, who the hell is Integrated Intelligence Devices?" Randy asked.

Doc's impatience was beginning to show. He pulled an M16 rifle off of its mounting cleats and handed it to Pat. "Seems like one of my patients told me these don't belong in the hands of the average citizen."

Pat stammered the beginnings of a response but Doc stopped him with an upraised hand. "Save it. You're not exactly average." He retrieved twelve 30-round magazines and placed them in the backpack. "Whatever your plan is, you need to get going. Take a couple more pistols."

Pat's grip on Doc's arm said more than words. He pulled two Glock 19s from their mounts along with matching sound suppressors that were lined up in a neat row below them, then gathered more magazines and stuffed them into the backpack. When he rose Doc was holding out four objects.

"These two are fragmentation grenades. The others are flash-bangs. Hopefully you won't have to use 'em."

"Doc, who the hell are you?" Pat said.

"Maybe I'll tell you over a drink when you get back." He prodded Pat forward.

When Pat got to the door, Doc called to him.

"You're dealing with a big-time cartel. You may start this . . . but you can't finish it by yourself. At some point you've got to call in the law, you do know that don't you?"

"I've got to find her first."

"You'll need help."

"I've got friends," Pat said. "I just don't know if they have enough tools for the job."

Doc winced and threw his arm back toward the closet. "Really?"

He pulled out a card and handed it to Pat. When they call Angel, use my old nickname to identify themselves." He pointed to the plaques on the wall and smiled. "'Johnny Glock.' That always did have a nice ring to it."

Pat turned to Randy.

"Look, I know you and Karen won't be able to sit on the kidnapping for long, but give me 24 hours, let me see what I can find. If you call Damron now the FBI will put out a BOLO and have a certain place surrounded, and I need a chance to check it out first. I'm pretty sure I've got a connection there. If the kidnappers contact you, tell 'em you'll get a message to me. Just keep me informed, OK?"

"Pat, this is all wrong and you know it."

"I got no choice, buddy. Twenty four hours?"

Randy nodded.

Within twenty minutes Patrick Grainger's motorcycle was pushing 90 on I-64, taking dead aim on North Carolina.

Chapter 21

THE FLY ON HER CHEEK woke her. It wasn't so much the annoying tickle as it was the involuntary swat that forced one side of the handcuffs to jerk away from the other. In the haze of a sudden awakening it took Aimee Grainger a moment to clear the cobwebs and recall enough for her fear to return.

Everything was out of sync: her palm resting against the coarse ticking of a bare mattress, a rough cotton blanket covering her, a pillow with no case. The steady ache from the wounds in her shoulder was still there and it slowed her movements as she rolled the blanket back, exposing the handcuffs and a light-duty chrome chain looped around the connecting links. She grimaced as she pushed up with her healthy right arm. Her eyes followed the trail of the chain to a metal post where the loose ends were wrapped and secured with a simple padlock.

The musty smell of mold and old wood was strong. She collected herself and surveyed her surroundings: a concrete floor dusted with grit and laced with hairline cracks that had opened up over the years; concrete block walls stained green and gray from poor drainage and untended leaks; two steel utility windows high in opposing walls, one with a broken pane, both duct taped over with cloudy plastic sheeting. The wood joists spanning overhead were overlain with diagonal cross planking that had been out of favor for 60 years. Other than an ancient oil furnace anchored off-center on the basement floor and a rust-streaked water heater on its last legs, the only other feature was a handyman special shelf unit leaning against one wall. Its fiberboard shelves sagged under the weight of gallon paint cans with the lids glued shut from the residue, plus assorted plastic jugs of paint thinner, antifreeze, and automobile fluids.

As she massaged her left shoulder she closed her eyes and tried to reconstruct the critical details: three men bursting in on her in the kitchen while she was making breakfast, binding and gagging her before she could scream; her immediate, paralyzing fear of being sexually violated; the methodical video recording taken with her own phone before they dragged her to the garage and into the van. The last thing she remembered was the rag being clamped over her nose and mouth, the sweet solvent smell, and a slow drift into an unconscious nether world.

She checked her pajamas and found no tears or rips. Then a frightening thought swept over her and she realized she was afraid to investigate, not even sure how. She felt no pain or discomfort between her legs. Tentatively she allowed her fingers to probe. When she found no tender flesh or blood a breath left her body, relief, even if only for the moment.

Footsteps and the creak of the wood floor above got her attention. *More than one person, heavy boots.* Then voices, unintelligible through the floor, coarse laughter, the clatter of dishes and utensils, a refrigerator door opening and shutting, more muffled conversation, the words chopped and indistinct. Finally a distinct trail of footsteps, the rattle of a drop chain, and the door at the top of the stairs squeaked opened.

Two sets of legs began a creaky descent down the wooden stairs. Her good right arm pulled the blanket back over her. Her eyes followed the men, their faces concealed behind black scarves. At the bottom of the stairs they stood over her, silent at first, dark eyes judging her like prized livestock. The second one held a bowl and spoon. The lead man, the taller one, broke the silence.

"Sleep well?"

Without looking at his partner he continued, his tone dripping with condescension. "I don't think we'll get a five-star rating." Then he shrugged. "At least we offer a free continental breakfast." He motioned with his hand and the second man set the bowl on the concrete floor next to the mattress. She glanced at the contents.

"It's not poisoned," the first one said. "Cheerios and skim milk. We're supposed to keep you healthy."

She deflected her gaze and pulled the blanket closer to avoid their withering stare. The standoff continued, the tension as thick as the dried paint on the rims of the cans.

"You need to eat," he finally said. "You're gonna be here awhile."

The shorter man finally spoke. "I don't think she likes us."

"She's a little young, but give her a couple of years, a little experience with—"

A stern voice from the top of the stairs interrupted the conversation. "What part about 'no contact' did you not understand?"

"I . . . was just trying to get her to eat."

The wooden stringers on the old stairs vibrated with each plodding step. When he reached the bottom he continued his forward progress and slammed his palms against the taller man's chest.

"She gets hungry enough, she'll eat," he said, the anger building behind his own scarf. The shorter man had already backed away from the gathering storm.

"Chill out, Sarge, I didn't mean nothin'—"

Bravo winced at the verbal slip up and glanced back to see if their hostage caught it.

"You fucking moron," he said. He stared at the floor and wallowed his head at the gaffe. "One more time. Who am I?"

He looked away, dreading the lecture that was coming. "You're Bravo."

"And you?"

"Charlie," he said.

"How about him?" he said, his head tilting toward the shorter man.

"Delta. Look, I know the protocol, I just forgot."

He fidgeted "You can't forget. Do you have any *fucking* idea who we're dealing with? He'd as soon cut your throat and piss down the hole as look at you. Forgetting can get you killed." He shook his head to clear his frustration, then closed his eyes, a purposeful delay to let the tension ease.

"You're lucky I don't have time to replace you."

He relaxed and backed away. A slight tilt of his head sent both men up the stairs.

When it was only the two of them he took a few steps toward Aimee.

"Eat the cereal."

He let the command sink in before he pivoted toward the stairs. His right hand was already on the railing when she broke her silence.

"Why?" she blurted.

Her captor pulled up short. She felt her own muscles tense up. The question had spilled out before she had a chance to weigh the implications.

Finally over his shoulder, "Why what?"

Even if this was the wrong time and place, she couldn't reel it back in. And she still wanted to know. So she finished it.

"Why did you take me?"

It took him a moment to decide. Finally he lowered his leading boot off the first stair tread and turned back to her.

"Because I follow orders. Because it will make me a boat load of money when this is over. Mostly because if I didn't, my life or yours wouldn't be worth what's in that bowl."

She glanced at the soggy cereal, and then back at him.

"You just broke your own rule," she said.

He cocked his head. "Rule?"

"No contact—that rule," she said with the coy innocence of a school girl as she rubbed her shoulder.

His eyes gave away the unexpected grin hiding behind the scarf.

"You *are* your old man's daughter, that's for sure." Too late, he realized his slip up. *Too much information. Not fatal but still . . . Why had he engaged her? Was she playing him?* The longer he stared the more he detected a subtle change in her, even tethered to the basement post. He wondered if her initial fear may have eased up, replaced with something else—curiosity? confidence? a cunning search for information? His controlled bearing fell back into place.

"He butted in. You should learn from his mistakes."

Instead of avoiding his stare, she had latched onto it. With her captor standing dominate over her holding all the cards and a loaded pistol, he sensed she was playing a psychological game of chicken.

"Anything else?" he finally said.

"I have to pee."

Without a word he slid a 5-gallon drywall bucket and a roll of toilet paper from under the stairs and scooted it beside her, then turned and took the stairs to the first floor two at a time.

Chapter 22

OTHER THAN A faint trail of tracks, the bed of pine needles had not been disturbed since Monday. His forced drive from Frankfort had given Pat Grainger time to plan, and he settled into his prone position in the grove of trees well before daylight, his binoculars trained on a familiar target. Lying impatiently on the ground beside him was one M-16 automatic rifle, a gunbelt stocked with pistols and grenades, and a half-dozen full magazines in a backpack. He'd wait until the feeding crew left for the day.

He was scanning the grounds when his cell phone in front of him blinked on. It surprised him to see Randy's familiar number replaced with 'Unknown.' He cursed them under his breath, the unscrupulous telemarketers who refused to obey FCC rules, and allowed the call go to voicemail. The second ring, same ID, was more a surprise than an annoyance. A third call from 'Unknown' forced him to lose patience and he picked up the phone.

The deep Hispanic-American dialect was unfamiliar. "Patrick, I was beginning to think you would not answer me."

"Who is this?"

"In due time, Patrick Grainger," the voice said, calm, confident. "All you should know is your daughter is safe . . . for now."

Pat closed his eyes. This was unexpected. A pivotal moment in his daughter's life, completely off script, and he wasn't prepared for it.

"How'd you get my number?"

"I'm surprised you had to ask. Your daughter's cell phone, perhaps?"

Damn it! He should have known. Careless. Gather yourself, Patrick, get it together.

This call was a hanging curveball dropping in out of the blue, and it had him on his heels. The beginning of a deadly cat and mouse game he hadn't anticipated, at least not so soon. It didn't matter. He knew what would come next and his instincts kicked in on cue. Men and women with far more intelligence had trained him during an earlier life how to do this. They'd drawn from a deep reservoir of experience gathered in the wake of successes and failures, of lives won and lost. They'd taught him precisely how to keep emotions off the field of play. During those early years, back when he had nothing to lose it had always worked. In the heat of battle, under impossible circumstances, always. Now, with his daughter's captor taunting him on what he had believed was a secure line, her survival depended on him dragging those old lessons back into play.

Focus! Get in his head. Win the mind games, Patrick. Win the mind games!

"Such a brave man," he tried, "taking a girl who can't fight back."

"Please, Patrick. It is no use trying to 'get my goat', as you say. You know it is not your daughter we want. She is merely a pawn in the game."

"Why not just come after me? You have resources. 'I am one, you are many.' Isn't that the way you scum-sucking mouth-breathers think?"

"Mouth-breathers?" he chuckled. "I have not heard that one.

I doubt it is a compliment. You are right, Patrick, we could have sent *professionales* after you. But it appears you are a formidable opponent. Even when we managed to kill you, it might draw attention to something that we prefer to keep, as you would say, 'under the radar.' Although in this case there are other things to consider. Personal things. Perhaps if you had not been so nosy your daughter would be in school today, flirting with a boy, complaining about the lunches, maybe even learning something scholarly. You see what meddling gets you?"

"You shot her in a public place. Innocent people died. You didn't give me much choice."

"Ahh, she was a mistake, I admit. Still if you had simply left it to your inept *policia* to muddle through, they would have never found us. The fact that you were able to do this on your own, it is to your credit, of course."

"Save the compliments. How do I know she's not hurt?" He stifled a shudder. "Or if she's even alive?" *Stay in the game, Patrick.*

"You don't. But you will . . . soon. She will be making a brief phone call to the State Journal after lunch. That should give you comfort that she is still alive."

"Let me talk to her."

"Sorry, my friend. Better the newspaper than you. Not so *emocional*. Besides, they have resources to make a proper recording for your FBI. That way you can play it back and listen to her voice tremble."

Put the pieces together, Patrick. Win the mind games.

"If I'm the one you want . . ." Pat said, scrambling for answers while random pieces tumbled and whirled in the spin cycle of his brain. ". . . who the hell are you?"

"You will know when I decide it."

"Cut the crap. Why her?" he pressed.

"*Familias*, Patrick. Family. Nothing is more important. "

Family? What the hell does that . . . ?

Without warning, a certain line from the kidnap letter jumped out and grabbed him by the collar. *We are civilized people. We too have families.* He recognized the last undeclared notes when they finally reoriented themselves and came together, all at once like those final half-dozen pieces in a Christmas jigsaw puzzle. The names came to him freely: *Family . . . Alejandro . . . El Capitán . . . We too have Families . . . Bingo! Winning the mind games.*

"Kidnapping my daughter wouldn't have anything to do with your shit-for-brains nephew, would it?" Pat asked.

A stilted silence filled the other end of the line.

"*El Capitán?* You still there?"

Finally a nervous response stuttered out, "You have no idea who I—"

"What was his name?" Pat interrupted. "Alejandro? Oh, wait, the ladies at University preferred 'Alex'. That's right." Pat repeated it for emphasis, his words dripping with sloppy, sing-song condescension. "The ladies at University."

Other than the nervous breathing gathering steam on the other end of the line, he heard nothing. Pat continued to prod his adversary. *Winning the mind games.*

"That self-centered jerk-off you sent to North Carolina, he was *your* family wasn't he? Too bad. He really was a loser. You actually thought he could show Diego how to do a man's job?" Pat scoffed into the phone. "He had his head so far up his uncle's ass—that would be you—he had no idea what it took to be a man. And you know what, because he wouldn't quit running his mouth he'll never know."

Hijo de Puta! ¡No chingues!

"Now, now, *el Capitán.* Hey, enough about your limp-dick nephew, let's talk about you, big shot. You feelin' all *mano a mano* kicked back in your safe Hacienda sipping pink drinks and getting another blow job while you send your Neanderthals out to do your dirty work for you. Murdering all those innocent locals and cutting off heads? That's how a real man does it. Were you going to let a cage-full of your knuckle-dragging suck-ups hold me down while you pulled another line of Coke before you found your balls and picked up that knife?"

The line went dead.

Pat pushed off the ground and slipped down the hillside toward the 10 warehouses.

Chapter 23

RENÉ LIT THE CIGARILLO and stalked across the gravel parking lot carrying his AK-47 down by his right thigh like a cheap briefcase. It puzzled him why they didn't send someone more skilled in matters like this.

When he approached the utility pole he squinted up at the camera. Like Enrique said, it wasn't moving. He turned south toward the rest of the complex. Even from a distance he could make out the two cameras behind Buildings 5 and 2 scanning and gathering video footage across their 120-degree sweep. Not only had the camera in front of him stopped moving but the video feed from it had gone blank. Perhaps the weather had shorted it out. Even so, how was he supposed to fix it? He used to be a farmer, not an electrician.

He took one last puff, pinched off the lit end, and tucked the stub in his pocket for later before he moved around to the back side of the pole. It took a second before it registered, the loose ends of the electric and video cables dangling free. He raised his rifle and reached out to examine the cables. A clean cut.

The distinctive ratcheting click behind him made him freeze. He recognized the slide of an automatic pistol engaging its first round.

"*Hablar Inglés?*" Pat said softly.

The guard hesitated, waiting for the shot he prayed would never come. His hand tightened around the front hand guard, a natural reaction but a useless one. It wouldn't change anything. His instincts forced him to at least look, a slow, methodical half-turn toward his unknown opponent, and he found himself staring down the barrel end of a silencer on a semi-automatic pistol. It didn't take an electrician to understand his options. Without prompting he carefully laid his rifle on the ground and raised his hands.

"*Un poco,*" he said, then translated his own words. "A little."

Pat made a precise move around to the guard's front, held up the duct tape to make his intentions clear, and motioned with his pistol to lie down. Within seconds he had the guard's hands and legs bound and a strip of tape secured over his mouth. Pat dragged him into the heavy brush. Behind an empty stare he placed an index finger in front of his lips and pointed the pistol at the man's head. "*Comprende?*"

The guard nodded and laid his head on the ground. Pat returned to his viewing station in the brush and waited.

Several minutes later the back door to Building 8 opened and a second guard appeared. He was on alert, his rifle raised and ready as he crept across the parking lot, scanning, searching for the first man.

"René?" he called out.

When he received no answer his caution level escalated. At the light pole he also recognized the cut ends of the two cables. His body language gave him away—sharp, jerky motions, wheeling to engage the parking lot and areas beyond.

"René?" he called out again.

Pat watched from his concealed position in the undergrowth. Attempting to peacefully disarm this second guard the way he had done the first was too risky. But allowing him to retreat to the nerve center and call for support was out of the question. A more permanent solution was still on the table.

Pat waited patiently, his pistol aimed, until the guard's position permitted a clean shot. The pop of the bullet leaving the Glock's silencer was, for all practical purposes, lost in the crunch of gravel under the guard's shifting feet. The round shattered the man's trigger hand, prompting a scream of agony. When the rifle dropped to the ground Pat stepped out of the brush and approached his victim, now on one knee holding his forearm and grimacing as blood dripped a small pool in the gravel. He recognized Pat's silent hand motions and, behind muted cries of pain, he staggered toward the thick brush.

Pat forced the man to the ground and examined his hand. The bullet had found a clean gap between metacarpal bones and blown completely through the palm. He pulled out a cotton handkerchief and wrapped the wound with tape to stop the bleeding. Once he bound the man's mouth, arms, and legs as he had done with the first one, he pulled the khaki ball cap off his captive's head.

He cast a sharp glance toward Building 8. Without any hesitation he hustled across the gravel parking lot to the back door and banged on it with the heel of his closed fist.

Seconds later an eye from inside appeared in the telescopic door viewer. It recognized the cap on the head outside, conveniently now turned away toward the parking lot. The second the doorknob clicked, Pat forced his body into the room with his gun drawn. As hoped he found himself standing face to face with an old man behind a white mustache and a startled expression.

"*Señor* Grainger," the man said. "What . . . why are you here?" His hand relaxed and fell away from the pistol on his belt.

"They took my daughter, Enrique." Pat reached out to touch the stitches on the man's forehead. "I believe she's here. Are you going to tell me what's going on?"

Enrique exhausted a deep breath and his shoulders sagged.

"She is not here. I can promise you that."

Pat's brow furrowed. "I don't believe you." His arm waved toward the room filled with computers and high-tech equipment. "None of this is for the animals. So what is it? Drugs? A processing center? Distribution? What the hell's going on in this building that requires generators and fire protection and food supplies?"

"*Señor*, you do not understand—"

"I came for my daughter. Be my friend or my enemy. Nothing in between."

"I would help if I could but I have my own reasons. I cannot give that up just to help you search for someone that does not exist."

"Whatever it is, Enrique, you're one man against many. You can't fight 'em alone."

"*You* are, *Señor*."

Pat fell silent.

"OK . . . OK, maybe so. But I have resources."

"Where are these resources? Why are they not here to help you?"

"I don't have time to explain. Look, maybe we could improve our odds by making it *two* against many." He straightened up. "With you or without you I'm not leaving until I find her."

"I would be risking my own family."

"Then we both have family that needs our help."

Enrique softened, a sigh of resignation as he looked across the room, burdened under the weight of circumstance. It had been a long, lonely two years. He turned back to Pat.

"There are four more inside. You will have to deal with them."

"Good men? . . . bad? . . . armed? . . .what?"

"Two are women. They are here against their will . . . simple cooks. The two men . . ." He stiffened. "They are devils without souls, no better than the ones who hire them." He nodded toward Pat's pistol. "That is the only thing they understand. They have automatic rifles."

"So, we work together?"

Enrique paused, then lifted the left sleeve of Pat's t-shirt and took a hard look at the Special Forces tattoo. "I hope you are worthy of this."

"Lead the way," Pat said.

Enrique wound his way through the desks and computer equipment to a solid steel door on the side of the room nearest the center of the building. Pat trailed behind him. He cracked the door and stuck his head through, a quick check both ways into a 10-foot wide hallway. On the other side of that hallway Pat could make out another room the same size as the high-tech room where he stood. Fixed glass windows revealed a small commercial kitchen where two women were busy cooking. When Enrique stepped into the hallway it got the women's attention. He shushed them with a hand signal, then waved for Pat to follow him and ducked left into the heart of the long warehouse.

Farther down the hallway they heard voices, two men chattering in Spanish. They turned the corner to find two men slouched over a table playing cards. When the guards saw Pat their chatter stopped. They lurched for the automatic rifles propped against the wall. Two silenced rounds from Pat's Glock dropped them.

"Any more?" Pat asked.

"No."

Pat turned and peered into the murky depths of the warehouse, and it hit him that in the dim light he had completely overlooked the large mass in front of him: a separate building inside a building. The inner enclosure was approximately 50 feet wide and structurally independent from the main warehouse. Other than the space taken up by the tech room and kitchen this structure ran nearly the entire length of the warehouse, approximately 250 feet, with a narrow walkway on both sides. No windows, only gangs of plumbing vent stacks and ductwork for heating, cooling, and ventilation, all punching through a flat metal roof. On the nearest end of the enclosure was a set of steel steps which led to a doorway, four feet off the ground.

"What the hell's this, Enrique?"

The old Mexican pulled out a set of keys and climbed the metal stairway.

Chapter 24

WHILE THE OLD MAN fiddled for the key Pat detected a gentle hum of activity coming from inside the enclosure. As soon as the key slipped into the lock Enrique drew his pistol and peered through the telescopic door viewer, then opened the door and ushered Pat inside.

Spread out before him, filling this chamber that ran the length of the building, was a milling crowd of young women. Some were engaged in animated conversation, all in Spanish; others sprawled languidly on mattresses on the floor, some staring at the ceiling, others at nothing, their eyes empty; a few drifted aimlessly across the concrete floor with no destination. Paper plates and cups and plastic utensils lay scattered among the living with scraps of food spilling onto the concrete.

Their abrupt entrance drew the attention from the girls nearest the door. One by one bodies and heads turned, each face a lifeless canvas, empty of emotion: no smiles, no gritty clenches of anger, no expressions of surprise or confusion. A landscape of lost souls gripped in the overarching grip of hopelessness, some lifeless notion that nothing could change their fate. Without realizing it Pat took a rough head count, mentally assembling girls in groups of ten.

"What's the deal, Enrique? There's 180 – 200 people here. Why are they—"

He halted mid-sentence. He didn't have to finish the question. It was right there in plain sight. His confusion slowly gave way to anger as he explained the obvious out loud to himself.

"I'll be damned," he said under his breath. "They're running a goddamn human trafficking ring out of Fox Hill Farm."

He didn't wait for Enrique to confirm it: two hundred young women, locked in a prison of despair, all hope gone, waiting for their turn to be shipped out with no more regard for their lives than the hogs being raised for slaughter in the other nine warehouses.

Some of the girls turned away with no more than a passing concern for the two men observing them. From their body language they had given up. They'd already acknowledged their destiny was sealed, no expectation for salvation, their future reduced in the next few short weeks to a grim, endless, daily routine of degradation where the men would stand in line like animals at the trough, steal a few precious, brutal minutes from once-promising lives, and then leave to make room for the next.

One girl separated herself from the crowd and walked toward them, hesitant at first. It was apparent that her body and legs had not yet developed. Her face was still that of a child— innocent, pure, perhaps not even a teenager, naive and uncertain of what unspeakable terror was to come. She stopped in front of them and tilted her head to one side as if to ask why, then dropped her chin and turned away. She knew enough. Another victim waiting for her turn in the meat market.

The shock of his discovery finally gave way to Aimee's plaintive voice calling to him from somewhere in the back of his mind and he leaned over the railing and anxiously began examining the girls in greater detail.

"She is not there, *Señor*," Enrique said, anticipating his question. "We have not had any new deliveries since Sunday."

Pat exhaled. He had disappointed himself, this gross miscalculation, his assumption that this would be the spot. *But if not here, then where?*

"Who's running it? The Captain?"

"Does it matter?"

"It might. He kidnapped my daughter."

Enrique winced and turned away, distressed, and leaned against the steel railing.

"What does that mean?" Pat said.

Enrique turned back to Pat and looked for a gentle way to explain. "*El Capitán's* real name is Lambito Suarez. He started as a street thug, a *matón*, and rose in the ranks *rápido* because he was so ruthless. Mutilations and beheadings were his trademark."

Pat felt his stomach turn.

"He gave himself his name *el Capitán*, but he is more like a top *teniente* in the organization, second in command behind the real *jefe*, Joaquin Costilla. Costilla is well known by the authorities—*el Araña*, the spider. A very dangerous man. More dangerous than the Captain. Costilla is the *líder* of *Cartel Independiente de Tlaxcala*. It is very powerful in central Mexico. They have managed to co-exist with many of the others: Los Zetas, Sinaloa, La Familia Michoacana. They thrive because they limit their activity in the drugs that the other cartels prize so much. They deal almost exclusively in trafficking people, mostly for the sex market."

"And Diego?"

"He runs their trafficking business here in North Carolina. There has been talk that he is not as popular lately because of some mistakes he and his men have made. Your capture and escape for one. He also made a mess of the *asesinato* in Kentucky––the murder of the woman."

"Why do you think I'm here? I was there when his men killed her . . . and shot my daughter."

Enrique stared aimlessly out over the girls on the floor as he spoke. "So you are the *gringo* he talked about."

Pat remained focused. "If they didn't bring my daughter here, where would they take her? Maybe they have other farms?"

"No, only this one. They grow pigs as a disguise for the girls. The money is in the sex. You saw my station. Their business, it is *gigante*."

"That day I met you . . . when I killed Alejandro, it looked like Diego and the Captain were not on good terms."

"Maybe not, but the Captain still needs Diego to run the farm and the girls. The cartel will never jeopardize the business over a personal disagreement."

"They talk on a regular basis?"

"Every day."

"Then maybe Diego knows where my daughter is?"

Enrique glanced at Pat. "What are you thinking, *Señor*?"

"You also speak with Diego often?"

"He would never tell me anything. I am a low level employee."

"You could get him here with one phone call."

"*Señor*, even if he knows something about your daughter he will never tell you."

Pat placed his hand on the old man's shoulder. "What about you? You're looking for someone. Who is it?"

Enrique lowered his head. He labored at the thought of reliving the nightmare. He felt his knees give a little as his eyes located a girl in the crowd that reminded him of her. His lips quivered as he struggled to get out the words.

"Two . . . two years ago. My granddaughter, Clio. Back in Pueblo, she always walked home after school. Then one day she didn't. It was three weeks before we found out from that they had taken her. Word on the street." He looked up at Pat, tears filling corners of his eyes. "Two years, *Señor*. She was in high school, not much more than a child. I do not sleep much anymore. My daughter and son-in-law complained to the *policia*. Gave them names they had heard. Their bodies were found in an alley a few days later."

He pulled out a handkerchief and tried to wipe away the pain that was eating him from within. Pat's hand did not leave the old man's shoulder while he went on.

"I thought perhaps if I could be around it, learn how they did it, I might be able to find what happened to her, where they sent her. Through a contact, I used a different name and managed to get this job a year ago. I watch them come and go, once a week, sometimes more. It breaks my heart, many of them like my Clio, and I can do nothing. And still I keep looking, thinking maybe someday I will hear a name, a city, anything that will tell me where she is. But, no."

Pat pulled the man close, a simple embrace between a father and grandfather, before he gently held him back and looked directly into his eyes.

"Maybe Diego knows where my daughter is. Maybe he knows where they took your Clio. Maybe not. What have we got to lose? *Two* against many, Enrique."

"Even if he knows he will tell us nothing."

"I'm not so sure," Pat said. "You asked if I was worthy?" He raised his sleeve and exposed the tattoo. "I earned this. Sometimes in ways I'm not proud of. Make the call."

Chapter 25

ON THE WAY BACK to the tech room Enrique darted into the kitchen and explained the developments to two frightened cooks. At the same time Pat dialed Randy and brought him up to speed on the trafficking ring, the inner chamber in Building 8 filled with girls waiting to be shipped out, the two guards bound and waiting for the police, and the two guards that only needed a coroner.

"Dammit, Pat, get the hell out of there," Randy said. "I can't sit on this any longer. I've got to call the cops."

"I need a couple more hours, that's all. Two hours."

"Do you know how much trouble you're in? And how much shit this is going to bring down on me? I might as well kiss my career as a journalist goodbye."

"I may be close to finding out where Aimee is. Two hours, Randy."

Randy shook his head and looked at his watch. "Two hours, but that's it."

"And I need some information."

"Why does this not surprise me?"

"Enrique told me a lot but I need more."

"Who the hell's Enrique?"

"A friend."

Pat dished out as much as he could remember about

Lambito Suarez, Joaquin Costilla, and *Cartel Independiente de Tlaxcala* in the few seconds he had before Enrique burst out of the kitchen and rushed into the tech room.

"Get what you can and call me back," Pat said. "or better still, send what you find to Enrique's email." He called to Enrique for his email address and relayed it to Randy. "Gotta go."

Randy stared into the blank screen on his cell phone and cursed under his breath. He hit the intercom button.

"Tracy! Get in here."

Enrique dropped into his chair and pondered for a second. He glanced up at Pat, a resigned shake of his head, and pulled out his cell phone. Two rings.

"Diego," he said, his performance Oscar-worthy. "We have problems here. The gringo we captured before . . . Grainger? He's back."

He listened to excited chatter on the other end.

"*Si*, we have him, but you must get over here. You remember the last time. Hurry."

When the line went silent Enrique looked up at Pat. "I hope you know what you are doing, *Señor*."

* * * * *

Eight minutes later Diego barged into the tech room. His anxiety flipped instantly to shock at the sight of Pat's Glock pointed at his head. A glance at Enrique sitting at the console told him enough.

"Are you sure you have chosen wisely, Enrique?" he said, his voice threatening.

"I have waited long enough, Diego," Enrique said. "My granddaughter has lived in hell for two years. It is time."

Pat used the Glock to guide Diego into a chair in the guard's sleeping room and shut the door while Enrique bound the man's arms behind him and his legs together. Pat slid another chair around to face his captive and sat down, leaning forward, arms resting on his thighs.

"So, Diego, did Doris serve *you* biscuits and gravy for your breakfast this morning at Hoagland's? I hear it is very tasty."

Diego's brow furrowed as he tried to place unfamiliar words.

"Never mind," Pat said. "Maybe you will remember something else you said to me once in this very room, something more important. You said my daughter was "expendable." I think that's how you put it."

Diego's eyes widened as he recalled the threats he had made a few days earlier.

"I thought that might ring a bell," Pat said, nodding his head dismissively as he stared off into space. Then his eyes locked onto Diego's.

"You see, your boss, the Captain, has done a bad thing." He waited for Diego to respond.

"I don't know what you mean."

"Let's hope you do, for your sake. Your Captain decided he would get back at me for killing his nephew. I know you weren't fond of the prick but you probably understand, being family and all, that the Captain would take it personally." He paused to let it sink in. "So he kidnapped my daughter."

There it was, out on the table.

"I assure you I know nothing about this kidnapping," Diego stammered. "It is something the Captain did on his own. He would not share his intentions with me."

"Somehow I have trouble believing you. You should understand it is in your best interests to tell me where she is."

"I tell you I know nothing. *El Capitán*, he is crazy sometimes. I am not one of his favorite persons. There is no reason for him to share a personal matter."

Pat sighed and stood up. "To be fair I didn't think you'd tell me right away." He grabbed a towel from the table and laid it on the floor next to him. Then he picked up a gallon jug of clear liquid and set it next to the towel.

Diego began to squirm. His protests came out rapid fire. "No! This is not legal! Your country's president does not allow this."

Pat was calm as he responded to the argument. "Kidnapping young girls is not legal either, my friend. Not those 200 girls in this building and especially not my daughter. Besides," he whispered as he looked around the room, "my president isn't around to ask permission."

"But I tell you," Diego protested, "I do not know where your daughter is. Even if I did, you know this waterboarding does not produce good information. You have been in the wars. You *know* this."

"Water? Who said anything about water?" Pat said as he turned the plastic jug around so Diego could read the label: *Muriatic Acid.* Pat picked up the jug and calmly read the tag lines. "Thirty-one percent, etches concrete, cleans stains off of metal." He was clinical as he continued. "There were several jugs in the building next door. Tsk, tsk, tsk. I guess all that hog blood must leave a lot of stains." He pulled on a pair of rubber gloves and began unscrewing the cap.

Diego's fear escalated to terror and he rocked the chair, a futile attempt to evade what he saw coming. "No! You can't do this! Enrique, stop him. You are not like this man."

Enrique was getting nervous as well. "Senor, this is too much . . . we cannot."

Pat looked up, his voice focused. "Enrique, this man sent your granddaughter to live in hell and didn't blink. Made her a sex slave to hundreds of men, a life she will never forget. Do you want to know where she is or not?"

"But Senor . . . this . . . I don't know."

"I'll tell you what. Let's give our friend here a chance to reconsider."

He took off the plastic gloves and leaned down and secured Diego's legs to the chair with duct tape. Then he untied one of Diego's boots and removed his sock. He placed a bowl of water and a sponge next to his feet and then carefully poured a little of the acid into a beer bottle. A few drops spilled onto the concrete floor, generating a hiss of tiny bubbles that signaled the beginning of the caustic chemical reaction. Diego watched wild-eyed and continued to rock the chair, out of control, unable to move away from the danger. Pat hovered the beer bottle over the foot and glanced at Diego.

"Where is she?"

Diego was apoplectic with fear. "I tell you I do not know. I do not know. Please!"

Pat splashed a few drops onto the bare foot. A torrent of screams erupted from the acid burning through the man's skin. Pat let the man rock for a few seconds before he soaked the sponge and wiped away the acid. He dribbled some water over the wound still stinging from the acid and sat back in the chair across from the captive.

"Is your memory getting any better?"

Diego's breathing was labored. "Grainger, I promise I do not know where she is. *El Capitán* would not tell me something like that. I would tell you if I knew."

Pat shook his head and knelt down again, then picked up the bottle and held it over the still squirming foot.

"C'mon Diego, make it easy on yourself. I can do this all day."

"I don't know! I don't know!" The screams came fast and furious. "I promise you I don't know . . ."

Pat recognized the raw honesty behind the man's full submission.

"Then think, my friend. Where could they have taken her? Is there somewhere else, maybe an office, a house, some other place that belongs to the cartel." He grabbed Diego by the collar and held the bottle within inches of his face. "Think!"

He backed off and poured water on the bare foot and dabbed with the soaked sponge to absorb any residual acid, then dribbled more water. He sat back in the chair to let the tension subside. Diego's head was rocking side to side as the pain slowly ebbed.

"Got any ideas for me?" he said as he wobbled the beer bottle in his hand.

Diego struggled, exhausted from the ordeal. "Maybe . . . I don't know . . . there is a slaughterhouse in Bledsoe not far from here. Perhaps they took her there, I don't know . . . I swear."

"I thought Fox Hill was the Cartel's only property."

"The slaughterhouse belongs to Sunspring. *Muy grande* industrial plant. As big as the town." He tried to catch his breath. "There's an old building in the back they used in the early days before the business became *gigante*. They abandoned it years ago when they upgraded their technology. It's empty but it's dry. The Cartel uses it sometimes to store the drugs they bring across the border."

"Enrique said your Cartel dealt in women, not drugs."

"The drugs, they are a small part but still profitable. Many millions. Like your American theaters. You go for the movie but you still buy the popcorn."

"But why would an international food company take that chance, allowing illegal drugs on their property?"

"They do not even realize that old building is even there. They are too busy with the business of meat. Except one man, a big shot high up in Sunspring. He makes sure Fox Hill remains a supplier of hogs and for that he gets a cut of the trafficking business."

"And now he's in so deep he couldn't stop if he wanted to?"

A nod.

"If you're running girls then you manage the drugs too?"

"*Si.*"

Pat backed away and pulled out his Glock. "Cut him loose, Enrique, we're taking a field trip to Bledsoe."

Chapter 26

ON THE WAY through the tech room Enrique checked his computer. One email from Frankfort, Kentucky. He clicked on the attachments and the laser printer kicked out nearly a dozen pages courtesy of Tracy at the State Journal. Pat scooped them up and the three men angled for Diego's SUV in the parking lot. A quick minute to bind Diego's hands in front of him and Enrique got behind the wheel while Pat slid into the back with his Glock poking Diego's ribs in the passenger seat.

On the road Pat took a quick run through the documents they had just received from Randy. Several were white papers on the more powerful drug cartels in Mexico along with a color map showing their areas of influence. Each page offered a brief history of each cartel, the number of states controlled, the main sources of revenue, and the most sobering statistic: the estimated numbers of murder and torture victims, 85,000 Central American civilians since 2006. A separate bio listed the most recent known kingpins and lieutenants in each organization.

As he continued to skim, a call from Randy lit up his cell phone.

"I'm here with Tracy," Randy said. "You get what we sent?"

"Looking through it now. Hey," he said, picking out one sheet, "what's so important about this little town in Mexico that qualifies it for its own Wikipedia page?"

"Tenancingo," Randy said. "A few miles south of Mexico City in the state of Tlaxcala. You're not going to believe this, buddy. The town has maybe 10,000 residents but the Department of Justice recognizes it as the leading supplier of sex slaves to the United States. I'm talking the whole . . . freaking . . . country. Dates back to the 1970s. DOJ claims as much as 10% of the town's inhabitants are sex traffickers—exploitation, pimping, forced prostitution—kids following in their daddy's footsteps. Generates more than $1 billion a year. That's straight off the DOJ website."

"Jesus."

"Yeah. According to Justice most of the victims are shipped to an unknown location in the US and then transported to New York or some other high-profile cell around the country. This is big business."

"Guess what, at least one unknown location is gonna get known real fast."

"That where you are now?"

"Not any more. I just got a lead on Aimee. Go ahead and call the FBI, send them to Fox Hill. The girls are there. Building 8."

"And where are you heading?"

"Let you know later. Can't take a chance on a show of force yet. Hey, do me a favor?"

"Do the requests ever stop coming?"

"Seriously, dig deep as you can on those two top dogs in the Tlaxcala Cartel. This Captain guy, Lambito Suarez, he has Aimee. I need to know anything you can find. *El Araña* too."

"So what else we looking for? Tracy's already pulled off all the available information from ProQuest, the GAO, all the news wires."

"Hell, I don't know. Personal stuff? Education? Illnesses? Family members maybe? Anything you can dig up."

"You're really not going to tell me where you're going?"

"Not yet. We're on the way."

"By 'we' that means you and Enrique?"

"We picked up one more straggler. Now that you mention it, see if you can find out anything on a teenage girl named Clio Aurenthes. She was kidnapped outside a shopping center in Puebla sometime in 2014. Her parents were murdered a few weeks later."

"Part of Enrique's family?"

"His granddaughter."

"That's a real long shot but we'll take a stab."

"By the way keep your eyes open for a message from Aimee. I got a phone call from the Captain."

"The Captain? Lambito Suarez called you? How the . . .? Were you gonna get around to telling me some time? That seems kind of important."

"I've been a little busy here, Randy. He called to taunt me. I know I pissed him off but before I did he said he was going to have Aimee make a call to the State Journal. If he does, try to record it, maybe see if the police can trace the call."

"Pat, we're a small town newspaper, not the CIA. Anything else you may have forgotten to tell me?"

"Give me a break here, Randy. I'm flying by the seat of my pants and my daughter's life's on the line."

"I know. Be careful."

* * * * *

Delta had no intention of stirring up trouble, especially after the close call a couple hours earlier with his partner. Bravo had nearly lost it. That's why they sent him down this time by himself. Deliver and leave. He watched her still huddled under the blanket as he descended the wooden steps. In some ways he felt sorry for her. She had no idea what her life was going to be like. *It could just as easily be his own sister.* He cringed at the thought.

With his last step off onto the concrete he avoided eye contact and laid the paper plate next to her. A roast beef sandwich. He placed a bottle of water next to it. When he stood up he noticed her watching him out of the corner of her eye and it made him uncomfortable.

"What's going to happen to me?" she said quietly.

He wasn't supposed to engage her. Deliver and leave. But the question threw him off. He stepped back and glanced up the stairs before he answered.

"I don't know."

It was a lie. He did know what would happen to her. They all did. Once they eliminated her father she'd be shipped off to a drop site like all the rest—New York, Chicago, L.A. He even heard them talking that Dallas was a hot spot lately. He didn't know how the system worked and he wasn't sure he wanted to. One thing he did know, it wouldn't take long for the men to start coming. Filthy men. Angry men with a little money and no conscience. He wondered if her handlers would at least give her a few days to acclimate or simply throw her to the wolves?

The first days would be the hardest. A brutal introduction to a world of pain and humiliation he couldn't imagine. He refused to let himself think about it. *She wasn't much younger than his sister.* A living hell for sure. How could a young girl tolerate it? It made his stomach queasy. He left her question unanswered and raced up the stairs to the safe comfort of the kitchen. Out of sight, out of mind. He'd feel better once he took a short walk. The paradox was the light stream of activity buzzing on the road less than a hundred yards away yet back here in the woods, nothing. They were practically invisible.

The sun splashing him in the face helped take his mind off the prisoner in the basement. He watched a butterfly light on the handle of a garden spade and admired the mottled pattern of browns and yellows. Beautiful.

Chapter 27

"HOW MUCH FARTHER?"

Enrique focused on his driving. "A few minutes."

Pat's fractured hope for Aimee made the 30-minute drive from Claxton seem like an eternity. Broad fields of cotton, soybeans, and sweet potatoes had dominated both sides of the quiet two-lane county road for the last two miles. It was when they made the turn onto NC 87 at the Minuteman Food Mart that the landscape took a noticeable change, from crops and the related agricultural equipment to the haphazard pockets of development that marred the roadside, the traditional indicators of low-country government, and the vehicle count immediately jumped. A sprinkling of local traffic jockeyed with refrigerated semi-tractor trucks on the four-lane limited access highway, some lumbering empty on their way to the plant for a new pickup, others leaving with a load of fresh meat bound for wholesale distributors.

"There, through the trees," Enrique finally said, as they rounded a sweeping curve. Over the hood of the SUV Pat glimpsed the first patches of dingy white, a city-sized compound of buildings and support infrastructure a quarter mile ahead on the left. Utility towers, conveying systems, steam and ventilation systems protruded awkwardly above building structures still partially hidden by the line of evergreens on Sunspring Foods' property line. The minute they passed the Plain Truth Holiness Church the enormity of the processing plant took on a new dimension. The farthest piece in the sprawling complex was barely visible in the haze nearly a mile down the road.

"OK," Pat said, prodding Diego in the ribs. "Where's this secret building you're talking about." His anxiety spiked at the thought of Aimee.

Diego flinched from the gun digging in his side. "The main entrance is there on the left," he pointed. "Go past it. Three more delivery entrances down the road for the big trucks."

"Which one?"

"Just keep going. There's a gravel access road at the far end that leads around back to the holding pond. That was the road to the old building years ago, back when they used it for butchering hogs. Now it's just a service road, a catch-all for all the worn out trailers. Nobody uses it much anymore."

"Uh, Senor Grainger?" Enrique said, the tension rising in his voice. Pat caught Enrique's scared eyes in the rear view mirror and turned in his seat to see a patrol car's flashing blue lights gaining on them.

"Shit!" Now was not a good time to be pulled over with a gun in his captive's side and Aimee so close. He glanced back, processing how he would handle the encounter, when the cruiser dodged around them into the left lane, its lights on fire and siren wide open, and sped down the road pushing 80. Pat exhaled and dipped his head.

"Up ahead on the left," Diego finally said without prompting. Enrique eased into the deceleration lane and turned into the service drive. Fifteen hundred feet ahead one person sat languidly inside a lonely guard gate.

"You have clearance?" Pat asked.

"Some guards know me. If not I have a gate pass."

Pat fished Diego's wallet out of his squirming back pocket and located the Sunspring pass tucked behind the driver's license. He switched the gun to his right hand and jabbed it around the car seat into Diego's other side. His words were menacing, even if they were a bluff. "Hide your wrists between your legs. I didn't come this far to get pulled over. I'm gonna find my daughter if I have to kill you and the guard. *Comprende?*"

Diego swallowed.

The guard laid down his magazine and forced himself to lean out the door of the gatehouse, unmotivated and, from all appearances, underpaid. With no interest in confrontation or their purpose he peered into the car and recognized Diego in the passenger seat. A casual pleasantry and he waved them through. Once the SUV cleared the corner of the building they crawled past gravel lots on both sides of the service drive packed with empty tractor trailers that had been parked and abandoned. Space was apparently in short supply since dozens more trailers lined the shoulders of the service road.

The pungent, earthy waft of the sewage treatment facilities gave them advanced warning well before it came into view. Finally, through a thinning grove of trees they caught a glimpse of the vast fenced-in area that Sunspring had set aside for the nightmare of sewage generated by their city-sized meat processing plant: pre-treatment basins, clarifiers, stilling ponds, anaerobic digesters, and more than six acres of brown scum that spread out across a putrid, malodorous lake of raw sewage.

At the fork in the road Diego gestured to the right. They dodged around one trailer that had been parked carelessly in the roadway. For several hundred feet ahead more abandoned trailers lined the drive in a narrow swath that had been cut through the forest years earlier. Finally Diego halted them.

"Here," he said.

The tires of the SUV crunched to a stop. A small gravel entrance drive peeled off to the right. It led to an inconspicuous gray metal farm gate, barely visible from the road, tucked 30 feet back into the edge of mature woods.

"There's nothing there," Pat said.

"You wanted to see," Diego said. "So look."

The SUV pulled off the road and nosed up to the gate. Pat got out and stooped down to inspect the tire tracks. With no recent rainfall it was impossible to tell if they were fresh or not. A few quick steps over to the gate and his eyes traced the drive as it continued 100 feet into the thick woodlands before disappearing around a bend to the right. He checked the chain on the gate. A heavy-duty padlock was fastened on the inside.

Pat drug Diego out of the car and over to the gate. Even with his arms bound together Diego had no trouble digging the ring of keys out of his pocket. When the gate swung open Pat shoved his captive ahead and motioned the SUV in.

Pat confiscated the key ring and forced him back into the passenger seat.

"If she's here what's the safest way in?"

"You are the cowboy, find your own way," Diego said. The defiant enemy was back.

Pat's hand dropped to his belt and unsnapped the sheath. He balanced calm against dramatic when he withdrew the survival knife and raised the eight-inch stainless steel blade within inches of Diego's left eye. The man tried without success to focus on the glistening steel and pulled away until his head was pressed against the headrest and he could retreat no further.

"Don't underestimate me, ol' buddy," Pat said, an intriguing mixture of good-ol-boy and ruthless psychopath. "It's in your best interests to stay a reliable source of information."

He punctuated his statement with raised eyebrows and touched the tip of the razor-sharp blade to Diego's eyelid. He scooped the tiny drop of blood on the blade and let it drip into Diego's lap.

"Now, what's the safest way in?"

Diego's bladder was on the edge of releasing but he held it back and let out a breath.

"A d-door around back, right side of the building, the mechanical room." He tentatively reached for the cluster of keys in Pat's hand and fished around for the right one. "That one . . . I think . . . I'm not sure."

Pat used three wraps of duct tape to bind the man's neck firm against the headrest.

"Stay here," Pat said to Enrique. "and close the gate. We don't want to attract any visitors. If he makes trouble, shoot him."

Pat crept toward the bend in the driveway before ducking into the forest. Twenty feet in he moved to the edge of the foliage to get a better look. There, a couple hundred feet away, the old cinderblock building welcomed them like an ill-tempered uncle. No fanfare, no glitz, just a sad, empty shell, forlorn and abandoned, an outdated slaughterhouse reeking of days gone by, now awkwardly tucked into a tangled clearing in the trees. From the haphazard straggle of scrub and volunteer trees that had encroached on the structure over the years it seemed odd to think that the building and its surroundings had been a player in former days. Mother Nature had taken over and for the last 40 years had worked her slow, steady magic, filling in, month by month, year by year, what had once been parking areas, turnarounds, access drives, outside spaces necessary to accommodate the traffic from trucks hauling in animals for slaughter.

At the right end of the building a three-foot metal door and a pair of metal frame windows suggested what had probably been a small office. On the opposite far left end of the building were two metal rolled-coil garage doors, sized to accommodate the delivery trucks of their day, noticeably too small for the refrigerated trailers that now roamed the four lanes of NC 87 a few hundred feet away. In between was the unobstructed mass of the building, close to two hundred feet in length, full-height cinderblock with horizontal slits of metal windows high near the roof line to allow light inside. It was behind these walls that the bloody and callous business of killing and butchering hogs had gone on for years and then ended when new technology and the runaway business of providing meat to the world dictated the complete and total shift to Sunspring's giant, modernized plant.

Then something else caught his eye. He hadn't seen it at first. Off to the right side of the building a white, late model pickup truck parked under a thicket of lilac.

Chapter 28

PAT DODGED his body through the tangle of forest undergrowth until he reached the lilac. He felt the cool hood of the truck.

His Glock was already out of his holster when he sprinted across a short open space to the end of the old slaughterhouse and flattened himself against the wall. The key that Diego had selected was the correct one. Pat was in the mechanical room in seconds, the murky haze of the windowless space broken only by the fresh streak of daylight sneaking through the open door. A flick of his finger changed his ring tone to vibrate.

Abandoned for years, the stale, lingering scent of mold and asbestos overpowered the room. He took aim on another steel door on the opposite corner and ducked around a congested maze of low-hanging pipes. As he brushed past, his shoulder dislodged a cloud of dust and fibers from the carcinogenic pipe-wrap insulation that had broken loose, dangling from the pipes like Spanish moss. Two ancient boilers—one for building heat, the other labeled 'scalding tank'—blocked his path. When he cracked the door he winced at the grating creak from rusted hinges and stepped into the eerie, vacant silence of a spacious room that occupied the bulk of the building. The line of high windows provided barely enough illumination to pierce the darkness.

Motionless, he listened.

Nothing.

The office and restrooms were thirty feet away to his left. Even careful, measured steps could not avoid the crunch from grit and broken glass underfoot. A quick check of both spaces found nothing.

Anxious, he turned toward the main chamber, his pistol raised, and eased into the gloom. On high alert for voices or movement, he dipped through the shadows, gliding quietly and efficiently from one end of the building to the other, dodging into each room and open space ready to engage. Within three minutes he had cleared the entire building. No signs that Aimee and her kidnappers had even been here.

Diego had it right: the slaughterhouse was a long shot. Still, finding no trace of his daughter made it a bitter disappointment. Maybe Randy was right. Maybe he couldn't find her on his own. He racked the pistol against the side of his head. Not at Fox Hill and not here. *Then where?*

The vibration in his pocket got his attention. A lengthy email from Randy. Despite his dejection Pat overturned an empty bucket and sat down to skim through the message. His mind raced, his attention split between Randy's information and his failure to find Aimee. He scrolled and read, compartmentalizing new information, the data fighting against his growing desperation.

Each email attachment dealt with one of the two leaders in the cartel: personal history, family members, education, arrest records. Medical information was non-existent. Nothing jumped out as useful.

At a loss, Pat rose and stared back across the long expanse of the chamber. The haunting reality of decades-old killing days, they were all there, and one by one he picked out the grisly details he had missed in his sweeping search. He was standing in the middle of the loading dock where thousands of hogs on the hoof had once been delivered by truck and herded into the low-walled concrete chutes directly in front of him. As he took his first tentative steps navigating back across the building a morbid curiosity urged him to follow the animals' final journey to slaughter.

The chutes emptied into individual concrete pens, the killing floor where workers would have picked them off one at a time and stun them before hooking them to the circular conveyor system, the backbone of the slaughterhouse that ran the length of the building. The conveyor and its macabre accessories still hovered like ghosts—the grappling hooks, the brutal chains used to hang each hog by one hind leg and lift them off the floor, moving them down the line, writhing and desperate for an escape which would never come. Then to the next station where another worker would make his callous, fatal jugular cuts. Dried stains still streaked the floor black, marking the path of the conveyor system, a forgotten trail of live hogs bleeding out on the way to the scalding tanks. Despite the unapologetic satisfaction he got from a good ration of bacon, as he walked and listened to the spirits of the past he couldn't help but acknowledge this memorial to an abandoned assembly line of cold slaughter.

The conveyor tracked into a larger open space where carcasses were halved and dropped to steel tables for butchering and separation into individual cuts of meat. Wayward butcher knives spattered with the brown and black of rust and blood still lay abandoned on the tables. When he turned back to survey the operation one last time, he saw it, the table against a back wall of the butchering room, loaded with bounty, its contents covered with clear plastic. He had missed it in the gloom.

He walked over and peeled back the 6-mil sheet of plastic. Heroin or cocaine, he couldn't tell, individual bricks wrapped in kraft paper and tucked a second time into plastic bags. The inventory was stacked a foot high and occupied the width and length of the eight-foot long table. It didn't take an accountant to recognize millions of dollars. Maybe Diego's prescient analogy made sense: *They still buy the popcorn.*

He dialed Enrique and called him in. While he waited in the semi-darkness his curiosity forced him to seek out the electrical panel in the mechanical room. With no expectations he pulled the switch in the main breaker box and a circuit of lights in the butchering room came alive. It should not have been surprising that the cartel had already done its due diligence, troubleshooting the old electrical systems.

As he walked casually toward the table of drugs ready to take a closer look in the fresh light he noticed the oversized safety switch assemblies scattered at intervals along the conveyor line. Without thinking he jabbed at the nearest large green button with the heel of his hand. A conveyor motor somewhere overhead came alive, a low hum at first, then a beleaguered groan as capacitors and rusted windings strained under the surge of its first stream of electricity in years. It surprised him that the fuses in the panel had held. The motor slowly gained momentum, finally shaking off the rust of time and energizing, then engaging the chain drive and propelling the conveyor line forward without any bloody cargo.

His curiosity satisfied, he threw open the front door, flooding the small office with a needed splash of sunlight, and watched the SUV crunching down the entry drive as it dodged around scattered saplings that had taken root in the gravel and pulled to a stop in front of the building. He cut Diego loose and dragged him into the large room and forced him into a musty chair he had retrieved from the office.

"Any more ideas," Pat asked, as the conveyor continued to grind in its steady, pointless circuit.

"I told you it was not likely," Diego said.

"You always meet them here. You must know something."

"I tell you I do not know any other place."

"How about Tenancingo?"

Diego's disinterest suddenly took a turn.

"How do you know about—"

He didn't finish the question. He was watching Pat's hand as it unsnapped the sheath on his knife. Pat moved closer with his hand resting gingerly on the butt of the knife handle. *A quiet threat is the most effective one.*

"They would not take her there," Diego said defensively, his eyes focused on the knife.

"They're using her to get at me," Pat said. "Maybe they took her across the border so I couldn't find her."

"No, they would not."

"Why not?" Pat said as his fingers tapped out a nervous rhythm against the knife handle.

Diego balanced the harsh truth against the consequences if he was the one to deliver it. He looked away, afraid to explain what his captor should have already figured out by now. Finally he turned back, his head bowed, then looked up at Pat.

"Because after they kill you," he said, "they will put her to work like the rest."

Chapter 29

"YOU ARE SURE the girl doesn't know where she is?"

"She's been in the cellar since she woke up," Bravo said.

"Then it is time. You have the little speech I sent you?"

"Yes, but I don't know why you want to take a chance making this call. It's risky."

The Captain reflected on his tension-filled conversation with Pat a few hours earlier. It hadn't gone as planned but he had calmed down now. If anything it reinforced how critical it would be to disarm a formidable adversary. Besides, Patrick Grainger had offered up a clear challenge, one he was not willing to concede.

"I want him on edge," the Captain said. "The more *desesperado* he is the more likely he will make a mistake. His daughter's voice, it will excite him."

"What if she goes off script?"

"What can it hurt? Perhaps a touch of fear will be good. I know this man. He won't play my game unless he is certain she is alive. Do it before the lunch hour is over."

* * * * *

They will put her to work like the rest. The words cut through Pat like tempered steel hot out of a blacksmith's forge. There had to be an answer, something he could latch on to, some clue he had missed. Pat paced as the grind of the conveyor chain continued in the background. *What had he missed?*

Diego was out of information. It was all on Pat now. He pressed his forehead against a block wall, searching for something, anything, banging his head against the stale, painted concrete, trying to jar loose the spark of an idea. Maybe something in the information Randy sent him? But he had gone through it already. *Do it again.*

Pat turned around, his back against the wall, and pulled out his cell phone. One by one he ran through the attachments in Randy's email. It did not surprise him that neither Lambito Suarez—*el Capitán*—nor Joaquin Costilla—*el Araña*—had any record of military service. Their arrest records, however, did take up several pages beginning with petty crimes in their hometowns and escalating almost overnight to robbery, arson, extortion, kidnapping, murder and torture as the stakes climbed. Still nothing in that long list seemed pertinent.

Suarez's family line had been a short and violent one. His brother, Marco, another high-flying climber in the cartel, had risen in the ranks along with the Captain and had been flirting with lieutenant status when his greed made him careless. In a highly publicized raid two years earlier he had been killed in a shootout with the Mexican police in Nuevo Laredo near the border, along with his wife and one son. His other son, Alejandro, away at university at the time of the shootout, had closed the final chapter on Suarez's family lineage this past week when he went up against Pat and lost.

It was the last attachment that made Pat jump away from the wall, rigid with the excitement of discovery. He'd missed it. One bit of personal data that might give the answer he was looking for. He digested this crucial information, this one last hope, then clicked out and called Randy. He ran down a short list.

"Why do you need this?" Randy asked.

"My last shot before I call in the Feds. I promise you nobody will know how I found out. Strictly between you and me."

"I'm not feeling good about this, bud. Am I about to be an accessory to something illegal?"

"I'm down to the nub, Randy."

"Take a breath, Pat. This could go south in a hurry."

"What would you do if it were Julie?" Pat said, playing his hole card. "You've asked me ever since the day I pulled her out of that barn if there was anything you could ever do. Well this is it. Time to even the score, Randy."

A long pause on the other end of the line.

"*If* I can get you this information," Randy said, his voice unsure, "you promise me you'll play it letter of the law?"

"Fire with fire, Randy. I got nothing left."

* * * * *

Bravo pulled the blindfold off and let her eyes adjust to the dim surroundings in the bedroom. "You have any idea where you are?"

She shook her head.

"If you want to get back to Kentucky let's keep it that way. You understand the rules?"

She nodded and glanced around—cheap paneling on the walls, windows with heavy drapes pulled shut, hardwood floors dulled and streaked with age.

"Don't waste your time. We've cleaned the room." He handed her the sheet of paper. "Read this word for word. It'll let your father know that you're alive."

She read the paragraph silently to herself, then waited for him to click on the pocket recorder and hold it up to her mouth. Her voice was shaky as she read the message aloud. Bravo clicked off the recorder.

"Now, would you like to add your own statement?" he asked.

She looked at him, puzzled.

"What . . . like whatever I want to say?"

"Sure. A personal touch. You don't know anything that could give us away. If you try to identify me or anything in this building I'll shut it off. Understand?"

She nodded as he held the recorder to her lips and turned it on. She reached out and cut it off.

"I'm nervous. Give me a minute," she said, as her mind churned. "Can I speak directly to my father?"

"I want you to, but remember I'll edit anything suspicious."

She nodded again and composed herself, looking for the right words. Finally, on her signal he turned on the recorder and she delivered her message. When she was finished he placed the recorder on the table and took her blindfolded back down to the basement and chained her to the post.

Back at the table he dialed the number of the State Journal. He disguised his voice when he announced his message from Aimee Grainger. Once the newspaper's recorder was up and running he played the recorded message into the phone and hung up.

As far as he was concerned the exercise went according to plan. The ad-libbed part of her message sounded a little convoluted, particularly her oddball comment about the ranch, but she was nervous. It gave nothing away. The personal appeal to her father at the end added just the right touch.

* * * * *

The driver's side door to the Ford pickup parked under the lilac thicket was unlocked. Pat rifled through the glove compartment, the door pockets, and behind the sun visors before he finally found the keys in the bottom of the console under a stack of lottery tickets. Sitting idle for a few weeks hadn't hurt the battery. While it idled he tossed Diego's ring of keys to Enrique.

"The FBI is probably taking Building 8 apart by now. We

told them you're innocent. Drop off this piece of shit and tell them everything. The trafficking ring, the cartel, what you were hired to do, even this old slaughterhouse."

"What about you, *Señor* Grainger? Why are you borrowing their truck?"

"Someplace I gotta be."

"Inside I heard you talking to your friend about more information. It is maybe something that will help you find your daughter?"

"Not sure, my friend. It's a chance. Just so you'll know, my friend is trying to run down information on your Clio. Now that the FBI is involved they have enormous resources. This may be your chance to find her."

"You don't really believe that, do you, *Señor*?"

"No guarantees, but yes, I do. If I get lucky I'll come back and help you myself. That's a promise."

Following a brief embrace Pat climbed in the white pickup and disappeared around the bend in the gravel driveway.

A minute later Enrique sat pensively behind the wheel of the SUV weighing the life-changing events that led to this pivotal moment when Diego, still strapped to the headrest, spoke.

"I heard the gringo's fine talk, Enrique, but the FBI will never believe you. The cartel will kill us both. It is time to be smart. We must both disappear." He took a deep breath. "I handle a lot of money for *el Araña*. It is in US banks and I can get to it if we move quickly. I'll give you thirty percent of everything. Your wife will love you for it. You can send for her and start over here in this country."

They sat quietly for a minute, the listless chatter and chirp of the old-growth forest barely audible over the steady drone of tractor trailers churning up and down the four-lane, and Enrique reflected on life.

"Perhaps you are right, Diego," he said as he opened the

door. "It *is* time to be smart."

He walked around to the passenger door and pulled the Glock out of his holster.

"What the . . . OK, OK, we will split 50/50," Diego said as he watched Enrique tear off another short piece of duct tape and open the door.

"Are you crazy, old man? If you turn me over to the Americans you will get nothing. Why would you not—"

His words melted into muffled gibberish behind the strip of tape that Enrique slapped across Diego's mouth. With a pen knife he cut Diego's tape harness loose and motioned the man out of the car, then pulled the ring of keys from his pocket and gave it a confident toss into the air.

"The FBI, they may be interested in my story, Diego. But I'm certain my granddaughter is not interested in your money."

He gave Diego a promising shove toward the slaughterhouse door.

Chapter 30

THE STEADY PULSE of the pickup truck nearly obscured the faint vibrations from the phone in his pocket. At the next exit off I-40 Pat parked on the shoulder of the rural county road and read the email. He typed a brief acknowledgement and was turning the truck around in a driveway when the phone rang.

"Is that what you needed?" Randy said.

"Perfect. Probably wasn't illegal after all, was it?"

"Public record. Look, Pat, I know you're desperate to get her back but you cannot get down on their level."

"This is not as bad as it looks. I have a plan."

"Please tell me nobody's going to die in this plan?"

"Not if I can help it. Have you called the FBI about Fox Hill?"

"Probably already on the way."

"I sent Enrique back to the farm," Pat said. "Tell Phil Damron to pass along to the Feds that he's not involved. He was just looking for his granddaughter."

"I'll tell him."

"He's bringing a bad guy with him. The guy who's been running the trafficking ring in Carolina for the cartel. I'm pretty sure the Feds can get some valuable information out of him."

"The way you said that makes me think you've already tried."

"Don't believe anything you hear from some lowlife that sells girls like just another prime cut of meat."

A distinct pause stapled itself into their conversation. "There's something else," Randy said.

"What?"

"Aimee finally called. A few minutes ago."

"You record it?"

"They *wanted* us to record it. Gave us time to set it up. I'll play it back into the phone."

Pat rolled up the window and plugged his open ear with one finger. "Go."

Her voice wavered a little at the beginning.

"My name is Aimee Grainger. April 22, 2016, 12:45 p.m. I'm being held in a secure location by people I cannot identify. I do not know where I am being held. I have been given food and water. I have not been harmed. The purpose of this call is to inform my family that I am alive and well."

A distinct click marked a stop and start in the recording.

"Daddy, I don't know none of these people and I don't know the town and ranch where they are keeping me, but they have treated me pretty good so far. I want to come home, Daddy."

Randy got back on the phone.

"Well?" Randy asked.

"It's two parts," Pat said. "The first half she's obviously reading from a script. The second half they let her ad-lib, probably to make it personal for me."

"You make anything out of it?" Randy said.

"It wasn't normal Aimee. She was stronger during the second half, almost like she was trying to tell me something. Not just that plea for help, but something. And she was using bad grammar on purpose. 'I don't know *none* of these people?' And 'treating her pretty *good?*' And what's with that 'town and ranch' part?"

"Oh, crap," Randy said. "Maybe . . ."

"Maybe what?"

Randy played the recording again. He'd missed it the first time, but now it made sense.

"There's a local paint manufacturing plant in Lexington—Town and Ranch. Pat, Aimee's not in North Carolina. She's still somewhere in Kentucky."

"Call Phil Damron, give him the recording. The haystack for my needle just got a little smaller."

Chapter 31

THE UPS DRIVER'S itinerary was routine for a Saturday: left off W. Pettigrew Street onto Erwin Road, a short burst past Sam's Quick Stop and under Durham Parkway, then cruise into the heart of Central Campus. Traffic was light so none of the occasional wise-guy taunts like "Hey Brown" or "nice legs." Too many important things in the world to worry about without mixing it up with college-educated dreamers who would soon be unemployed or, in a fitting turn of irony, considering an entry level job with UPS.

As always his handheld Diad device spit out perfect directions. He'd blow on past Oregon and Alexander and hang a left on Anderson. Even if their screen delivery system wasn't as personal and soothing as that GPS lady living on the dash of his car at home it was efficient and never wrong. She was in her early thirties, he guessed, maybe more, and her voice wasn't that sexy but then neither was his handheld. As soon as he crossed the intersection at Yearby the screen displayed a final command and he turned into the parking lot and searched out a spot to park. They weren't supposed to use up double spaces but with such a large van if he stopped in the aisle it would block someone in. He decided to grab two empty spaces at the end and left the engine running.

He usually didn't lock up while he was out of the truck but since this was a college campus, leaving it open seemed risky. He reached over to slide the passenger door shut and locked it. He read the ticket information on his handheld, picked up the package on the floor beside him, then stepped out and locked the driver door behind. A quick visual survey across the grassy courtyard and he found the building number he was looking for.

As he navigated down the sidewalk toward the front door with the package under his arm he thought it unusual that a venerable institution like Duke would house nationally recognized sororities in buildings that resembled decades-old student dormitories rather than the grand, multiple-columned plantation homes he pictured in his mind. Maybe that explained the large signs announcing the Central Campus Overhaul Project scheduled to begin in the summer. None of that mattered as long as he had the right address today. He entered the unimposing front entrance, passing beneath oversized Greek letters announcing Chi Omega in brushed brass.

The tile foyer was nearly empty other than one young lady checking her mailbox. In the open gathering room beyond, girls lounged on couches, a few watching a golf tournament on a wall-mounted flat screen, others engaged in conversation, most of them staring at their cell phones or typing messages. The single sorority member at the mailbox looked up from her loose stack of mail and walked over.

"Got a package for Teresa Sandoval," the driver said, as he read the screen on his handheld over the top of his glasses.

"I'll take it for her" she said, holding out her hand.

"I need her signature."

"Oh . . . right." She glanced as her watch. "Uh . . . I'm not sure if Teresa's here. She has soccer practice on Saturday. Can't I sign for her?"

He checked the screen again. "Must be something important. The delivery ticket requires a signature from the recipient. If she's not here I'll have to come back."

"OK, hold on a minute," she said as she bounced away.

She drifted through the gathering room with a couple of questions, then glanced back at the driver with her index finger raised, mouthed a few words he couldn't make out, and disappeared up the stairs. A minute later an attractive young lady appeared on the landing, her creamy bronze skin and shoulder-length black hair a dead giveaway, and with a few athletic strides that telegraphed her soccer background, bounded into the foyer.

"I'm Teresa."

"Package for you," he said holding up the corrugated cardboard box with his free hand, "but I need an ID. It's marked 'personal'." He glanced at the screen again. "It's from . . ." he stumbled through a labored attempt at pronouncing it. ". . . Jo-a-kwinn Cos-tilla?"

She laughed at his mangled pronunciation and her eyes lit up with excitement. "Joaquin Costilla," she said, her pure Mexican accent throwing an exaggerated, almost theatrical emphasis onto the name. "He's my dad. Can I just sign?"

He pulled the package back. "ID."

Her eyebrows crinkled, a faked pout, and she bounded away and up the stairs. In less than a minute she was back standing in front of him with her wallet. She held her driver's license up for him to read.

"Thanks," he said.

He scanned the barcode on the package and offered the handheld and stylus for her signature. He handed her the package and pivoted toward the door. He was ten feet down the sidewalk when he heard her calling to him as she was running out. When she caught up to him she was holding out the box.

"This isn't my package," she said, reading the address. "It's for someone named Barker, on Marchmont Drive."

His eyebrows furrowed as he took the package and read the label, then tapped the keyboard on his handheld and compared the information on the screen and the label.

"I must have . . . I guess I picked up the wrong package. It's in the truck. Come on, it won't take a second."

As they walked toward the brown van he shook his head. "I'm really sorry."

"Don't worry about it," she said, excited. The thought of receiving a rare package from her father made the inconvenience of the mix-up seem trivial.

He smiled as he unlocked the passenger side door of the van, then stepped up into the front compartment and slid open the door to the rear package area. A half minute later he popped back out with a discouraged frown and double-checked the screen on the handheld again.

"It says here it's for Teresa Sandoval. Fragile. Were you expecting it?"

"Fragile? No," she said, uneasy. The idea of something breakable shipped all the way from Mexico and rolling around in the back of a UPS truck was unsettling. "You can't find it?"

"Not yet." He laughed, a quick glance out the front windshield. "Obviously I'm not that good with Spanish names. You think you'd recognize it?"

"I hope it didn't get broken," she said as she climbed the steps and turned toward the package area. The sight of a man on the floor in his underwear, blindfolded, his legs and arms bound and a gag taped cross his mouth, made her freeze just long enough for the driver to clasp the rag over her mouth and drag her back into the depths of the van. He held her, writhing in a desperate, reflexive attempt to escape until the chloroform worked its magic. He laid her gently in the floor of the van next to the real driver now struggling to free himself.

"Don't waste your time," the man said. The bound driver laid his head back on the floor.

Pat Grainger took off his Dollar Tree glasses and the fake mustache he found at the costume store and tossed them aside. Once the doors were closed and locked he backed out of the double parking spaces and turned onto Anderson Street, heading for the nearly deserted parking lot six minutes away where the Ford pickup truck was waiting.

Chapter 32

THE CALL went straight to the Kentucky State Police detective's desk.

"Phil, it's Randy. Did the FBI make it to Fox Hill?"

"It's only been a couple hours. They don't exactly live-stream every move to me."

"No, but I fed you dynamite information which you passed on to the Feds, so I know they're at least keeping you in the loop, as a professional courtesy."

He heard Damron shifting in his chair.

"You know I can't talk to the newspaper about an ongoing investigation."

"C'mon, Phil, they wouldn't have an investigation if Pat hadn't handed it to you. Besides, there's something I need to talk to you about."

"Like what?"

"You first. Fill me in. It's not for print, I'd just like to know."

Detective Phil Damron settled back in his chair and weighed working relationships against protocol. "Off the record . . . the agent in charge emailed me a few minutes ago," he said finally. "The Carolina Field Office mobilized a half dozen agents to the site. That's the best they could do on short notice but more's on the way. They called in help from the local sheriff, and a few SBI agents are en route."

And the girls?"

"Like you said. A couple hundred immigrant girls. This is a huge bust. By this time tomorrow they'll have Immigration and Customs involved, Homeland Security, DOJ, who knows who else."

"There'll be another man coming in, a farm employee named Enrique. He's not part of the ring. The cartel trafficked his granddaughter and he's been looking for her. He's bringing in the man that ran the whole operation in North Carolina for the cartel."

"You mean he and Grainger are bringing him in."

"No, just him."

"My contact agent didn't mention him."

Randy frowned. "Guess he hasn't made it back yet."

"Now that's it over we need to talk to your buddy, Grainger. You know where he is?"

Randy debated how much of a lie to tell. From the information he just forwarded to Pat, he could make an educated guess, but with 'absolute certainty'? Not really. It wasn't over, not by a long shot.

"No."

"Look," Damron said, "we all know Grainger wanted to get back at whoever shot his daughter at the shopping center, I get it, but we've got the bad guys now. He can come in and help us fill in the details."

"Actually, Phil, that's the other thing I need to talk to you about."

Phil Damron released a groan. "Why do I get a bad feeling here?"

Randy squared himself in his office chair and braced for the storm.

"His daughter, Aimee, she went home from the hospital two days ago."

"That's your new information?"

Randy took a deep breath. "Aimee Grainger was taken out of her home yesterday morning."

"Taken? Meaning what?"

"Like in kidnapped. By the cartel."

"Are you *freaking* kidding me?" Damron screamed into the phone. "Somebody kidnapped the man's daughter and you're just now getting around to letting me know? That's been, what, 24 hours? Hell, longer than that. What the hell were you thinking?"

"He made me promise I'd wait."

"For what? For them to kill her? To mail her head in a box?" He was fuming now. "How do you even know it was the cartel?"

"A top lieutenant in the cartel, a man named Lambito Suarez, called Pat."

"How could Grainger know it was him?"

"We don't have time to split hairs. Trust me, it was him."

"Jesus, Randy. These cartels are nothing to play around with. Grainger may be a bad ass but this ain't the wild west. He can't just go hunting bad guys like rabbits."

"They left a kidnap note. Promised to kill her if he went to the police."

"They all say that. Once we get plugged in it doesn't mean we let *them* know it. We actually have a few professionals in our employ that do this for a fucking living, Randy."

"I know you're pissed, but Pat made me promise I'd wait. He just turned me loose this morning to call you about those girls."

"Yeah, and in the meantime, where's his daughter? Grainger's out there somewhere trying to find her on his own, isn't he? Look, I can read between the lines. We have rules to follow. He doesn't. I haven't forgotten this man was on a secret assassination squad back in the first Gulf War. They didn't have any rules. Hell, Grainger still doesn't have any rules."

"He's getting better, but he does make me nervous."

"Nervous? I'd be shittin' in my goddamned pants if I were you, especially if you have any first-hand knowledge of where he is or what he's doing."

Randy thought back to the barn in rural Georgia last year, the day Pat left the rules behind and rescued Julie from a living nightmare. When Pat brought their daughter back to him and Karen, when things looked hopeless, Randy knew then it was a debt he could never repay. It'd be a fine line he'd have to walk over the next few days and weeks, now that Pat had charged headlong into a pissing contest with an international human trafficking cartel. But with Aimee's life on the line, like Julie's was that summer day, he saw no other way than to drive on and pray for divine intervention. That or the unrelenting determination of a father who had no boundaries.

"There's more," Randy finally said.

Damron sighed. "There's more, he says."

"We got a phone call. From Aimee."

"Who's 'we'?"

"It came in to the State Journal a little after lunch. They gave us time to record it. They're holding her somewhere in Kentucky, Phil. Don't ask me how we know. When you hear the recording you'll understand."

"Send me a copy. I have to put out a BOLO on Patrick Grainger in Kentucky and North Carolina, who knows where else. Let's just hope it's not too late."

Chapter 33

THE BROWN BLENDED IN, inconspicuous for all practical purposes, just one more UPS delivery truck lumbering through an unwary neighborhood of duplexes and low-rise apartments. Once it left the Durham Freeway at the Blackwell Street overpass it caught the sweeping boulevard between the Lofts at Southside and the St. Mark Zion Church and turned into the first entrance at the half-empty shopping center, a dingy, fading, last-ditch holdout in the war on neighborhood blight.

He ignored the crude, oversized mural painted across the side of Food World and took the van down the rear service drive past loading docks and open dumpsters and turned into the secluded corner lot that separated Food World from Family Dollar. The dozen parking spaces there were empty with the exception of one lonely white Ford pickup.

Pat Grainger stepped down onto the blacktop and scanned the area. Windowless block walls framed two sides of the small service lot while spotty tree lines outlined the other two, screening it from the empty church grounds and the Durham Freeway. All clear, no reason to delay.

He unlocked the passenger side door of the pickup truck and

left it open while he retrieved the girl, still unconscious on the floor of the van's package compartment. He carried her over to the truck and deposited her limp body in the seat.

Back in the van he changed into his jeans and t-shirt and covered his face with his navy blue bandana. A little anonymity seemed prudent. He raised the real driver up into a sitting position and pulled down the blindfold.

"You've been very patient—he reached for the name tag on the UPS shirt's breast pocket—Barry. Don't be too hard on yourself. I'm a professional. You really didn't have a chance."

Barry shrugged silently behind the gag. Arguing seemed pointless.

"Once I'm clear of Durham I'll call one of your distribution centers." He glanced at the colorful stripes on the man's boxers. "It might be a little embarrassing when they pick you up but I'll let them know you were overmatched, so don't take it personal."

Barry nodded, grateful for the encouragement.

Pat unscrewed a bottle of water and set it on the floor of the van. "I can't untie your hands, but you'll figure something out, necessity being the mother of invention and all that crap." He started to push up but a thought stopped him. "You have any kids, Barry?"

Considering his circumstance Barry found the question odd, maybe a little threatening, but with his options limited he decided to go along. He nodded yes.

"I realize your participation today was involuntary but for whatever it's worth your contribution to this little exercise could help me shut down a major human trafficking ring. It's a nasty business, Barry, nasty people. Read up on it."

Barry's puzzled response was apparent behind the gag.

"I'll crack the window and leave the keys on top of the front tire, passenger side." Pat retrieved a packing blanket from the topmost shelf and folded it into a makeshift pillow and laid it on the floor. "Take a nap, Barry, it may be a few hours. If it's any consolation I'll tell them you were instrumental in keeping this from blowing up into a public relations nightmare. Anything else before I go?"

Barry shook his head.

Once Pat locked the van he stripped the bandana away and piled into the Ford pickup. He taped the unconscious girl's hands and legs, and placed a strip across her mouth, then fashioned a makeshift nest in the passenger seat with a second UPS packing blanket. Within minutes he was back on Durham Freeway on the way to Kentucky.

* * * * *

The petite brunette couldn't tell if it was an outright flirt or if he was just being polite. She returned his toothy smile, just in case, and scurried to the first landing and called up the stairs. "Tell Teresa that Brandon is here."

She glanced back at the handsome Lambda Phi standing in the foyer in his button-down pinpoint oxford and khakis and offered another playful glance, one he couldn't help but notice despite his lukewarm efforts to downplay it, and rushed up the stairs to deliver the message.

Twenty minutes later Brandon was back in his car, wondering how she could have forgotten, while a puzzled clique of sorority sisters went through the half-hearted motions of a search party—calls to her cell phone, checking her calendar book, text messages to friends that might have known. There had to be a reasonable explanation, they felt sure. Still they laughed about how they would milk it for all it was worth. Meanwhile, exchanging phone numbers with Brandon had given the brunette credibility as a good point of contact and if things somehow didn't work out with Teresa, bruised feelings and all, who knows what might come of it. Spoils of war, even among Mu Kappas.

Two hours later, when all reasonable attempts to find her

had been exhausted, they made the first tentative call to the police. Even then they might not have placed that call if the girl at the mailbox had not remembered the UPS driver.

It wouldn't be until the next morning, Sunday, that the Durham police would piece together the unlikely connection between the UPS stolen van report, the missing Chi Omega, and the be-on-the-lookout bulletin issued by the Kentucky State Police two days earlier. Nothing in the BOLO had made any mention of a late model Ford pickup truck making an anxious trip up I-40 on its way from Claxton.

* * * * *

"I'm on the way home," Pat said

"I've got the Kentucky State Police on my ass. You happy?"

"My ol' buddy Phil Damron?" Pat said.

"You should see the huge bite he took out of my ass when I told him that Aimee had been kidnapped."

"TMI, Randy. He'll get over it. I bet he did wonder why you waited."

"He knows why. He's no dummy. You're playing loose with the law. It's going to catch up with you, Pat . . . and me too. Where the hell are you?"

"What you don't know can't hurt you, OK?"

"Damron's got cops in Kentucky and North Carolina looking for you."

"Of course he does. They're looking for a man on a motorcycle."

"And . . .?"

"I'm not a man on a motorcycle."

"Great, so you found another vehicle. You want to tell me what you're doing?"

"Let's just say I needed a way to transport more than one person."

Randy hesitated long enough for the pieces to slide into

place, to come to grips with why the specific information on Joaquin Costilla's immediate family was so important.

"Pat, please tell me you haven't done what I think you've done," Randy said, nervous anticipation hanging on each word.

"Like I said, what you don't know won't hurt you. In a court of law you know nothing."

"Jesus Christ, Pat."

Randy fell back in his chair and swallowed this latest revelation and the implications it could have. Kidnapping was a felony. It wouldn't take a thousand-dollar-an-hour attorney to make the connection. Whether or not it was justified in the court of public opinion didn't mean a thing. He felt a slight shiver at this disturbing turn of events. Yet the fact remained: Aimee was being held by a Mexican cartel kingpin in some unknown location, likely in Kentucky, and her life was in jeopardy. He blew out a breath as his career, his family, his whole life whizzed by, waiting for him to make the right decision. Pat's one-man show wasn't one man any longer. Randy heard the tinny rasp of Pat's voice on the phone in his lap. It brought him out of it and in a haze of renewed conviction he returned the phone to his ear.

"So what's the plan?"

Chapter 34

A FEW MINUTES after I-85 merged into I-40 Pat noted the girl stirring in the passenger seat. A glance at the gas gauge showed the needle dipping below a quarter tank. He couldn't take a chance on her drawing attention. Steering with his legs, he slowed down and dabbled more chloroform onto the cotton rag and covered her nose again until the twitching legs went still.

The Graham-Pittsboro exit at Burlington looked the most promising. No motel chains, no shopping centers, no traffic jams. The Exxon station immediately off the exit ramp was nearly empty. He pulled to the pump the farthest from the door and set the nozzle on automatic fill before walking around to the other side of the truck. As he blocked the half-open passenger door with his body and adjusted his sleeping cargo he saw the locket dangling from her neck. The clasp unhooked easily. Inside the locket were pictures of an adult male in the right half, a woman in the left. Apparently even a murderous cartel leader and his wife could be loved by a daughter. The inscription engraved on the back brought a wistful smile. He dropped the locket into the cup holder and leaned back against the truck until the pump nozzle clicked off.

Back on the road, he waited until he had escaped the charge

of late afternoon traffic at Winston-Salem before he made the call.

"What is it now, Diego?" the Captain said.

"Well, if it isn't my old friend," Pat responded. "I bet you weren't expecting *me*."

The lengthy pause on the other end of the line was palpable. "Grainger?"

"*Si, si, señor*." He made no attempt to hide his sarcasm.

Within seconds two adversaries were vying for position, sizing each other up, a dangerous game on the fly with no rules and an ending neither could predict.

"You have Diego's phone," the Captain said. "I assume he has met an untimely end?"

"I'm afraid your boy is out of commission for good."

"He has made many mistakes lately. This does not surprise me."

"Bet you're wondering why I'm giving you a shout on a Saturday afternoon."

"You do surprise me. I assume you have listened to your daughter's phone call by now?"

"I have. Thank you for letting me know she's still alive."

"I thought it might touch you as a father."

"You also thought it might be a good way to get me out in the open."

"Possibly," the Captain said. "I knew you would not give up without a fight. So, here we are."

"It's too bad," Pat said, "you went to so much trouble on account of your arrogant nephew. He's not worth all this, you know."

"He had his faults, but still he was family. And now that we have your daughter I'm sure you understand. Family is everything."

"I do understand. I wonder if *el Araña* feels the same way?"

A slight pause. "I see you have been doing homework. You have learned things about *el Araña*, yes?"

"About you too, Cap'n. By the way, now that we're getting to be such good friends, can I get rid of all the Captain bullshit and just call you Lambito?"

"You should show some respect, Grainger," he said, his contempt obvious. "Do you not worry with your daughter in such a dangerous position?"

"Actually it's you who should be worried. I know more about your boss than you think."

"I doubt that, but it does not matter. This is between you and me. He does not even know we are playing this game."

"He will when you tell him how much I've learned about *his* daughter."

Lambito Suarez squirmed in his chair and pushed his drink back as he tried to get a handle on this new strategy and its threatening implications. This was not part of his script.

"You know nothing of his family."

"I know his daughter, Teresa's a proud Dukie. Go Blue Devils."

"Even if you have found these things," he sputtered, "it means nothing. You are playing a dangerous game, Grainger. I could have your daughter killed with a phone call."

"That's why we're in this pissing contest, Lambito. This is the only chance I have to level the playing field."

"You waste your time, these threats. One call and Teresa is safe."

"Too late," Pat said with a casual lilt in his voice.

"You could not . . . there is no way . . ."

"I'm looking at her as we speak, Lambito. She's sleeping now. A beautiful young lady."

"*Lo que la cogida!*" Suarez held the phone speaker against his belly to muffle his voice and screamed a command to the maid in the next room. "Marcela! Call Horatio, have him contact Teresa in Carolina *inmediatamente*! Send one of the local bodyguards."

Marcela hesitated, the words incomprehensible, the orders clear. She wasted no time, on her cell phone in seconds, an excited conversation in Spanish, arms flying in animated gestures, before she ended the call and threw a concerned look back at Suarez.

Pat heard heavy breathing when Suarez came back on the phone. "You're wasting your time, Lambito," he said, calmly. "The girls at Chi-O are probably already looking for her. Just check with the police. I'm sure they've gotten the call by now."

"Do you have any idea what you are doing, Grainger? Are you trying to kill your daughter?"

"I'm hoping you're concerned enough about your own hide that you won't do that."

"It is not me in danger. It is your daughter that—"

"When I notify *Araña* what has happened, that you've put *his* daughter's life in danger because of your personal vendetta against me, let's just say I'd hate to be there for that conversation."

"There is no way you can contact him. Only a very few—"

"I found you, didn't I?" Do you really think I'd let Diego off the hook until I'd gotten every email and phone number out of him."

Suarez was growing more agitated by the minute, his responses abrupt, defensive. "His only contact is through me. He would know nothing about *el Araña*."

Pat had carried the ball this far with facts, a few plausible details, snippets that filled in gaps of disbelief, even a real-life kidnapping to back it all up. Now he was out of facts and out of time. He had no choice now but to dive headfirst into deception and pray he could convince his opponent he wasn't out of ammunition. *Winning the mind games.*

"You remember Enrique, don't you?"

Pat waited while the pause lingered on the other end of the line.

"A common name," Suarez finally said. "It means nothing to me."

"It should. This particular Enrique manages your security system at Fox Hill Farm. Ring a bell?"

"He can communicate only with me."

"Ah, Lambito. You underestimate so many people. Your security at the farm is tied into your entire communication system. It's sophisticated, I'll give you that, but with a year to play around with it and with angry young family members back home who are savvy in ways that old warriors like you and I could never understand . . . finding a back door was not that difficult. Revenge is a powerful thing, Lambito, you of all people should know that. Once we got Diego's passwords, which were not hard to acquire—that was my job actually—do you really think hacking contact information for *Araña* was so hard. Personally I have trouble sometimes with my own email. But Enrique and his extended family . . .?"

"You bluff, Grainger."

Pat laid the phone on the seat and picked the locket out of the cup holder. With one eye on the road he read the engraved inscription into the phone.

"*Dios y la familia.* It's on the back of Teresa's locket. You probably ought to pass that along to *Araña* before I do. He'll recognize it. I don't think that's something you want to keep from him."

He waited a few beats for Suarez to process his next move, then offered his own suggestion.

"You read my file, Lambito. For Teresa's sake you better convince *Araña* that a trade is in his best interests. And if anything happens to my daughter . . . I'm coming for *you.*"

Chapter 35

RANDY LAID THE RECEIVER in the cradle. This latest report from Damron was not what he expected. A day after Pat's promise, Enrique still hadn't made it back to Fox Hill. It wasn't so much his value as a source of information as it was the priceless cargo in his custody. The FBI, along with a swelling cadre of support personnel, still had its hands full at the command post processing 200 immigrant girls, although the appearance of Immigration and Customs Saturday morning had smoothed the process. As the sweep continued over the last 24 hours, random pieces of the cell had fallen into the net— perimeter guards, cooks, undocumented workers showing up for feed duty, personnel discovered at the downtown office. But the Feds were getting anxious to lock down the man who directed the cartel's American operations, a key player with a trove of information that could do serious damage to the cartel.

Randy placed a hurried call to Pat but the line was busy. He had no way to anticipate the tense exchange of threats and promises ongoing between enemies two thousand miles apart. Four busy signals later he finally connected.

"Your man Enrique still hasn't made it back," Randy said. "Something happened, either he cut a deal with his prisoner or the cartel got to him. The Feds are getting antsy."

"I'll call you back."

Enrique finally picked up on the fifth ring.

"*Señor*," he said, a hopeful ring in his voice. "Did you find good news about your daughter?"

"Maybe. I'm more interested in you. Are you OK?"

"*Sí*."

"The FBI's waiting for you. What's going on?"

"I decided not to go back."

"I know that. You can't be afraid, Enrique. I told them you weren't involved in the trafficking. They can help you find your granddaughter."

"Maybe yes, maybe no."

"Enrique, where's Diego?"

"In a safe place."

A curious answer, one that forced Pat to briefly re-visit the picture in his rear view mirror yesterday when he pulled out on the gravel drive at the slaughterhouse. Enrique was standing stoically next to the SUV, Diego bound in the passenger seat, a promising end to a grandfather's unforgiving search, and with the FBI's assistance, the beginning of a new one. And hopefully a reunion if it wasn't too late. But something had changed after he turned the corner.

"You didn't take him back to the farm."

"No, *Señor*."

"What'd you do with him, Enrique?"

His answer was calm, unconcerned. "It was time to find out where my Clio was."

"Even if he knew where they took her, I don't think he'd tell you."

"You have been a good friend, *Señor* Grainger. I will not forget that. I have watched you, learned from you. It is sometimes difficult for an old man, learning new things."

"What've you done?"

"Only what I had to."

"Enrique?"

There was no anxiety, no reluctance in his explanation, more a simple recount of events from one friend to another.

"Diego was very helpful. He knew more than he let us think. You already know this but these people, they think of the girls the same as the pigs. To them they are not humans, they are things to be bought and sold."

He was on a roll, now, anxious to share his discovery with a trusted ally, especially one he knew would understand.

"The week Clio disappeared? I remember it like yesterday. It is remarkable, *Señor*, this business of theirs, how they kept such good records, the local *proxenatas* in Tenancingo. They find handsome young men to pose as salesmen with nice clothes and fancy cars to lure the girls to their security houses. '*Calcuilchil*' they call them . . . 'houses of ass'. They rape them, beat them. Sometimes the mothers of these men would feed the girls, teach them how to give in."

"Diego told you all this?"

"Eventually."

"Where is he, Enrique?"

"They would round up small groups of girls in the backs of trucks and send them from Tenancingo and other towns around Tlaxcala to the border, and from there to different stopping points in the States, and finally to Claxton. Once they gathered enough girls to make one large delivery Diego would ship then off in FedEx vans to . . ." he caught his breath as he tried to get the rest of the story out. ". . . work houses." He took a minute to gather himself, his breathing labored, before he continued. "The girls, they were pieces of meat, shipped to market."

"Enrique . . ."

"No, *Señor*, listen. You will be proud of me when you hear."

"Is Diego alive?"

He ignored the question, his mind locked into his narrative. He had done a lot of homework over the last year and now with the help of his new friend from Kentucky, he was closer to finding his granddaughter.

"It was smart for me to take my laptop when we left the farm. With Diego's passwords, I was able to find the shipping order for the girls that were at the farm when Clio disappeared. All girls that month went to New York City."

"That's a big place, Enrique. The FBI knows their way around. They will be able to use that information to . . ."

"I am already on the way, *Señor* Grainger. I know the neighborhood where they sent her, an old hotel in Queens. It is a local business, much like the way they do it with your McDonald's. What do they call it?"

"Franchise," Pat said, the word bitter on his tongue.

"That is the word Diego used. I know the 'franchise' where they sent my Clio. And now I know the man who runs it."

Pat was squirming in the seat of the truck. His friend was on a fool's mission, a dangerous one blinded by unconditional love for his granddaughter and his first legitimate chance in two years to rescue her from hell.

"Enrique, do you trust me?"

"Of course. It is only with your help that I would have this opportunity. Clio would not have had a future. And now when I find her she will."

"Enrique, listen very carefully. The men that run these houses in New York, they don't work alone. They are gangs. Very dangerous. Even I would not try to get into one of those houses without the law to back me up."

"It did not stop you at the farm."

"That was different. I had no choice."

"How is it different? You were looking for someone. I am

looking for someone. This is even better because I know she is there."

"Maybe, maybe not, but you haven't been trained in these things. They will kill you. More important, it will let them know the house is no longer safe and they'll move Clio. Then how will the FBI find her?"

"If I know where she is I cannot leave her there, *Señor*."

"Then let me send the FBI to help you."

"Your FBI, they will maybe not be on my side now. Perhaps *you* can come help me? Do you remember what you said back at the farm? Two against many?"

Pat was having difficulty talking sense into a man driven off the rails of common sense by his thirst for revenge. It sounded too familiar. He shook his head as he dispensed advice he had not been able to take himself. Maybe letting his friend in on his plan would buy some time.

"Enrique, I'll come and help you. I promise you. But not yet. I'm still trying to find my daughter."

"You see, it is impossible to wait."

Pat debated how much to share, how deep to involve him in the details.

"Enrique, I'm on the way to meet *el Araña*."

"*Señor!* But how could you do this? Why would this man agree to meet with you?"

"He hasn't yet, but I have something he values."

"This man loves only money."

"I have his daughter."

Pat heard the grind of road noise growing louder while the SUV slowed down somewhere on the road to New York. The slight thump of a window rolling up and a fresh quiet invaded the other end of the line.

"*Señor*, what are you doing?"

"Like you, what I have to. I'm going to trade his daughter

for mine. If this works then I'll come help you find Clio."

He could almost hear the wheels turning in the old man's head.

"I will find the house," Enrique finally said. "And I will wait, but not long."

"I'll hurry, I promise. Now where is Diego?"

"I could not bring him with me, *Señor*, so I left him where he belongs, in the slaughterhouse."

The connection ended.

Chapter 36

LAMBITO SUAREZ paced under his covered veranda, the late afternoon sun bouncing off stucco the color of brushed suede, when the tires of a black Mercedes crunched to a stop in the gravel driveway. A swarthy driver got out of one side and the *líder* of *Cartel Independiente de Tlaxcala*, his hair still wet from a late afternoon swim, stormed out of the other. Both strode quickly across the lawn and through the deepening shade of the loggia.

"What is this business about my daughter that is so important it could not wait?" *Araña* said. His scowl was a perfect fit for his leathery complexion and the deep lines that decades of violence had stamped into his face. He settled onto the upholstered divan across the large glass table from Suarez.

His bodyguard quietly drifted off to an inconspicuous spot next to the bar, physically and emotionally detached from the conversation. The guard's apparent lack of empathy was deceiving. Even though these meetings never involved him he always paid attention in case things took a wrong turn.

Suarez had been struggling over the past half hour with how to manage what would be a testy encounter. In retrospect it was clear he had been impetuous, even careless in his decision to seek revenge against the American who killed his nephew. Maybe

Grainger was right. At this critical moment with the vultures circling he had no argument: Alejandro was definitely not worth it. If he had simply left it alone, written it off as a loss to a superior opponent, maybe even to the karma of arrogant conduct, he would not be standing here in this predicament. No matter what the reason, the situation was volatile and it wasn't going away without a confrontation. Joaquin Costilla had earned his reputation as a ruthless sociopath and the not-so-subtle title given him by the government and the liberal press—*el Araña*, the spider—was dangerously appropriate. Suarez felt a slight shudder.

His rise to first lieutenant in the cartel had been swift, in no small measure a result of his own violent psychopathy. It was a trait *Araña* had admired and because of that had rewarded him accordingly. Despite the considerable resources of the Mexican government, his ability to deliver brutal, cold-blooded retribution against their enemies, even against the judges and newspaper reporters that opposed them, had carried the cartel a long way, especially given their success in the business of trafficking women and labor. His tactics had helped make them both rich beyond their ability to calculate such wealth. Now, standing here, wondering how to break the news, his wealth seemed fleeting compared to life. He still hadn't found an easy way to diffuse the tension that was coming.

The rumors and innuendo had always been there, the reported infighting, the hints of power struggles, the parry and thrust of those inside the chain of influence who tried to gain footholds, tried to make names for themselves and move up the ladder. These diversions had always been fodder for the newspapers, planted perhaps by the forces that sought to bring them down from within. But he had always tamped the struggles down, kept them at levels where they could be managed. And despite a few heated exchanges through the years on policy or strategy or how far to carry their ruthless measures, he had always deflected final decisions to *Araña*. He never retreated from openly and forcefully stating his opinions but it was *Araña's* show. He kept it to himself but subconsciously he eyed a change in power some day. Today was not that day. He'd admit his error, duly chastised, and walk away.

"I told you about this *Americano* in Claxton," Suarez began, "The one threatening to expose our operations there."

"We have discussed it already. You said you would fix it. I take it that plan is not working or we would not be here. The bigger question is why does it involve Teresa? Marcela said you sent the bodyguards for her."

"I did."

"Good. Then it is no longer a problem. My question is how did you let it get this far?"

"It seems the American, Patrick Grainger, is not only a dangerous man but a man with considerable resources. He has found out some things about you and me. Personal things."

"And Teresa as well? Have you contained the situation? I assume the *guardaespaldas* have her protected until we can dispatch others to find Grainger and deal with him?"

Suarez's hesitation gave him away as he fiddled with the half-empty glass in his hand. *Araña's* eyes narrowed into slits and he pushed back from the table.

"What about Teresa!" he growled. "You had better tell me she is safe."

Suarez did his best to hide his growing apprehension. "She is safe," he said reluctantly. Until he heard differently from the bodyguards, technically that was true. He could only hope that the phone call from Grainger had been a bluff, although the inscription from the locket was unsettling.

"Then what is the problem I had to rush over here?"

"We are still waiting to hear from the bodyguards."

The tirade began immediately as *Araña* stood up and kicked

the potted plant next to the table and began pacing, his cursing rising to levels that could be heard on the far side of the spacious lawn. His own man standing passively by the bar never changed his expression.

"How long has it been since you talked to them?" *Araña* blared.

The ringtone on Suarez's phone interrupted the conversation. He snatched it off the table and listened.

"You have checked the sorority?" A pause.

"The police?" Another pause, longer this time.

"File the report now. Do not wait 24 hours." Another pause.

"Because I know. Just do it."

Finally he clicked off, his eyes fixed on the colorful flower arrangement in the center of the table as he weighed the implications. Finally he threw a cautious glance at *Araña* staring back with blood in his eyes.

"She is not at the sorority," Suarez conceded. "They have not seen her since this morning when she received the package from you."

"I sent no package."

"They claim a UPS driver delivered a package from you, Joaquin."

Even though the Captain's mouth continued to speak, his mind was busy processing what he suspected had taken place over the last six hours in Durham, North Carolina. The ominous message from Grainger was looking more legitimate by the second: *I'm looking at her as we speak.* The lecture pouring out of *Araña's* mouth had already broken apart into an unintelligible word salad while Suarez tried to walk step by step through what would certainly come next. It was his *lider's* rough grip on his shoulder that brought him out of it.

"Maybe she is just out riding around," *Araña* ranted. Then he remembered Suarez's half of the phone conversation.

"What did you mean 'because I know'?"

Suarez stood up and faced his *lider*.

"I got a call an hour ago . . . from Grainger." He waited as long as he could to finish it. "He claims he has Teresa."

Araña's jaw dropped. "But . . . that is impossible. He couldn't just take her . . . our bodyguards . . ."

"They watch after her, Joaquin, but not every minute of every day. She is a young woman in college. You agreed to that, I remember the conversation."

"Yes, but . . ." He paced in the veranda as he studied it. Then he turned. "You said he had a history. Is he capable of something like this?"

Suarez recalled the pages of information, Grainger's background, the newspaper articles about his daring rescue of the newspaperman's daughter, the detailed history he had reviewed in some detail before he set out on his vendetta.

"He has dangerous skills, yes."

"Kidnapping is a serious crime in the States."

Suarez nodded.

"Why would this man take a chance on going to prison? He discovered the farm. Why not call the FBI and let them handle it?"

There was no way to avoid the consequences of what had turned out to be an extremely bad decision. Suarez squared up to *Araña*.

"It is not the trafficking that drives him. It is personal with him now."

Araña looked away, thinking through it as he spoke. "His child was wounded in a crossfire. That would piss him off, maybe even make him search out the ones that did it, but kidnapping? No, he would not go to such extremes. Why would he do this?"

"Because we have *his* daughter."

Chapter 37

WE DID NOT take his daughter," *Araña* shot back. "She is probably still in the Kentucky hospital recovering from her wounds."

He waited for the Captain to agree with him but the blank expression staring back offered a different answer. *Araña's* head cocked but his eyes never left Suarez's face.

"Who would order such a thing, Lambito?"

Suarez looked away, his eyes sweeping across the soft expanse of the manicured lawn toward two gazelles grazing peacefully in the low-slung glow of a Tlaxcala sunset, unaware of the storm that was brewing a few hundred feet away. He had already considered throwing blame onto someone else in the chain of command, build the case that a lesser lieutenant looking for a way up the ladder had gone rogue, stepped out of the chain of command, misjudged the fallout, and given an ill-advised order without necessary approvals. If deception and betrayal could get him out of this jam, he had no problem with that, even if it meant sacrificing a friend or two. Over the years the deceit and treachery had often given him a rush, turning lies into truth. In all that time he'd never missed a minute's sleep over it. He might have been able to make it stick if he'd only had a little more time.

But with less than an hour's notice by Grainger, there was no way to lay the necessary groundwork. He saw no way to dodge the truth, to make the facts any less damning. Alejandro was definitely not worth any of this.

"It seemed like a good idea," Suarez said, as he braced himself for the back and forth that would come.

"A good idea? What possible good could come out of it? What made you decide this kidnapping was justified?"

"The American," he said. "He would not quit. His meddling, it threatened to expose us. We have worked for so long, Joaquin. I did not want to lose it."

"And by kidnapping this man's daughter you thought it would make him stop searching? Does waving a red flag make the bull go away?"

The argument snagged a loose thread in Suarez's brain and suddenly it came to him, a flicker of new strategy. *Drawing out the enemy.* It was a stretch but it seemed plausible and it might get him off the hook.

"I thought if we could draw him out he would be easier to kill. That would solve the problem. So yes, I decided the kidnapping would be useful."

"And such a strong decision, you made it without me? That is not like you, Lambito. Always when something threatens the business we discuss it together. And you should have learned I make the final decision. Now it turns out that this American is suddenly not so helpless. Your reckless decision has put my daughter in jeopardy."

Araña paced, staring blankly at an imaginary circle on the tile floor. The wheels were turning. He had not been educated at University but he was as cunning as they came and his ability to think through difficult problems had been underestimated over the years by far too many that never lived to regret it. He stopped in his tracks.

"This is what does not make sense, Lambito. Why would you not discuss it with me? We could have sent men to eliminate him. We could have found ways to turn him away. This order, I would not have given it, kidnapping the American girl. I think you know this but you did it anyway. Is there a reason you decided without me?"

"I don't know what you mean," Suarez said. His nerves cranked up a notch. "I only did what I thought was best for—"

"No, I think it is something else."

Araña walked to the edge of the veranda and watched the sun continue its slow dip behind the forest on the distant hillside. The gazelle had disappeared into the forest and the warmth of the day was gradually giving way to dusk. His mind traveled back to the events of the past week: the botched shooting at the shopping center, the American's capture and escape at the farm, the disastrous truck demolition on a back road. He turned back to the table.

"Has this American embarrassed you, Lambito?"

"Not an embarrassment, a threat," he said unconvincingly, "to us and everything we have built."

"What does your nephew think about this fiasco, Lambito? You said you were sending him up there to help Diego."

Suarez had hoped to deal with this later, once he had time to prepare. A later day would give him breathing room, time to weather the storm. Only not now. But *Araña* had gone there and there was no way to avoid it any longer.

"Alejandro is dead."

Araña's head snapped around.

"Dead? You told me nothing of this. When?"

Suarez blew out a breath. "Monday."

Araña reflected, then took a few methodical paces toward the Captain. "That's the day you sent him to Carolina."

Suarez nodded.

"And the same day Grainger escaped from the farm," *Araña* said. The pieces were beginning to come together. "Did Grainger have something to do with Alejandro's death?"

"He shot him . . . in the head."

The final piece of the puzzle fell into place. The storm started low and built.

"You kidnapped Grainger's daughter to get even for killing your brother's son?"

"To avenge his honor."

"That worthless *pedazo de mierda* had no honor. He was an embarrassment, Lambito," he said, his voice rising in disbelief. "And now, because you wanted to avenge his honor Grainger has done the only thing he could and kidnapped *my* daughter?"

"No one ever thought that could happen, Joaquin."

"*You* didn't think it could happen. But you didn't consider the consequences. You underestimated this man. I would never have allowed it, you *know* that, this vengeance for Marco's arrogant son, and you did it anyway?" He was shouting now.

"But the business, Joaquin, it is what I have worked for. I could not let it fall apart because of one—"

"What *you* have worked for? I brought you in, Lambito, when you were *nothing*," he screamed as his arms flailed the air. "Nothing! This fucking vendetta of yours has put Teresa's life in danger."

El Capitán was watching his empire falling apart in front of him. *Araña* had brought him in but it was *his* own hard work, the endless hours and days, those six months rotting in jail waiting for reprieve, the ceaseless threats over the years from law enforcement, the never-ending stream of enemies waiting around every corner, all of it leading to this inescapable specter of a life. Now that *Araña* was aware of what he had done, his misguided mistake, the future looked shaky. The thought of losing it all made his decision easy.

His hand crept near the pistol on his belt. Out of the corner of his eye he had already sized up the bodyguard by the bar, hands clasped in front of him. The instant *Araña* looked away to gauge his next move Suarez's pistol was out of the holster. He fired one shot into the bodyguard's neck, then swung around in time to meet *Araña* leaping across the table.

The momentum from the charge carried both men to the floor, the crack of heads and shoulders landing hard against the tile. *Araña's* left hand gripped Suarez's gun arm as they fought, rolling and punching, the cascade of grunts and curses punctuating unexpected combat between desperate *compañeros* turned adversaries. They wrestled for position, kicking, throwing damaging jabs, until Suarez finally managed to leverage his greater weight, and forced *Araña's* back hard against the floor. He'd gained the advantage, his eyes blazing with jealous hatred, not unlike dozens of times over a violent career. His chance had finally come, whether he was ready for it or not. The pistol in his hand twisted toward *Araña's* head with his finger poised over the trigger.

The fire in his eyes suddenly went empty. He froze, one brief, unanticipated moment in time, caught in the throes of a final tremor before his body went limp. *Araña* felt the release and shoved Suarez sideways onto the floor. When the body slammed against the tile the steak knife protruding from the side of his neck twisted and sank deeper. In the shadow of the ceiling fan that hovered over them, rotating silently, he saw Marcela leaning over, her face splashed with the blood that had gushed from Lambito Suarez's jugular when she drove the knife home.

Chapter 38

"C'MON, RANDY, it's Saturday night," Phil Damron said, "The wife and I are out to dinner."

"How long's your wait?"

"Maybe twenty minutes."

"Then you've got time to call your FBI guy. I just got off the phone with Pat. That farm security worker that never showed up? . . . he got scared and took off. Before he did he dumped the guy that ran things at Fox Hill and I know where he is. You want this asshole, trust me."

While Randy relayed the information Phil Damron wrote directions down on the back of a dry bar napkin. His wife rolled her eyes and shrugged off his lip sync apology. After thirty-three years she'd gotten used to it. Things leveled out when a vodka and cranberry appeared on the bar in front of her. Damron knocked down the first sip of his Woodford and water before he made a hurried call to his FBI contact in Lexington.

* * * * *

An hour and fifteen minutes later in Bledsoe, North Carolina a team of four agents cut the chain on the gate at Sunspring Foods and, in the fading twilight, swept across the tangled yard at the abandoned slaughterhouse. A string of ceiling lights produced a faint glow inside the building. They jerked opened the front door to the sounds of machinery, a rusty grind of metal on metal, and slipped through the tiny front office into the large open space.

They thought it unusual, the old conveyor line running with no one else around. It droned on, the motor laboring under the strain of age, drive chains clanking in a steady, endless circuit as it circled through an abandoned building guarded, curiously enough, by a locked entry gate two hundred feet away. Hooks and chains from a bygone operation slithered by with no cargo other than the porcine ghosts from the past. The agents had been tipped off about the building's undistinguished history and they watched with interest as worn, outdated production machinery, out of service for the last forty years, cycled past carrying nothing but empty memories.

The female agent was the first to see it when it turned the corner and emerged from the loading dock area. The shape was hanging from a hook, inanimate and lifeless. They watched slack-jawed as the conveyor transported the carcass past the original gutting station into the open expanse of the butchering room. An agent jabbed the heel of his hand against the large red button on the nearest safety switch and the conveyor line came to a grinding halt. Like gullible audience members staring mindlessly at a shiny ornament dangling from a magician's hand, the agents found themselves mesmerized by Diego's body, clad only in his underwear, hands bound behind him, swinging ponderously back and forth in response to the conveyor's abrupt halt. The hook twisting in the conveyor slot, its metallic grind in rhythm with the sway of the chain, provided an eerie, haunting sound bite.

The slices across his chest and the blood streaking down his face and neck got their attention first. Then the odd rash of blackened marks on his legs and chest. When they approached the victim they recognized a chain wrapped around his neck and secured to the steel meat hook. His face was bloated, eyes bulging like golf balls, his pants soiled in a final release. Two agents stood on chairs and lifted the weight while another climbed a ladder and unhooked the chain.

Once they laid the body on the concrete floor a quick once-over revealed deep pockets of burned flesh and the familiar, accompanying scent of leather tanned over a flame, a nauseating combination of sweet and putrid.

A call to headquarters mobilized the nearest coroner and an ambulance. While they waited, they checked out the rest of the building. In the middle of a concrete pen near the loading dock they found a single chair, and under it, patches of drying blood plus a few lingering pools that had congealed but not yet crusted over. Next to the chair was a butcher knife and tangled lengths of cotton cord. One agent noticed a slender rod that had rolled into the corner. With plastic gloves he picked it up and flicked the switch. A sharp blue sizzle of electric current jumped the gap between contact points at the tip of the cattle prod. He glanced back toward the dead body on the floor at the far end of the room.

"I wonder how long he lasted."

Chapter 39

"WHOSE IS IT?"

Both bodyguards looked at each other and shrugged. They laid the body on the gravel driveway and traced the phantom ringtone to Lambito Suarez's pocket. The smaller of the two men fished it out, glanced at the unfamiliar name on the screen, and handed the ringing phone to his boss. Joaquin Costilla released a half-hearted smirk. *Sorry, Diego, your boss can't come to the phone anymore.*

"Finish it," he told them as he walked away.

The men picked up the limp body and swung it into the bed of the truck with no more regard than if it had been a sack of fertilizer. Costilla deliberated whether to answer the ringing phone. *Why was Diego calling Suarez now? Was he in on the decision to kidnap the girl? Perhaps he knew where the girl was being held?* The decision came on its own when the rings stopped. He pondered what would come next. If Suarez was to be believed, Grainger's daughter was being held prisoner by someone in Costilla's own cartel. For the kingpin of one of the largest cartels in Mexico, being the last to know in any matter was unfamiliar territory. He cursed at this unexpected state of affairs. Maybe Lambito's phone log would turn up a location. Regardless, it was a dangerous game and he didn't know enough about his opponent to engage him, not yet.

While he stared at the blank screen the men lugged the fallen bodyguard from the veranda and laid him on the grass.

"What about Max?" one asked.

"Put him in the back seat of the Mercedes. I know his mother. I'll take him to her."

As they carried him away Suarez's phone rang again. Costilla responded with a resigned shake of his head, touched the green icon, and listened to a voice that didn't belong to Diego after all.

"Did you give him my message," Pat said, "or do I have to do it myself?"

"Why don't you do it yourself," Costilla said.

Pat hadn't heard this voice before but from the sound and tenor he made a calculated guess.

"*Araña?*"

"You must be the mysterious Patrick Grainger."

"Not so mysterious. Just a father, like you."

"I have been told you may have someone who belongs to me," Costilla said.

"*Belongs* to you?" Pat said. "Why doesn't it surprise me, Costilla, thinking of your own flesh and blood as something you own, like your pigs. She's not that different from the girls you sell and trade like pieces of meat."

"Save your lectures, Grainger. Why should I believe you have her?"

"I'm sure you know by now she's AWOL from the Chi Omega house." Pat waited for an answer. It surprised him when none came. "The Captain didn't tell you everything?"

"Only that you claim to have her."

"I'd let you talk to her but she's snoozing right now," Pat said as he sped up and passed an older lady in a slow-moving tan Corolla, her eyes straight ahead, both hands gripped on the steering wheel. As soon as he pulled into the right lane in front of her he fished the locket out of the cup holder.

"*Dios y la familia.* Ring a bell? Engraved on the back, but you knew that. Is that you and your wife on the inside? Must have been younger pictures."

There was a noticeable delay before he spoke. "You should have not done this."

"Sorry, but you have someone of *mine*. It only seemed fair."

"I don't suppose it makes any difference if I tell you I had nothing to do with such an unwise decision."

"None."

"I have no grudge against you, Grainger. This was Lambito's choice, his way of getting back at you for his worthless nephew. He should have left it alone. The years have taught me to keep business and personal matters separate."

"Like those young teachers you burned and dumped in the river at Guerrero? How about those bodies in the mass graves at Michoacán? How many was it . . . sixty, seventy? Business to you, maybe, but to their families it was personal."

"You have read too much, Grainger. Those were other cartels, different men, very *violento*, no restraint. They do not seem to understand that advertising their brutality for all to see only strengthens the opposition. We do not operate like that."

"No, you operate in the shadows, like cockroaches. These girls you sell like pigs are no different from your daughter or mine. They have dreams and you take them away."

Costilla brushed off the lecture as easily as a fly on his sleeve. "We aren't here to debate morals, Grainger. Or business. We are in a dilemma, yes? We have your daughter. And apparently you have mine."

"Where is she, Costilla?"

A lengthy hesitation filled the other end of the line.

"Well I'll be damned. You *don't* know, do you?" Pat said.

"The Captain really did this on his own."

"I told you it was his decision."

"Then there's no problem. Get him to tell you where she is. You and I can meet, swap out our daughters, and be on our way."

"Unfortunately that option is no longer possible."

Pat flinched at the news. It explained why Suarez didn't answer his phone.

"How you going to find her, Costilla?"

"Give me some time, Grainger. Lambito's body is still warm. Locating your daughter is the least of my problems. I didn't get to this place in life without resources."

"Maybe it'll help if I tell you she's somewhere in Kentucky."

"How could you know this?"

"He let her call the local paper. Something she said tipped us off."

"Obviously you don't know where in Kentucky she is or we wouldn't be talking," Costilla said.

"Sharp as a tack."

"This is no problem. We have people there."

"In Kentucky?"

"We have people everywhere. Our business, it is not what you would call Mom and Pop."

"For Teresa's sake, Costilla, you better find my daughter."

"Would you really harm an innocent girl, Grainger? Even if she is my daughter?"

Pat already knew the answer to that. Innocents never paid the price. Even back during the most desperate moments of that furtive, violent conflict in Iraq, a covert war orchestrated by ambitious politicians and carefully hidden from the public, it was an unspoken code on the ground. Their own personal law at a time when no law existed. But here in this unpredictable dance of wills if he allowed even a sliver of compassion to show it would signal weakness, especially to a man like Joaquin Costilla. Aimee's life depended on the charade.

"You'd be smart to read my history, Costilla," he said, firm, steady, convincing. "I left that life behind. But if anything happens to my daughter . . ." He paused and his voice picked up cadence and tone. "Then, my friend, you could listen in your dreams to your daughter's screams during her last agonizing moments, calling your name begging for you to save her. That's when you'll realize too late that underestimating me was the wrong choice." He waited before he finished it. "There's no more dangerous place in the world, Costilla, than between a man and his child."

Costilla shifted uncomfortably in place, and his boot scraped out a meaningless path in the gravel. "Is this what it has come to, Grainger. A trade, one for one?"

"Nothing else."

Costilla was not a man easily rattled. If it had been a friend or a cousin, or even his mistress they were discussing, he would have been less likely to agree to a trade. But even a cold blooded killer can find purpose in the comfort of a daughter's eyes.

"If we make this trade, what is to stop you from trying to shut down our operation?"

"Shit, Costilla. I guess you haven't heard by now," he said, dismissive. "The Feds are on to you, bud. There's more FBI agents at Fox Hill tonight than there are pigs. You're gonna need to find a new line of work."

Costilla bristled at this news. But he didn't miss a beat. "If this is true, we will start over. It will not take long."

"Not my worry. My daughter is somewhere in Kentucky. When you figure out where, call me back. This is between us. No police, no bodyguards. I'm on the way back there. She was taken from her home in Frankfort, so Frankfort is where we'll make the exchange."

"You are in no position to set the terms, Grainger. I decide what—"

"It's not a dick-measuring contest, Costilla," he snapped. "A simple trade. You want your daughter, I want mine. Call me when you find her."

The line went dead.

Chapter 40

PAT NUDGED ASIDE the locket's chain and picked his ringing phone out of the cup holder.

"The FBI's sending a team to the slaughterhouse," Randy said. "I can't figure out why your man, Enrique, disappeared. Maybe he was more involved than he let on."

"He wasn't."

"Then why'd he run?"

"He had a change of plans."

"Speaking of plans, you want to share yours with me? I'm flying blind here, Pat. Considering I may be spending a few years in an adjoining cell I need a little more information."

"You know Frankfort pretty well, don't you?" Pat finally asked.

"Um . . . yeah. Running a daily newspaper helps a little. Why?"

"Where'd be a good place to meet someone, out in the open, no crowds, no traffic, no opportunities for passersby to get shot?"

"If you're sending me feel-good vibes, that wasn't a good opening."

"Sorry."

"I'm going to take a stab here, given all the information I've funneled to you and knowing how desperate things are with Aimee. You've gone and kidnapped the daughter of the head of Tlaxcala Cartel, haven't you?"

"It's best you didn't know that, for your own sake."

"How about, blink once for yes, twice for no. Look, I know what you've done and why. I passed that class in intuitive journalism. And now you're setting up a meeting with some cartel rep to try and get her back, I get it. But don't you think this is finally something where you get the police involved. There comes a point when you can't take on all the bad guys all by yourself."

"I wish this was that time. And it's not a cartel rep. It's the head man himself, Joaquin Costilla—*el Araña.*" He heard Randy's deep breath of surprise on the other end. "So if you think *you're* flying blind . . . I mean, shit, Randy, this whole thing's a gamble. If it goes south and something happens to Aimee . . ."

Pat exhaled and leaned back against the headrest, giving the tension a chance to ease off, when he noticed that in the heat of his own anxiety, with demons and daggers swirling like gnats, the speedometer had crept up to eighty-five. He let his foot off the pedal. With a drugged girl in the seat next to him there couldn't be a worse time to get pulled over. He let the truck settle comfortably back to seventy and restarted his confession with Randy.

"That little exercise back in that barn last year, that was vintage Grainger. Other than my little PTSD side trip, I knew what I was doing and how to handle those guys. This . . . it's a whole 'nother animal."

"Which is why you need help. How do you propose to trade kidnap victims? I don't think it goes down like the movies. You just going to let him walk away? What's the playbook here?"

"No freakin' idea yet. Hell, these guys don't even know where Aimee *is.*"

Pat spent a minute explaining how the second in charge who engineered the fiasco was now dead and that the leader of one of the largest cartels in Mexico was still trying to locate the cartel's half of a kidnapping tag team.

Randy had been giving it some thought. "Pat, Aimee's got to be in a fifty-mile radius of Frankfort. I mean how far would somebody drive just to buy Town and Ranch Paint? Hell, she might be somewhere here in town."

"But why Frankfort? They'd have to establish a base of operations. Have some kind of organization."

"It's already here, bud. Our little town is one of the largest hubs for drug trafficking in this part of the US."

"That's hard to believe."

"Think about it. We're dead center in that regional triangle—Louisville, Lexington, Cincinnati. And out past that it's a quick hop to Atlanta, Kansas City, Detroit, Chicago, Philadelphia, Washington, Miami. Pat, we're the hub for all that drug traffic. If the public only knew how many major drug gangs our local police bust every year. So, if it's that way with drugs, why not human trafficking. I read the police reports every day. It's already a serious problem right here in our little river city."

"That's interesting but I just want my daughter back. They could be hiding her right there under our noses. That's why I'm bringing my cargo back home."

"Where do you plan on keeping your guest once you get here? You thought about that yet?"

"I was hoping you might have some ideas."

"So *now* I'm part of the team?"

"You said you wanted in."

Randy leaned back in his chair. "What's your ETA?"

Pat checked his watch. "I'm guessing around 11:00 or so." He detected movement in the passenger seat. "Let me get back to you."

The girl was stirring, first her legs, tucked and jammed against the door during the last couple of hours now searching for room to stretch. Then her body, cramped and bent double in the seat, her head lying on the console padded with a roll of the shipping blanket. He watched her wake up as she slowly took notice of the tape bindings on her arms, then her ankles, then a cautious glance back up at him over her shoulder, her eyes wide. When she recognized him without the glasses she slumped back into the seat and tried to put the pieces together. Finally she struggled up on one elbow, a brief look at the dashboard, then at him when she sat up in the seat. She glared at him and waited.

"Take the tape off your own mouth. It may not hurt so much that way," he said. "But you even hint at yelling for help or, heaven forbid, try to open that door at seventy miles an hour, well let's just say you don't want to do that. Understood?"

She nodded, then picked at the corner of the tape. Slowly, painfully she peeled it off and wrangled her lips and chin in contorted twists of newfound freedom. A few gentle massages with her fingers to get the blood flowing in her jaw again before she spoke.

"Where are you taking me?"

"Sorry, can't tell you that."

She reached for the switch in the door and closed the whistling gap in her window so it would be easier to hear. "Why are you're doing this?"

"It has nothing to do with you and everything to do with my daughter."

Her brow crinkled at this strange, illogical motive as it circled inside her head. Her confusion didn't stop the questions from coming.

"What's her name?"

He debated whether or not to answer. Maybe injecting a real name of a real human in a very real predicament might help if things got dicey later on.

"Aimee."

"I don't know Aimee, do I?"

"No."

She struggled with it. "I don't understand. Why would someone I don't even know give you a reason to kidnap me?"

"It's your father." The question marks over her head grew larger and wouldn't go away so he finished it. "His organization kidnapped her."

She threw her head off to the side and rolled her eyes in frustration. Finally she began to shake her head, slowly, deliberately, as she stared at the floor mat and cursed under her breath in her native tongue.

"Why did they take her?"

"Another man in the cartel, *el Capitán*, got a burr under his saddle. I killed his nephew."

"Suarez," she confirmed, her disgust in the open. "I knew he would make a big mistake someday." She continued to think it through, twisting and turning the pieces until they finally came together.

"And now the only way you can get your daughter back is through my father. And me."

Pat caught it out of the corner of his eye, the look she gave him, not so much fear as it was grudging appreciation for a well-executed plan.

Chapter 41

SOMETHING FELT WRONG, this unfamiliar voice on Suarez's phone. Training and old habits told him to hang up, destroy his phone and any chance for someone to trace the call. But the speaker's accent was similar. And authentic. And if he tossed his only line of communication, what then? He'd give the call a few seconds, not enough time to triangulate his position, before he made a decision.

"How do you know my code name?"

"It is here on the screen, *idiota*. And the settings on his phone, there is more information . . . Robert Miller, Sergeant First Class."

Miller cringed. They had agreed from the start, no names. Not in their communications, not on paper. Not ever. It was a flimsy attempt at a firewall but it might serve as a temporary shield if things went to pieces. This unexpected turn of events left Bravo feeling uneasy. Or more to the point—exposed. He'd spent too much time setting it up, the protocol, the team, the cover, the abduction, all by the book. Now one phone call brought it out in the open.

While Bravo was weighing the implications of the call

Marcela handed Costilla a folder. It took only a few seconds scanning the pages for Costilla to gather all he needed to know about the man running scared on the other end of the call.

"I am looking for a girl, Robert Miller. Do you have her?"

Even for a military man with his rigid background and by-the-book sensibilities, the question threw him. His mind raced as he analyzed the caller and his reasons. *Who would know? Where is Suarez?*

"Do you know who this is?" Costilla said, his impatience flaring."

"Should I care?"

He brushed aside the impertinence. "You have had many communications with Suarez over the last few days. You may know him as *el Capitán*. I am his boss. Now do you care?"

"I . . . when you say his boss—"

"Does the name *el Araña* ring any bells in your Sergeant First Class brain? Tlaxcala Cartel? Listen carefully, Miller. Your *former* business associate, Lambito Suarez, made some decisions without me, most notably one where he directs you to kidnap a girl. I suspect the many calls between you and him that I found on his phone pertain to this girl."

"I'm not sure . . ."

Costilla interrupted and read down the list. "Robert L. Miller . . . Minot, North Dakota . . . parents Walter and Shirley . . . Basic Training Fort Campbell . . . AIT Fort Bragg . . . MOS infantry . . . Army Rangers . . . specialist in Sniper Warfare . . . three tours in Afghanistan and Iraq. You want me to go on?"

The silence on Miller's end of the line was his answer.

"I don't have time to waste, Miller. Suarez is dead. For reasons you do not need to know, I must locate this girl tonight. Now where is she?"

For the next several minutes Bravo recited the necessary information on Aimee's location while Costilla wrote it down on the back of Miller's bio page. When they were finished, Costilla took over.

"There is a small private airfield in Eastern Kentucky a few miles north of Whitesburg. A former strip mine site before they turned it into an airport. It's abandoned now but we use it from time to time. I'll text you coordinates. Pick me up there in the morning around 8:00. Your time zone is EDT I think. You will drive me back to the place where you keep the girl in Frankfort."

"You understand I was only acting on orders from Suarez," Bravo said. "Our arrangement was purely financial. If he made a bad decision I had no idea."

"I understand but you work for me now. Do you have a problem with that?"

"No, but the money . . .?"

"The arrangement you had with Suarez, I will honor it. Besides, you bring something useful to the table."

"I was a good soldier."

"Were you a good shot?"

* * * * *

At 11:15 on a Saturday night, Moore's Mill Road was empty other than the white Ford pickup that slowed at each entrance, the driver on alert for the small wooden sign. In the field off to his left a pair of headlights flashed, his beacon in a sea of darkness. He pulled off the paved county road onto a gravel driveway and followed it eighty yards to the black hay barn where a lone figure was waiting with the end doors open.

Pat pulled inside and cut the engine while the barn door slid shut behind him. A Coleman lantern perched on a 55-gallon drum cast a lonely glow in the center of the aisle. He checked his cargo. Her blindfold was still snug. As a favor to her he had replaced the strip of duct tape over her mouth with a gag fashioned from the bandana he found in the console. She'd complained about the musty flavor, but in his opinion a stale handkerchief was an improvement over the solvent-based adhesive and the skin cells that would be ripped off along with the tape.

Randy walked around to the passenger door and helped the girl out. He gave in to the natural instincts of a blind captive and allowed her to take tentative steps as he led her to the stall where he had prepared a dusty but comfortable bed of hay. Pat walked in while Randy was settling her into the fluff.

"If you promise not to move around," Pat said, "I won't tie you up. But try and get away or nudge your blindfold off, I'll hogtie you. You understand?"

She nodded.

Pat tilted his head toward the barn door and Randy followed him out in silence. Once they slid the door shut, Randy had questions.

"OK, now what?"

"Not sure. It's a work in progress."

"We can keep her here all night, Pat, but tomorrow something's got to give. Is Costilla on board with this?"

"He agreed in principle. I just hope to God he loves his daughter enough."

"You said yourself he didn't know where Aimee was."

"Suarez didn't operate in a vacuum. He sent people, he used his phone to communicate with them. There's a trail. Costilla probably already knows where Aimee is by now."

"Let's assume that Aimee is being held somewhere near Frankfort. When Costilla finds the location that means he's coming here to get her, right?"

"Why do you think I brought Teresa back to Frankfort? He'll do whatever it takes to get her back."

"So, do we take shifts? Tie her up? What?"

Pat looked at his watch.

"Go home. Karen's worried enough as it is. I'll watch her

awhile. I've got help coming."

"What kind of help?"

"I called a few buddies. They're on the way. When they get here we'll throw a few ideas around, come up with a plan. I have an idea, but it's a little rough on detail. It could use a little input from you if you could run back out."

"Jesus, Pat, you make it sound like a country brunch. There's a kidnapped daughter of a Mexican kingpin in my barn and you want me to 'run back out'? This is serious business." He looked away and sighed. "What time?"

"Make it close to lunchtime. Middle of the morning my guys will be out paying a visit to a mutual friend or ours."

Chapter 42

DAWN WAS BREAKING when the Gulfstream V made its approach to the runway from the south. It had shut off its transponder and dropped to a 200-foot ceiling when it passed over the Cumberland Gap at Middlesboro, one more way to avoid detection by local airports, especially those few that were awake at this early hour. The instrument-rated pilot had already switched to visual flight rules, VFR. With no rain in the forecast, a minimal cloud cover, and three-mile visibility, the chances for mid-air engagement were unlikely.

From the air the forested terrain of Eastern Kentucky spread out for miles, a dense, verdant blanket undulating and sweeping in a graceful rise and fall, the softened shapes appearing to flow as if carved into the landscape. It was captivating, an artful creation by a grand sculptor's hand during a moment of glorious upheaval. But its grace was illusory, this image of land masses in gentle, fluid proportion and scale. It made a lie out of the stark reality of plunging valleys and soaring peaks and the inaccessible, challenging topography that dominated the Appalachian mountains.

The aircraft skimmed over the landscape at Mach .7 on an east- northeast heading, passing over Wallins Creek,

Leatherwood, Blackie, Jeremiah, other tiny communities named for heroes and scoundrels, before changing course past Isom and turning due north. Its target had no instrument landing system, no glide slope, no localizer signal, just a narrow 5,000-foot runway on a former mountaintop removal site. It was by all measures a conspicuous, blighted scab surrounded by a sea of old-growth forest hanging on to the past.

Once the plane touched down the wheels danced and bounced over ragged, weed-choked construction joints in a long-abused strip of asphalt as brakes fought for purchase. Tall, unchecked prairie grasses blurred both edges of the narrow runway. The aircraft finally came to rest a few hundred nervous feet from the edge of the rock slide that dropped off the mountainside like a sandstone waterfall. The plane turned and taxied to an empty staging area next to what had once been a makeshift terminal, now a block building in serious need of repair, or more likely demolition. A rangy man in jeans and t-shirt was waiting for them.

Costilla descended the stairs and engaged his new employee face to face for the first time.

"You have any trouble finding this place?"

"Not too bad. Without GPS I'd have been lost for sure. You weren't wrong when you said it was out of the way."

The pilots carried two bags from the plane and stashed them in the back of Bravo's SUV. Within fifteen minutes the vehicle was crawling its way down a steep gravel road, dodging tree limbs and washouts on the way back to the tie-in point at County Road 2547. The polite but businesslike voice of the GPS lady pointed them in the right direction.

"The girl, she is in good shape?" Costilla said.

"She's fine. Kinda spunky, if you ask me."

Bravo was unsure how much to question, or even how much he wanted to know, given the circumstances. But his military bearing called for answers. Better to know too much than not enough.

"Why is she so important to you now that . . . now that Suarez is no longer in the picture."

Costilla didn't often divulge sensitive information to underlings unless it was necessary to complete their mission. In this circumstance, with Suarez gone and him in Kentucky with no backup, this was one of those times.

"This girl, the one you are holding . . . her father has done something very bold, and in my opinion, very dangerous. He has decided—how do you say it—turnabout is fair play. He has taken my daughter."

"Shit! You mean kidnapped?"

"Yes."

Bravo watched every treacherous curve in the road while the details fell into place. "So let me guess. He's offering to make a trade . . . his daughter for yours."

"Exactly." Costilla mused on the irony. "In a way, I have to give him credit. Without this he would have lost his daughter. He would have tried to save her, of course, but he would have failed. We are too strong, too many. In the end we would have to kill her too."

Bravo winced. "That's not exactly how Suarez put it," he said. "He always claimed the girl was just a way to draw Grainger out in the open."

"It was. But then what? We gain nothing by releasing her. She had to die."

Bravo's internal moral compass twitched. Even from the beginning he'd been playing for keeps. In any war, foreign or domestic, the risk of casualties was always part of it. Like many dedicated soldiers he'd taken lives before. But he'd always considered Patrick Grainger the only target. It had never been spoken but he'd always assumed they would return the girl when

Grainger was eliminated. Just like that the stakes just got higher.

When they passed through Hazard they grabbed coffee and biscuits at the Hardee's drive thru. Back on KY 15 more questions.

"What's the story on the old airport back there?"

With a two and a half hour drive staring them in the face Costilla saw no reason not to answer.

"It was the old Whitesburg Airport. An abandoned strip mine at one time. It was fine for fixed wing aircraft but times change, even in the sticks. Regional airfields popped up and in the eighties they abandoned Whitesburg. When our business started growing we needed a way to travel in and out of the States. We couldn't fly commercial so we found this place. It is out of the way, not exactly a secret, but still not in the public eye. It's close to the regional triangle and, most important, to our operations in Carolina."

"You bought your own freaking airport?"

Costilla looked at him as if he were a child.

"We purchased the airport for the tax bill. They were glad to get rid of it. Unfortunately the runway, it was only 2,800 feet. Bizjets need close to 5,000. So we bought the knob next to it and sold the timber. The real cost came when we bulldozed the top of that knob and filled in the hollow."

"That cost a few bucks."

"Six million. Drop in a bucket. The real problem was the permitting. Too many state agencies in Kentucky." He held his head in his hand as he rattled off the ones he remembered. "Abandoned Mine Lands, Division of Reclamation, Environmental Protection, Division of Water. You Americans require a permit to take a shit. And it wasn't just the cost of the permits but the time, the engineering. The Fiscal Court in Letcher County was easy to work with because we created jobs and a tax base for the new property, even donated to local causes. It was the inspectors that were the problem. We spent another half million paying off those greedy bastards."

Once they reached Jackson another curious thing popped into Bravo's head.

"What about your pilots? They flying back?"

"They will wait for me. They have food and drink to last them three days."

"When you get your daughter back, are you taking her back to Mexico with you?"

"That, my friend, is where you come in. Those items the pilots put in the back? There is something there for you. I think I might be taking two daughters back with me."

Chapter 43

DOC WAITED in his MINI Cooper parked behind his office. He was running down a long list of things that could go wrong when a red 4x4 pickup truck, the custom detailing streaming across the hood and down both sides to the tailgate, pulled in twenty feet away. A .30-30 lever-action Winchester rifle and a fiberglass hunting bow hung on a rack in the back window.

The driver's head swiveled slowly toward Doc while two men exited the other side. Doc's hand felt for the reassuring touch of the pistol on his belt before he stepped out of his car. The second he closed the door a fully-dressed motorcycle rumbled into the parking lot on the other side of the truck and killed the motor. The rider was an imposing figure, a hulk in a denim shirt cut to the shoulders, dusty jeans, an unkempt gray beard that grazed his chest. His muscled arms were layered with faded blue tattoos. He took his time dropping the kickstand and joined the other three men as they approached Doc's car.

They had closed to within ten feet when both sides came to a halt. The oldest in the quartet raised the simple question.

"Johnny Glock?"

Doc broke a smile. The nickname still had a nice ring to it after all these years, especially when it came in the course of a real mission. He tendered an abbreviated handshake to each man: Pike, the spokesman, short on stature and hair; Granville, the grizzled veteran with a gray pony-tail; Axle, the driver of the red truck, cocky and the youngest of the bunch; and Montgomery, the menacing biker, Mongo to his friends. Doc pivoted toward the back door and led the men inside, flicking on banks of lights as he passed switches on the way through the waiting room. Once they made it to his private office the four of them waited patiently while he unlocked the door to the closet behind the desk. When the lights came on four jaws dropped at the same time.

He didn't bother waiting for questions and comments. He entered the room and began pulling weapons from the hanging clips, dealing them to Granny who passed them along the assembly line to Pike, Axle, and Mongo: two M16 automatic rifles, one AR15 semi-automatic, four Glock pistols with sound suppressors. He filled up a navy blue carry bag with the appropriate magazines, all fully charged.

While they were examining weapons Doc opened a large drawer off to the side and selected an array of electronic devices, some still in their boxes, and handed them to Granny.

"Put these on the desk," he said. "They need fresh batteries." He returned for a small armful of two-way radios with hands-free headsets. "These too. They've been in their chargers but it's been awhile. I need to change 'em out." When he returned to see if he'd missed anything he noticed Axle staring at one item off by itself, high on the back wall.

"Uh . . . Doc, you do any deer huntin'?" Axle said.

Doc admired the weapon. "Not with that. I don't think Fish and Wildlife would approve."

"That's not an M24 by any chance, is it?"

"Yep, but it's a variant, an A2," he said. "The Army phased it out in '14." He led his fellow admirer of weaponry back into the room. "Five-round magazine, adjustable stock, barrel mods for a sound suppressor which I don't have. You know this rifle?"

"We used the M40 in the Corps in Afghanistan, but I've fired this one too. What's a chiropractor doing with a standard issue Army sniper rifle?"

"We never know who's coming for our guns," he deadpanned.

Doc led them to a back room where they loose-wrapped the rifles in kraft paper. Once all weapons were secured behind the seat in Axle's pickup, three men piled in the front seat and took off for the barn on Moore's Mill Road with Mongo trailing on his Indian Chief, the muffler blasting.

Chapter 44

FIFTEEN MINUTES OUT OF HAZARD, Costilla checked Suarez's cellphone: one missed call from Diego's number. He tried twice to return the call and both attempts failed . . . no signal.

"Your country, it is nothing but hills and valleys," he said. "How do you people communicate?"

He removed the empty coffee cup from the holder on the console and replaced it with his phone, face up. Once they made it through Campton and caught the Mountain Parkway the wooded hillsides that crowded the narrow KY 15 corridor changed to pastures and wide rights-of-way and he tried Diego's number again.

"Grainger? . . . You called?"

"Just checking in. When are you coming?"

"I am in Kentucky now."

It caught Pat off guard. "We just talked last night. How'd you get here so fast?"

"Let's not beat around the bush, Grainger. For the moment I have three bars on my phone but in this God-forsaken country who knows how long that will last. You wanted to meet . . . so we meet. I am on my way to your little town. Have you dreamed up a safe way to make this exchange?"

Pat gathered his fragmented thoughts. There was no plan, not yet.

"I'm working on it."

"Working on it," Costilla said, a trace of annoyance. "Be smart, Patrick Grainger. Any trickery and it will not end well for your daughter. You bring the *policia*, you even mention this to them, your daughter will not see her next birthday."

"Guess that means you found her?"

"Did you really think that would take long?"

"She still OK?"

"Yes, Grainger, your daughter—what is her name, Aimee?—is unharmed. I trust that you are treating Teresa the same. This dangerous game we are playing, you know it comes down to trust. I trust you, you trust me." A malicious sneer spread across his face when he glanced over at Bravo in the driver's seat and his thoughts drifted to the weapons in the back of the SUV. "If we trust each other then we both go home with our daughters. Happily ever after, isn't that the way you say it?"

"I'll get back to you this afternoon when I've found a good place for the exchange. A place with no bystanders."

Once they signed off, Bravo stared in silence at the road ahead before he finally spoke.

"Do you really think he trusts you?"

"Of course not. But as long as he doesn't know about you it doesn't matter."

Costilla glanced as his watch. In a couple of hours he would finally get to meet the girl at the heart of the controversy. He was almost looking forward to it.

* * * * *

Pat watched Teresa resting quietly in the stall, bound and blindfolded, when the end door to the aisle slid open. Randy motioned to him. Pat exited the barn to the sound of Mongo's bike pulling in behind Axle's truck. Pat refreshed Randy's memory, pairing names and faces from their encounter a year and a half earlier. Then they dropped the tailgate on Axle's truck, a strategy table of sorts, and Pat got to it.

"Costilla's got to believe he's got a clean escape route or he'll never show. Easy in, easy out. A public place, out in the open," Pat said. "Limited traffic, no bystanders. A shopping center or parking lot is no good. We have to be able to manage traffic that comes out of the blue. A spot in the country is too remote, too many variables. We lose control if there's no civilization."

"So let's say we come up with a place. Why are *we* here?" Pike said. "It's going to boil down to you delivering his daughter and him delivering Aimee. Isn't it that simple?"

"We're dealing with a psychopathic liar," Pat said.

"Guess that means you don't trust this guy?"

"Not for a second," Pat said. "He's a cold-blooded killer who traffics girls for money. No, he's got something up his sleeve, I just don't know what, yet."

"So basically we're playing defense," Granny said. "Making sure he doesn't pull a fast one."

"Why not tip off the State Police?" Pike said.

"I can't take that chance and he knows it. He's bringing Aimee in with a gun to her head."

"That means no long shots?" Axle said.

"If his finger's on the trigger, muscle reflex and all . . ." He didn't have to finish the obvious. "Even without that, if it wasn't a perfect kill he'd have time to retaliate."

"I know one thing," Granny said. "Your buddy, the chiropractor, is one unusual dude." He snickered. "The man gave us enough weapons to fight off a small army. What's with this cat?"

"I don't know yet," Pat said, as he recalled his introduction to Doc's arsenal, "but if we get out of this thing with our skin I plan to find out."

Randy raised his hand, almost apologetic. It seemed the best way to enter the conversation with a bit of information and a suggestion.

"Doc's got a past and it's not just firepower. In his early career he was involved with some high level CIA programs. He created some of them himself. Pretty well known in inner circles. By the way, I invited him to join us as soon as he gets his equipment charged."

"What's with all that equipment?" Pike asked. "I don't even know what some of that shit is."

"That's because his former company invented it, sold a lot of it to the Feds."

The hum of tires rolling down Moore's Mill Road interrupted them. Doc's MINI Cooper turned into the gravel driveway and came to a stop behind Axle's pickup. He got out, ambled over to the truck with a confident grin, and dropped a nylon bag in the bed of the truck. He offered no comment to the six faces staring at him.

"So, anybody got any bright ideas?" Axle finally said.

The discussion drifted into a gallery of random thoughts, all hitting the bed of the truck for review and rebuttal, a comment here, a contradiction there, until Doc finally found a pause in the dialog.

"Controlled Psychological Disposition."

The puzzled looks and a total lack of response gave him permission to continue. He spoke with authority and a calculated confidence as he hit the bullet points.

"Costilla's got his own set of problems with this deal. He doesn't know where the meeting's gonna take place yet. He has to make sure he's got a way out. The one thing you can be sure of is he won't come in passive. He intends on screwing you, he just doesn't know how yet. So . . . it's up to you to give him some direction.

"If you wait for him to come up with his own plan you're working on his terms. You'll have no idea what his plan is until it unfolds. Or . . ." he said, holding his index finger in the air as a point of focus, "*you* could dictate what you want him to do."

All heads were still, their eyes focused on the lesson unfolding in front of them. "Create a scenario of your own making. If it's the right one with limited variables you can predict with reasonable certainty what his response will be. Human nature. He'll believe it's his original idea when in fact it's the *response you forced him to take.*"

"If it's that simple . . ." Pike said, waiting for someone to finish it.

"The only thing simple is the situation you set up and his reaction to it. After that there're dozens of variables and they're all up for grabs. You may know *what* he's going to do, you just won't know where and when."

"A controlled reaction," Granny said, "like Pavlov's dogs."

"Controlled . . . psychological . . . disposition," Doc said. "Make it your game, not his. I'd rather be the one dictating the parameters and then figure out how to plug the holes."

Mongo had been quiet until now. He picked up the bag and unzipped it, then pulled several pieces of equipment out and, belying his massive stature, gently set them on the bed of the truck.

"Are these supposed to help?"

"I hope so," Doc said.

Pat looked at Randy. "You got any suggestions where we can do this?"

Randy pursed his lips. "I might."

Chapter 45

"OVER THERE, what is that?" Costilla said, as they slowed to turn off the West Side Connector in Frankfort. "Many boats, a covered dock."

"Benson Marina. It's a local hangout. Burgers and beer."

"After that long drive from Whitesburg a cold Dos Equis would taste good if we didn't have business to tend to."

"Sorry, boss, 'The Most Interesting Man in the World' don't hang out there. It's a Bud Light kinda place."

Costilla snorted his disapproval.

The SUV began its climb out of the valley and settled in for the tedious drive out Bald Knob Road, a sinuous two lane county road that wound its way around and over the knobs of northern Franklin County on its way to Monterey and Owenton. Seven tedious, curvy miles later they hung a right onto Flat Creek and eased past single-wide trailers and open garages until they slowed and turned into a gravel entrance that led into the woods.

"Could you have picked a more out of the way place?" Costilla said. "The airfield in Whitesburg would be easier to find."

"Isn't that the point?" Bravo said as he got out and swung the unlocked rusted farm gate out of the way.

When he got back in the car and pulled into the trees, Costilla asked, "Any nosy neighbors?"

"Everybody out here keeps to themselves."

The SUV advanced along the crushed stone driveway through a narrow passage in the trees until the drive opened into a modest front yard littered with plastic bottles and windblown trash.

"The house isn't much," Bravo said, sweeping his hand toward the yard, "but it's got a cistern and electric, and it's secluded. Your local crew wasn't using it right now."

"Where's the girl?"

"In the basement."

Costilla opened the car door and surveyed the grounds of the dilapidated drug house. He thought it ironic that, in this land of plenty, the self-proclaimed greatest country in the world, the old farmhouse in front of him wasn't that unlike thousands of rundown hovels back in the more poverty-ridden areas of Tlaxcala. He joined Bravo in a slow plod around to the back door, bypassing the rickety front porch and the barricaded front door where one glass pane was replaced with taped-in cardboard.

Inside, two men at the kitchen table watched them enter, unsure whether to acknowledge the kingpin of the international cartel or simply remain an unobtrusive part of the furniture. Bravo led Costilla to the cellar door and both men descended the stairs to the basement where Aimee Grainger, shackled to the basement post, was lying on the mattress. She made no effort to acknowledge him. He stopped near the edge of the blanket that spilled onto the concrete floor.

"It appears your father has gone out of his way to rescue you."

That got her attention. She rose on one elbow and scrutinized him. He was dressed no better than the others, his vocabulary no more impressive, but his demeanor and the way the other man deferred to him told her he was different.

"Who are you?"

He debated whether to answer, but with things coming to a head he saw no disadvantage in an introduction.

"Joaquin Costilla. Mean anything to you?"

A simple shake of her head.

"Well, Aimee Grainger, it is a pleasure to meet you finally. Your name has been mentioned a lot lately. Have your ears been burning?"

She ignored him.

He reached out to touch her wounded shoulder. "May I?"

Her first reaction was to pull back. But since he had requested politely she decided to give him some latitude. She allowed him to raise the edge of her sleeve and observe the bandages.

"You were not supposed to be involved," he said, a concerned shake of his head. "Especially not getting shot. For that I apologize."

He noted the puzzled look on her face while she tried to sort out his meaning.

"For reasons you would not understand," he continued, "I'm afraid we were responsible for the incident at the shopping center in Lexington."

It startled her. She remembered the details of the victims, read their obituaries. Whoever this man was, his apology was worthless.

"You murdered them."

"Only one. The other, she was an accident," he said with no trace of remorse.

"Only one? You talk about them like they were nothing! Bailey Callahan was a person—a good woman—and you killed her. Why?"

He shrugged. "We had good reasons."

"And the other woman? She had a family. Since she was an accident that makes it OK?"

"That woman, she was not the reason. It was . . ." he searched for the right words. ". . . her time."

"You killed two people!" she screamed, springing up from the mattress until the chain caught her and jerked her back.

Costilla recoiled. Her advance had startled him, this innocent girl, chained, defenseless, completely at their mercy, coming at him packed with rage. He admired her for her passion, even if he couldn't agree with her reasons.

He'd tried in his younger days to understand it himself. He'd read the textbooks, the accumulated analyses from professionals that explained in clinical terms why he had no remorse for killing even when he knew it was a crime against nature. He'd never been able to accept their logic. Obviously nobody wanted to die, that part was easy to grasp. He had the same instinctive sense of self-preservation, the desire to live. But in the end it always came down to what it meant for him. Sometimes taking a life was merely one more step in the pursuit of his goals. It was always about that.

The Regency killing was not so much taking another life as it was the elimination of an obstacle. Logical, necessary, justified. He could almost understand her feelings about the other woman, the innocent bystander. But he knew this girl in a rage in front of him would never understand him. And as he watched her with anger boiling in her eyes, her clear, moral sensibilities of right and wrong made him wonder: could this girl's father, the genetic sponsor of her morals and values, really be the ruthless killer he professed to be? If not, was Teresa really in jeopardy? And despite his sudden concern, could he take the chance?

"I wonder if your father is really so dangerous."

"If he finds you, he'll kill you," she said.

"If seeking justice for the things we have done were his only motivation, I would not be worried. And, sadly, you and I would probably not be having this conversation," he said, looking away. "But he is a smart man. He has found something I value as much as he values you."

She stared at him, the words swirling in her mind. She glanced curiously at Bravo and back again.

"You see, I have a daughter also," he finally said. "You actually remind me of her a little. She is also full of fire."

"And my father knows where she is?"

His deep sigh was unusual for a man of such a violent background. "As it turns out, he has taken her. Like we have taken you. So you see, as much as you may hate me for the bad things I have done, do you think your father is any better?"

He spun on his heel and took the stairs two at a time with Bravo behind him. Once the door closed behind them, the emotions of his meeting vanished, bottled up only inside the girl in the basement. Back to business. Now it was all in the details.

"Bring the bags in the back of the car. There is something I want you to see. We must prepare."

Chapter 46

THE FOUR-LANE DIVIDED HIGHWAY that links the busy east and west sides of Frankfort, Kentucky is officially KY 676 but to the locals it's simply the East-West Connector. Built to relieve the commercial traffic and congestion on interior streets, its traffic is moderate and steady and, other than five well-spaced stoplights and the busy morning rush five days a week that feeds State Government offices, relatively uninterrupted. It wasn't ideal. But in Randy's mind, the road adjacent to it met all of Pat's criteria.

Sunday afternoon at 4:10 two vehicles veered off the Connector onto Coffee Tree Road, bypassed the city water treatment plant, and turned into the long, winding entrance drive leading to the State Library and Archives. Less than a hundred feet in they pulled into a small 23-space parking lot where five cars were docked. Four men exited Randy's SUV and another three got out of Axle's truck.

"What is this place?" Pike said, as he stared at the fourteen-foot-tall stainless steel sundial on a raised platform thirty feet away where a dozen people were milling around. Several were stooped over, their eyes focused on the walking surface.

Axle was reading the limestone monument that guarded the

entrance. "Kentucky Vietnam Veterans Memorial," he answered with a touch of reverence.

"Eleven hundred Kentuckians died in Vietnam," Randy said. "The sundial arm—they call it a gnomon—throws a shadow on the granite stones. Every person who died has their own block. As the sun moves through the day and the seasons, the shadow touches their block on the anniversary of the day they died."

The men were caught in a brief moment of nostalgia and awe when Pat brought them back. "We've got work to do."

Ignoring the dwindling swarm of visitors that roamed the site, reading plaques and taking pictures, Randy unfolded the aerial map on the tailgate and handed a Sharpie to Doc who was already surveying the surrounding countryside.

"This won't be a simple trade. He'll have backup. Maybe not out in the open but it'll be here just the same. Once you tell him this is the meeting place he'll have somebody out here within the hour checking it out. You're giving him an open invitation to plant somebody up there in the trees with a rifle. This is good."

"Are you crazy?" Pike said.

"Controlled Psychological Disposition," Doc said, rambling on as he continued to survey the countryside. "You set the table. He responds."

"Yeah, with a rifle," Pike said.

"Costilla's going have a gun to Aimee's head. This is the only way."

Doc splayed his arms behind him to the north toward the Capitol building. "That tree line between us and the Connector, too sparse. Not enough cover."

Then he turned in the opposite direction, looking off to the south past the shiny steel sundial arm.

"There," he pointed. "That's where he'll have someone in the woods."

"Where?" asked Granny, as he scanned the old-growth

forest that stretched across the top of the hillside until it finally disappeared behind the Library and Archives building.

"That's the big question," Doc said as he compared the tree line in front of him to the aerial map laid out on the tailgate. "See that little grove of trees in the field off to your left all by itself? Those trees block everything to the left of it." He marked a line with the black marker on the aerial map and hash-marked out a section of the forest.

"That area to the right behind the Library, that's no good because the building blocks the line of sight." He marked that section of the forest off the map and then used a ruler to measure the distance.

"That still leaves over a thousand feet of tree line to hide in," he said. He gathered them around the map and marked off broad circles of responsibility. Granny, you cover this area. Pike...this is yours. Axle...you're in the middle."

"Where the hell you expect me to be?" Mongo said, indignant.

"You're our big diversion. You and Karen."

"Karen? Randy's wife?"

"Bear with me. Costilla's no dummy. He's got to believe this is on the up and up, just another day in Frankfort. And he has to think he's got a quick exit with no cops. If he thinks it's a trap, Aimee's in trouble."

Mongo waited for Doc to go on.

"You're going to be our token veteran, cruising in on his bike to pay his respects to fallen comrades." He gave Mongo a quick once over. "You look the part."

"And Karen?"

Randy interrupted from behind. "She's your biker chick."

"You're kidding, right?"

Randy interrupted. "Nope, she's all in."

Mongo turned away from the group and paced, running his

fingers through his shoulder-length hair as he weighed the possibilities. When he returned to the truck he looked Doc in the eye.

"This ain't Mission Impossible, Doc."

"It's all on the fly, I admit, but Costilla's expecting a showdown. I didn't have time to stage a big production. You're our failsafe in case something goes wrong."

Mongo blew his cheeks full and exhaled. "How about you, what are you doing?"

"Jackie and I will be tourists at the Memorial."

Mongo was still skeptical. "Tourists? Great. Doing what? Even if you had a weapon, I thought you said we couldn't take a chance with Costilla holding Aimee."

Doc picked a video camera out of the bag.

"I'll be taking pictures."

Mongo, Granny, Pike, and Axle all winced at the same time.

"It's a TIV camera," Doc said. "Thermal imaging video. It can detect a person by the heat that radiates from their body. A range of maybe 500 yards."

Axle looked off into the forest at the top of the hill. "Like somebody concealed in the woods," he said. The pieces were starting to come together.

"Precisely."

"So," Granny said, "even if you pick up an infrared image of this guy in the woods, assuming he's even there, then what?"

"Not infrared . . . thermal. There's a difference. And I guarantee he'll be out there waiting to take a shot." Doc pulled another device from the bag.

"This is a range finder. When I pick up his thermal image, I hope I can get a brief line of sight to the shooter through the foliage. This thing is accurate to within a yard. Once I locate him plus each one of you from your thermal image, I'll know who's closest."

Then Doc reached into the bag and pulled out a pair of two-way portable radios and five sets of hands-free speaker/receivers. "They're all synced to the same frequency. Randy gets the hand-held radio. Each of you will have ear buds and lapel pins. Mine's a full speaker/headphone so I can keep an eye on the camera and give directions."

"No offense, Doc, but where the hell'd you get all this stuff?"

"My company developed it a few years back. Had a pretty good deal going with the CIA for a while until I got burned out. Of course most of this stuff you can get on Amazon now, only not with the accuracy and range as mine."

Doc turned to Pat. "Well, we have a plan. You think you can sell it to Costilla?"

"I don't have much choice."

Pat pulled Diego's cell phone out of his pocket and dialed as he walked away. The crew watched the conversation from a distance, picking up a word here and there, while Pat's arms swirled as he laid it out to the man who held Aimee's life in his hands. More than once they watched his eyes roll skyward as he tossed around details, and then stared at the ground while he listened intently to the other side of the conversation. His head would nod, then a second later shake in disapproval. Finally the conversation ended and Pat shuffled back to the truck.

"He's worried about how he's going to get away after we make the trade. Said he'd think about it."

"What that really means is he needs an hour or two to send a man out to recon the site," Doc said. "You gave him the plan. Now he's coming up with a response. We need to get the hell out of here. We don't want to be around when they show up."

Chapter 47

"WHAT YOU GOT FOR ME that you're so proud of?"

Costilla unsnapped the package.

"Is that a Barrett?" Bravo said, as he reverently plucked the 48-inch-long .50-caliber sniper rifle out of the soft case.

"I thought you'd like it. You ever shoot one of these?"

"No, man. Just the Remington. But I've always wanted to try one," he said as his hand stroked the perforated black steel upper receiver, trailed along the fluted barrel, and came to rest on the signature squared-off muzzle break.

"I've been told," Costilla said, "that there are differences in these weapons—the weight, the grip, the recoil. I think maybe you should fire it few times, just to get comfortable. Unless you think it'll draw too much *atención*."

"Are you kidding? Out here shots go off all the time. This baby may be a little loud but none of our whack-stick neighbors would know the difference."

In the back field approximately a hundred yards from the house Bravo set up a cardboard box in front of a hollowed-out dirt backdrop. Back at the house next to the cistern he found a level area and unfolded the Barrett's bipod front supports. Before he dropped down into a firing position he popped the obvious question.

"Is this for Grainger?"

"I assume you don't have a problem with that."

"Not him, no. I'm not crazy about taking out the girl, though."

"You won't have to," Costilla said as his hand grazed the grip on his pistol.

* * * * *

Bravo had fired six rounds into the cardboard target, cleaned up his brass, and was back in the house packing the warm rifle into its case when Costilla's phone rang. The raw power of the Barrett had been intoxicating and it provided a renewed sense of dominance as he plowed through the conversation he'd been waiting for. While Patrick Grainger laid out the meeting location Costilla put his phone on speaker and motioned for one of the men to open his laptop. The man followed along with the conversation and brought up the Veterans Memorial site on Google Maps. A silent question to Bravo got an affirmative nod. Costilla filled the rest of the conversation with fake concerns but he already knew what he was going to do.

When he hung up he asked Bravo, "You are familiar with this place?"

"I've been there a couple of times. I may be an asshole, but I'm a veteran asshole. A lot of men died back then . . . for nothing," he said, spitting the words onto the table. "It's a tribute to them."

"Save your bleeding heart." Costilla said, as his finger traced the roads in and out on the laptop screen. Finally it settled on the large band of forest above the site, and he nodded his head as the plan took shape in his mind.

"You are comfortable with the weapon?" he asked.

Bravo acknowledged with a confident nod.

"Good. Gather up the girl and your new toy. It's time to make a trade. And perhaps make Patrick Grainger sorry he tried to cross *el Araña*."

* * * * *

Teresa had been quiet in the stall while they were gone. Karen greeted them with a cooler of bottled water, green tea, and soft drinks and they debated the plan's shortcomings and refined the details. Doc appeared nervous and shook his head as he paced.

"If I had more time I could have set up a GNSS system and synced my range finder with an aerial map on my laptop."

He recognized the silent question on Randy's face.

"It's a one-man robotic system. Bounces signals off navigation satellites. Land surveyors use it, the ones who can afford it. That would've let me pinpoint the guy within an inch."

It was a little over two hours before the call finally came. Pat walked away from his crowd and answered. He listened for a few seconds before he began throwing arguments back into the phone. Several exchanges back and forth, a few words of clarification, and it was over. When he walked back to the gathering he had a scowl on his face.

"Well?" Randy asked.

Pat addressed Doc. "He went for it. I hope you know what you're doing."

"When?" Doc asked.

"An hour."

"An hour?" Doc said. "But . . . this was supposed to happen sometime tomorrow. We can't set up that fast."

"It was take-it-or-leave-it. He wasn't willing to give us time to set a trap. Can't say I blame him."

"OK . . ." Doc took a deep breath. "Randy, you drop Granny and Axle off behind the Library. The parking lot will be empty on a Sunday. But stay out of sight. Their man will be out there, somewhere. Find some way to drive Pike around to the other end without being seen."

Randy eased over to Karen.

"You sure you're up for this?"

"Hell, yes," she said. "After what he did for Julie?"

She was nervous, no question, but now wasn't the time to show it. She turned to Mongo.

"Let's do it, big boy."

Mongo cocked his head at Randy, his helpless look out of character for a man of his size. When he got nothing but a shrug he surrendered and mounted his bike and offered his hand to Karen. One foot on the mounting peg, she slid in behind him and the bike dug a small trail in the gravel on the way down the driveway.

Back in his MINI Cooper Doc was on the phone with his wife.

"Plans have changed a little. It's going to happen in an hour. Can you meet me at the McDonald's at the top of the hill?"

"But I've got Jonah and Tali with me."

"No time. Just bring them. We'll leave 'em in the car. It'll give our grandson a good story to tell at our funeral."

* * * * *

The near corner of the parking lot behind Library and Archives was blocked off: a staging area for the coal tar bitumen rolls of glass-fiber roofing felts stacked in a classic pyramid, a loose pile of round river rock ballast, and the roofing contractor's inventory of propane-fired kettles and hand tools. By the end of the week most of the materials would be used up, but for now it provided good cover. Seconds after being dropped off Bravo disappeared into the woods and Delta took off for the Elder-Beerman parking lot to wait for the pickup signal.

As Bravo weaved through the trees he kept an eye on the Memorial's stainless steel sundial. The slope of the hillside wasn't severe but he couldn't find any flat areas to lie spread eagle for the shot. That made the bipod front supports on the Barrett useless. It wasn't a problem. He was less than six hundred feet from the Memorial, a relatively short shot. He'd find another way to brace the barrel.

He located a small clearing with a decent line of sight to the granite plaza. One pine tree with low-hanging limbs fit the bill. He sat cross-legged next to the trunk and selected a branch. A few hacks and slices with his survival knife and the limbs above and below it were gone. He unzipped the soft case, pulled out the Barrett, and slid the upper receiver into the crook where the branch joined the trunk. It required only a minor adjustment of his body for the angle to work. A cluster of locust branches between him and his target was a possible distraction. He skidded down in front of his station and made a few select cuts with the knife. Now he had a clear line of sight.

His text to Delta was brief: *Be ready. I don't want to be around when the cops show up.*

While he waited for the rest of the party to make an appearance he nestled his butt into a hollowed out scoop in the leaves and reflected on the circumstance of this final engagement. It was perfect. Almost too perfect, the more he thought about it. Grainger had picked this location for a reason. A public platform out in the open. A hillside with good cover, a great place for a marksman to hide. It was almost like an open invitation for him to be at this particular spot. Bravo felt a twinge of nervous energy.

He double-checked the woods behind him. From the aerial maps he already knew that access from that direction was difficult. The other side of the hill was much steeper with no vehicle pull-offs on Glenn's Creek Road. Still, his defense mechanisms were sending out alerts. As he took in the panorama spread out in front of him—the glistening stainless steel sundial of the Memorial out in the open six hundred feet away, the broad expanse of grass between it and his hiding spot, the empty field to his right, the Library building to his left—his discomfort grew. It was too perfect. He decided on a slight change in plans.

Chapter 48

TWO CARS WERE LOADING UP when Mongo glided into a vacant space and killed the motor. Karen swung off the motorcycle onto the blacktop and dusted off her jeans.

"Your first time on a bike?" he asked as he dismounted.

"Not since college. Your . . ." she stooped to read the scrolling chrome logo on the side of the tank. ". . . *Indian* is a lot more bike than the ones I rode on back then. I think Craig Massey had a Honda 350."

Mongo allowed a half-hearted snort. "Maybe after this is over you can get Randy to take you shopping." He turned toward the Memorial, then hesitated.

"Is any of this legal, counselor?"

She didn't bother making eye contact. "Don't ask."

Together they strolled to a tri-panel display where the text and graphic diagrams etched into stainless steel plates detailed the Memorial's ideology, the unique physical features of the sundial and how it worked, and the methods and materials of its construction. While they pretended to take in the history, Mongo's eyes drifted up toward the woods at the top of the hill. *He's up there somewhere.*

After a minute they made their way up the sloped walkway

to the plaza and more than eleven hundred individual pieces of blue granite, each one engraved with the name and death date of a lost warrior. Tombstones of sorts placed in memoriam.

As they played out their charade a MINI Cooper pulled into a free space. Three tourists and a Russian wolfhound got out, late afternoon visitors. While the boy took the dog for a long safe walk in the grass at the far end of the lot, the two adults headed for the Memorial. They stopped briefly at the display before strolling up to the plaza. A camera bag was draped over the man's shoulder. He took a digital SLR camera from the bag and began the pretense of taking pictures—some shots of the names sandblasted into the granite blocks, some of his wife posing beside the oversized stainless steel sundial.

Two minutes later a Ford Explorer entered the lot and parked. Pat Grainger removed Teresa Sandoval's blindfold, reached across the seat to open the passenger door, and scooted her out with him on her hip. He held her close, his arm draped around her shoulder, while his left hand dangled in front of her neck. The other hand held a semi-automatic pistol tight against her ribs. Together they awkwardly made their way up the ramp to the plaza and waited by the flagpoles at the far side. It was no coincidence that Pat kept his hostage between him and the tree line.

Nine minutes later a black SUV turned off Coffee Tree Road and stopped in the middle of the Library drive. It idled in place while Joaquin Costilla checked out the scene. He was aware the Veterans Memorial was open to the public twenty-four hours a day but at this late hour he had hoped all visitors would have been gone by now. For the biker and his girlfriend this place of honor would be a time to linger and think. Between them and the man in Bermuda shorts and flip flops taking more touristy pictures of his wife than he would ever show, he had no way to predict how long they would hang around.

Finally, Costilla caught a glimpse her on the far side of the plaza standing upright and rigid, the man's arm tight around her, something held tight against her side. Caution fought against his natural instincts to charge in, but he decided to wait. He held his position, idling in the drive lane. After a minute with no one making a move to leave, his anxiety got the best of him and he pulled into the parking lot. As he shifted the car into park and shut off the engine his eyes never left his daughter.

It was an odd feeling for him, something he hadn't anticipated, this paternal glow creeping over him one strand of conscience at a time. Until now this whole exercise had been a battle of wills, a rancorous competition between adversaries, two men with too much to lose. But as he stared at her on the far side of the plaza, vulnerable and helpless, it came to him in an unexpected fit of candor that perhaps his handling of the matter may have been distorted by the pure challenge, an ultimate test of how he might recover his daughter—his possession. The sensation was unexpected, this fear, a father's fear, watching her standing there clutched in the grips of a man who could spare her life or end it.

He had read the man's bio in Suarez's file. Patrick Grainger had killed before, notably in the name of country. Perhaps he'd left it behind on the battlefield. He said as much on the phone. But the newspaper reports had alluded to other incidents, recent ones. Three rapists in the old barn in Georgia. A standoff with kidnappers in Richmond. With those on his resume had he really left it behind? And could Costilla take that chance? She was his flesh and blood, a product of his own making, the mother of his future grandchild standing on the other side of the plaza with hopes and dreams of her own, waiting to see what her fate would be.

Costilla blinked and broke away, then glanced at Aimee Grainger in the passenger seat, blindfolded and frightened, her arms bound with cotton cord. And at once he realized she was not so much a vulnerable human being as she was his bargaining chip, the one thing that would let him win. The paternal instincts that had made him flinch began to back off, and as predictable as the sun that would set in an hour, his competitive edge surged back to the forefront, as if his rare moment of conscience had never happened.

It was time.

He leaned his mouth into the hands-free microphone attached to his collar.

"Are you in position?"

Through the static: "Affirmative."

"Can you get off a safe shot?"

"Negative. She is between us. Too tight."

"Get ready."

Costilla removed Aimee Grainger's blindfold and dragged her out of the SUV. With his pistol tight against her side he forced her toward the display board and the sundial beyond.

Doc had already activated the TIV camera. By now he'd located clear thermal footprints of Pike, Axle, and Granny. Their positions were very close to those marked on the map. He'd confirmed each one by their waving arms when he locked onto them. Now he was scanning the broad spectrum of woods looking for the shooter. Jackie kept the forest at her back while Doc slowly panned the camera.

Finally he saw it glaring like a neon sign, the thermal image of a man, the gauzy white from the heat of his body in direct contrast to the dark background of the cooler foliage behind him. With his eyes glued to the screen Doc spoke into his hands-free mike.

"Axle, he's in your sector. Sixty, eighty feet to your west, maybe forty feet higher up on the hill."

"Got it."

Axle climbed the slope with his pistol drawn. He maintained a low profile and cover. Doc kept him updated in real time as he watched one thermal image closing on the other.

"Thirty feet."

Axle slowed his approach. A killer with a rifle would be in no mood for an unexpected visitor. Axle traded large strides for small, measured steps, concealing his body behind tree trunks and undergrowth.

"Almost there. Twenty feet straight ahead."

Axle could see the man through the foliage now. He raised his pistol. At the edge of the clearing his simple command broke the silence.

"Put it down."

On the other side of a small clearing the man with his back to him froze. Then both hands slowly rose into the air. No rifle, no pistol, only a 35-millimeter SLR digital camera clutched in his right hand.

"I . . . I'm not armed," the man said.

"Turn around, slow."

He was in his late sixties, with a dark blue windbreaker and a camera bag slung across his shoulder. When he turned it was obvious the fear stamped on his face was not that of a killer.

"Identify yourself," Axle said. His pistol was pointed at the man's head.

"G . . . Gene Burch. I'm a photographer," he said. "I'm taking pictures for a calendar. I can show you a card."

Axle grabbed the mike on his lapel.

"Wrong man. Wrong man."

Chapter 49

FIVE MEN, ALL ON THE SAME FREQUENCY, received the
message at the same time.

"How do you know?" Pat stammered into the mike.

"He's a local," Axle answered. "A photographer. Trust me.
He's not our guy!"

Pat and Doc's heads turned at the same time toward the car
door slamming in the parking lot and watched Joaquin Costilla
leading Aimee toward the Memorial.

Doc was on the camera again. He panned the forest again,
left to right. As expected, he picked up Pike first, the white
thermal image already on the move. Then twin images in the
middle sector, Axle one-on-one with the photographer, every
movement of arms and bodies showing up on screen in real time
while he checked the contents of the man's camera bag. Doc
panned to a third image beyond the Library and the construction
area. Granny was making his move as he scanned the forest for
the other man.

"Where the hell is he, Doc?" Pat said.

"I can't find him. Maybe he's not . . ." Without thinking he swung the camera over to the Library and the stockpile of roofing materials in the rear lot. Nothing there either. It was when he pulled out his range finder that he saw the ladder leaning against the wall. He raised the TIV camera's line of sight and spotted the tiny blotch of white, the thermal image of a man's head barely visible sticking out above the low parapet wall.

"He's on the roof! On the roof! Anybody see him?"

Three voices came back within seconds of each other, "Negative."

Doc glanced behind him again. Costilla had reached the Memorial's front display with his hand gripped on the back of Aimee's neck as he pushed her forward. It was impossible to mistake the pistol planted in her back. With a sociopathic killer approaching from one side and a sniper in the woods Doc knew that Mongo, Karen, Jackie, and Aimee were in danger.

"Mongo, get her out of here," Doc said into the mike.

"What . . ."

"Just do it."

Doc hurriedly shoved his camera in the bag and got Jackie's attention.

"Let's go honey," he said in a cheery voice loud enough for everyone to hear.

He glanced at Pat and whispered in his mouthpiece mike. "Buy some time. I need five minutes." He slid the hands-free headset off his head and onto his neck. Hopefully it would pass for earphones when he met the kingpin and his hostage.

"What's going on?" Pike said into the two-way's frequency band.

Everyone heard his question but Doc. He had already grabbed Jackie's hand at the sundial and was heading for the ramp with Mongo and Karen moving out in front of them when Costilla turned the corner with his hostage. Mongo was faking a conversation with Karen as he passed, but his hand was poised, ready to grab the pistol tucked in the back of his belt if things went to hell.

Doc recognized the fear in Aimee's face as she approached, her body stiff and inanimate. He decided not to avoid Costilla's glare, instead offering a courteous greeting.

"Have a good one," he said as they passed.

Costilla nodded without comment, returned a forced smile, and turned back to face Patrick Grainger.

As soon as Doc turned the corner out of Costilla's line of sight he slipped his hands-free headset back onto his head and spoke in a low, clear voice.

"Mongo, make sure we don't have any visitors on Coffee Tree. Randy's already got the west end, you take the other. Everybody else, hold your positions."

Pat still had a firm grip on Teresa. He kept his face behind her head to screen his conversation.

"What the hell you doing, Doc?"

"Five minutes. And take that receiver bud out of your ear. Costilla sees it, he'll know something's up."

Mongo revved his motor, an obvious effort to draw attention, then turned onto Coffee Tree and roared east, tailpipes blasting. The boy and dog were already back in the MINI Cooper and Doc and Jackie followed the motorcycle onto Coffee Tree before they slowed five hundred feet down the road and turned unnoticed into a small parking lot. Both departures were lost to the drama that was playing out at the sundial.

With the last of the general public out of the way Costilla gave Aimee a gentle shove forward. Pat locked onto his daughter's eyes and his stomach tightened at the prospect of the life and death encounter.

"Hello, sweetie," he finally said. His calm outward composure was doing its best to mask the terror growing in the pit of his stomach. "I'm here. It'll be OK, I promise."

He thought he perceived a subtle reaction, a nod perhaps, and he wondered if he sensed a greater courage in her than he did in himself.

Costilla nudged her forward again, one step. His face showed no emotion when he raised his pistol and placed it against her temple.

"Well, here we are, Patrick Grainger, this trade you insisted on."

"I thought you'd be taller," Pat said.

Winning the mind games.

Costilla cocked his head, unsure whether to be amused or offended.

"I hope I didn't come all this way just to trade insults. Surely two men with such lovely *hijas* see the wisdom in doing this the way we agreed."

"Keep it English, Costilla. I'm not that smart."

"Smarter than you let on, Grainger. I must give you credit. This was the only way you could save her. I'm not sure how you managed to figure it all out."

Buy five minutes.

"Google is my friend. Everything is right there for all to see. Your daughter's college, her sorority, the thousands of innocent people you murdered over your *illustrious* career. I'm sure your daughter is proud of her daddy." Teresa flinched at the gentle poke in her back with the Glock. "You are proud of him, aren't you?"

She stared ahead, no answer.

"I would not be so disrespectful if I were you, Grainger."

"It works both ways. I see you have no respect for my daughter with that gun to her head. It could go off accidentally."

"Nothing I do is by accident, I assure you."

Pat raised his Glock to Teresa's temple.

"Oh, I understand . . . completely."

Even though both men had played this scene out in their minds dozens of times, all the what-ifs, the changes in plans, the bluffs and back-downs, the irrational behavior by the other party, it seemed different now, a surreal moment suspended in time. No mediator, no judge to render fairness, no God almighty with his finger on the final outcome, just this moment. And it could all go to hell in a second. Lost on all of them was the fact that while hard men with guns stared at each other, so did their daughters. Aimee Grainger and Teresa Sandoval had already found each other's eyes, had read the fear and hope in the other, and understood it was out of their hands.

"You realize," Costilla finally said, "there's no way for this to end well as long as we both have the other's daughter."

Pat saw it coming—the trade—this one vulnerable moment when his only leverage would take a short walk to the other side. He knew Costilla saw it the same way. The difference was that a shooter was out there somewhere. *Where the hell did Doc go? Why did he need five minutes?*

"There's only one way this can play out, Costilla. I release Teresa, you release Aimee, both at the same time. We keep our weapons aimed at the other's daughter. You can back out to your car with Teresa. I'll back into the grass with Aimee. The only way. Agreed?"

Costilla grinned. *Exactly according to plan.* "Agreed," Costilla finally said.

Pat released his grip on Teresa's shoulder, Costilla did the same for Aimee, and the girls began the slow walk, pistols still aimed at their heads. At the midpoint it surprised them when they both slowed and came to a stop, took one last look at each other, and then began walking again. Aimee was almost within reach when Pat heard the shot.

Chapter 50

PAT GRABBED AIMEE and swept her to the ground, an automatic, instinctive act of self-defense, and he shielded her body with his. Then he shuddered as his worst fears ripped into him. His adrenaline took over and he lifted her face. It shocked him to see her eyes wide, frightened, filled not with the empty void of every parent's worst nightmare, but with life. He tensed and leaned her away from him. No wounds, no blood, nothing but a shaken daughter still in wrinkled pajamas and a trembling smile.

"Are you hurt?" he heard himself asking.

She looked down at her body, as if she had to check to be certain.

"No."

Over his shoulder Pat fired a look at Costilla huddled on the granite with his own daughter, going through the same quick, choppy motions, the same hurried words. The one other common denominator was the reality of loaded pistols still gripped in their hands, and in a response befitting men who had instinctively battled for their lives before, both raised their weapons toward each other in the same instant. A standoff. Only now with one variable—a gunshot and no apparent victim. The confusion in Costilla's face matched that in Pat's.

Deliberately and with extreme caution they shoved their

daughters out of the line of fire and pushed up off the granite slab, both with weapons aimed at the other, poised for some unknown resolution, and they began to circle, wishing for cover that didn't exist, strategically naked and exposed. They both understood the reality: any first shot would be followed instantly by a reflexive second. While they jockeyed for position Aimee and Teresa smartly crawled out of the way.

Costilla made the first move. He leaned his mouth down to the microphone on his lapel.

"Shoot him."

Pat braced for the shot that never came.

"Shoot him, now," Costilla repeated. Still nothing.

Doc was right, Costilla had made plans. And now it was obvious those plans were off the rails.

"You talked so much about trust," Pat said. "Did I misjudge you?"

"No time for jokes, Grainger. Nothing has changed. I take my daughter, you take yours. I think I won't get to kill you. I will have to live with that disappointment."

The sound in the distance of four rounds from an automatic rifle forced both men to jump. It came from the east end of the hillside. Then another three-round burst from the west end. Neither Grainger nor Costilla could stop themselves from jerking toward the sounds. Walking across the empty field toward the Kentucky Vietnam Veterans Memorial sundial were two men, each with an M16 automatic rifle pointed at Joaquin Costilla. Pat was never so glad to see Hanley Pike and Granville Mullins in his life.

As the men made the slow but steady trek through the grass Doc's MINI pulled into the parking lot. He hustled up the ramp, his pistol pointed at Costilla. When the kingpin recognized the tourist, the pieces of the puzzle started to come together. Mongo's bike roaring into the lot put an exclamation point on it.

When Pike and Granny stepped onto the granite slab Costilla found himself staring down the barrels of two M16s and three Glock handguns.

"What's it going to be, Costilla?" Pat said.

"You know I could take you with me, Grainger," he said, his pistol still pointed at Pat's head.

"If you wanted me that bad you would have already done it. The only question now is do you want to spend the rest of your days in an air-conditioned cell or are you ready to cash it all in. I'm betting the thrill of trying to run your empire from prison sounds better."

"You are not police. You can make no promises."

"Trafficking people is serious business these days, Costilla. With the extradition laws between us and your country being what they are, I'm betting you'll spend your days in some supermax." He nodded his head toward the M16s. "Or you can be food for worms."

Costilla kept his weapon aimed at Pat. "What about Teresa?" he finally asked.

"She can go back to being a Dukie if she wants. You know, I'm a Kentucky fan and I really should hold a grudge, but can I really blame *her* for that Christian Laettner shot? I say let bygones be bygones."

"What you are talking about, this Christian shit? Promise me you will not hurt her."

"You have my word."

He waited for the leader of *Cartel Independiente de Tlaxcala* to make a decision. It took longer than he expected but finally Joaquin Costilla laid his weapon on the ground.

Jackie had followed Doc to the plaza with a roll of clothesline cord. She cut off a length and Granny and Pike secured Costilla's hands behind his back and propped him against a low wall. Teresa was in shock and sat next to him on the capstone, resigned to the ending. Jackie joined her and draped her arm around the girl. Pat searched out Aimee leaning against the sundial arm and wrapped his arms around her. He'd kept his promise. They held each other for a long time, the sway of familial ties ultimately more powerful than the treachery that threatened to end it. The odd gathering had settled into an awkward quiet when Mongo's booming voice broke the silence.

"What'd you find?"

Pat broke away from his embrace with Aimee and watched with some surprise as Axle sauntered onto the plaza from his long walk through the field. The mystery shot—Pat had almost forgotten about it.

A broad grin spread across Pat's face. "You got him, didn't you?" he grinned at Axle.

"Nope."

"Whaddya mean—nope."

"I mean, I couldn't see the dude from where I was. He was too low behind that wall on the roof."

"Then . . . who?"

Axle turned to Doc with a crafty smile. "You brought your M24, didn't you?"

Doc shrugged. "I really didn't think I'd need it, but . . ."

Pat stared dumbfounded at Doc. "The M24's a sniper rifle." The pieces started to fall. "*That's* why you needed five minutes. But how . . ."

"That little parking lot over there," Doc said, his thumb pointing across the field. "I'm a little rusty but it *was* only three hundred yards. Hard to miss, that close."

"I dunno, Doc. You might need some practice. The round caught him over his left eye, way over here," Axle said, pointing to a spot on his face.

"If there weren't young people around I'd answer that."

"I found something else," Axle said as he held up a cell

phone. "On the walk over I checked the call log, but it's the text log that was interesting." He read Bravo's last text out loud, then looked up. "Whaddya say we invite this Delta cat to our party."

Eight minutes later an SUV pulled into the Library's rear parking lot. The driver had no chance to get out of the car before three men appeared from behind stacks of roofing materials with pistols drawn. It didn't take Mongo long to convince young Delta that the precise location of the safe house wasn't a secret worth keeping.

Fifteen minutes later Karen and Jackie were transporting Aimee and a newly-blindfolded Teresa Sandoval back to the barn on Moore's Mill Road while a two-car caravan wound its way out Bald Knob. Their cargo: Joaquin Costilla, the impressionable and helpless Delta, the body of a man with a 51mm bullet hole over his left eye, and four men armed with Glocks and M16s.

Chapter 51

THE TWO MEN holding down the fort in the safe house weren't prepared for this new man walking across the yard behind Delta. Bravo hadn't mentioned it. If he was bringing in additional manpower they had questions. Their curiosity turned to regret for their lax security when Axle pulled the gun from his pocket and backed the three of them down into kitchen chairs. A few minutes later a second car pulled up the gravel drive behind the first. Pat escorted the cartel leader inside while Granny and Pike lugged in Bravo's body and dumped it on the floor.

Pat forced the four men to the basement where the remains of a half-eaten roast beef sandwich lay scattered on the floor beside the mattress. Aimee had already told him about the chain and padlock but the sight of them made his temper flare.

A half hour and two rolls of duct tape later the men were bound and strapped four-square with their backs to the steel basement post. As a precaution Mongo made several full wraps around their necks to hold their torsos erect against the post. In the kitchen Granny snagged Bravo's pant legs and unceremoniously dragged the body down the wooden stairs. The skull hammered against every tread.

"So this is how you *Americanos* treat your prisoners?" Costilla said.

"Oh, we could try the cartel way. How's that work? . . . we skin one of you alive? cut off a head? Whaddya think?"

The terrified shakes of three other heads made it clear that was not a preferred option. Pat squatted down in front of Costilla, forearms resting on his thighs.

"You don't deserve my sympathies but I suppose your daughter does so I'll make sure she gets a ride back to Carolina." He breathed a satisfied sigh of relief. "But you, old boy . . . you're done. I expect the next faces you see will be pretty excited to see you."

"Perhaps we meet again, no?" Costilla said.

Pat smiled and stood up. "Let's go, guys."

As he turned to follow his crew up the stairs he caught a glimpse of the shelf unit on the opposite wall. A quick glance back at the cheap mattress where Aimee had been held and he made the connection. When he sauntered over to the shelf unit he saw the seven partially used cans of paint, dried up and the rims sealed shut with time: *Town and Ranch*. He couldn't ignore the chance for a little mockery. He took all seven cans off the shelf and placed them in a semi-circle around the four men strapped to the basement post, offered one last sarcastic smile, and retreated up the stairs.

* * * * *

"You ready?" Axle said, as he leaned against the three-board fence.

"Let's go," Pat answered. "I need to get her back before Randy makes the call to Damron. No trail."

"It's a good eight hours, plus stops. If we push off now, we can get there before they wake up."

Inside the barn Karen checked Teresa Sandoval's blindfold and helped her from the stall to the truck. No one talked. Pat backed the Ford pickup out and turned around in the gravel drive. He nodded to Axle waiting in the pull-off and took off down the driveway in the dark.

* * * * *

On I-64, a few minutes past the Georgetown exit, Teresa finally broke her silence.

"Where are you taking me?"

"Back to campus. Wouldn't want you to miss any Monday classes."

"What did you do with my father?"

"He's in a safe place," Pat said. "By tomorrow he'll be in a safer place."

"You know they'll arrest you for taking me."

He'd been expecting this conversation since they left. He was surprised it had taken so long for her to work through the pieces.

"I'm betting that won't happen," he said.

"I know who you are. I've seen your face."

"So?"

"So, I'll tell them what you did. You kidnapped a college student."

"No I didn't." His tone was dismissive, bordering on casual, maybe even argumentative.

"What do you think this is," she said, frustrated behind her blindfold at his refusal to acknowledge it.

"Beats me. I've been hanging out with friends all day."

"Very funny. I saw the big sundial. The men with the guns. All the stuff that went on. My father was there."

"Sweetheart, your father's a drug dealer. He buys and sells young girls. He kills people for sport. He's not your best choice for a character reference."

"He'll tell them the same thing, that you kidnapped me."

"Of course he would, he's your father. He'd say anything if he thought it'd get him off the hook."

"So? . . . he's done some bad things but that won't keep you from going to jail for kidnapping me."

"You're not listening. I've been with my buddies all day, playing cards, drinking beer. You know, guy stuff."

She was silent for awhile as she worked through the details over the last two days.

"My sorority sisters saw you."

"No, they saw a UPS driver in glasses and a cheap mustache delivering a package. Does anybody ever pay attention to the UPS guy? I don't think so. *You* may know what I look like but they don't."

"The UPS driver. He'll recognize you."

"Never saw my face, dear. And if you're wondering about gasoline and credit cards, that's the beauty of cash."

"But all those other people at the sundial. I saw them."

"Really?" he said. His sarcasm was blatantly transparent. "Unless you're that one person out of ten thousand, I doubt you paid much attention either, not to faces, not with all the guns pointed at you. Tense moments like that tend to make us nervous, forgetful."

She sighed as she thought back to all the people she knew she would never be able to pick out of a lineup. "And the barn where you kept me . . . I don't know where it is either, do I?"

"I sure hope not."

Teresa Sandoval had asked and he had answered. He could almost hear the wheels of disappointment grinding in the passenger seat.

"Look at it as a grand adventure," Pat said. "Maybe after you get back you and your gal pals can celebrate your freedom with a few tequila shots."

"You Americans, always profiling us. I don't even like tequila," she said.

"Yeah? You're a college girl. What's your preferred drink?"

"Bourbon. Why?"

"Just making conversation."

A few minutes later Pat took the Lexington exit at Paris Pike and pulled into a darkened corner of the parking lot at Liquor Barn Express. He walked a dozen steps away from the truck and waited, pacing on the sidewalk while Axle made the purchase. He made sure he gave Teresa Sandoval plenty of time to rifle through the glove compartment and locate the registration and license number of the Ford pickup that was taking her back to Duke.

Chapter 52

THE DARKNESS was his ally. Other than one halogen pole light in the parking lot there'd be no way anyone could tell he was even there. It had taken only a few seconds for the chloroform to do its work. She had resisted but, as always surprise was to his advantage. He opened the passenger door and glanced around to make sure there were no campus cops, then lifted her out of the seat and carried her down the sidewalk to the front porch of Chi Omega. What was the point of a night light in the foyer if no one was awake?

He lowered her gently in the recliner and propped her head on a cushion. It didn't take long to unscrew the cap on the half-pint of Jim Beam and dribble some on her lips. He splashed a few calculated drops on her shirt, then emptied all but the last few ounces in the grass next to the porch before he wrapped her hands around the bottle and tucked it against her body. He wasted no time getting back to the parking lot where Axle was guarding the truck.

* * * * *

The carrier despised his route. Delivering the Herald-Sun to privileged sorority girls, the ones who were too good for him, making all those unbelievably tiring rounds before class that no one would appreciate, it was a humbling thing. But it was unavoidable if he wanted to finish his degree as a Blue Devil. One more year and he'd be in the hunt for a real job.

He allowed the Ford pickup to pull out of the parking lot before he turned in. Twelve housing units in the court, each with a dozen or more residents, and he only had sixteen hard paper subscriptions? It was a sad state of affairs, the newspaper business now that journalism had gone digital. He couldn't blame them, though, he'd done the same. Cheaper, convenient, everything right there at their fingertips. He did miss that stack of newsprint that always seemed to come in handy, but it was just one of those unfortunate byproducts of progress. Regardless, he was glad to have his customers. It wasn't big money but it'd help pay for tuition until he scored a killer job in information technology, and that field was wide open.

He'd made deliveries at four units and was laying three rolled up papers by the door at the Chi Omega house when he noticed her off to the side in the dark, curled into a comfortable position on the recliner. When he moved closer he picked up the strong scent of the bourbon. The half-pint bottle tucked against her stomach told the story. Another one that couldn't hold her liquor.

Maybe he should check to see if she was all right. He approached her, his sneakers quiet on the concrete, and gently rustled her shoulder. Dead weight. Passed out cold. She was beautiful though. Even in the dark he could tell—the long black hair, soft creamy skin shimmering in the faint glow of the foyer light.

The stunning ones like her were the ones he could never have. They seldom returned his shy smile when he passed them on campus. It wasn't so much an obvious disdain as it was their insensitivity, their cavalier acceptance that he wasn't on their level. It hurt, those feelings and the deep insecurities behind them. It always got to him. He felt those same feelings sweeping over him now before he knew it. He jostled her again. Nothing. He peeked into the window, no one in the foyer, then glanced nervously around the grassy courtyard. Just him and her. She would never know.

He laid a tentative hand on the leg of her jeans. When she didn't move, not even a reflex response to his touch, he nervously glanced around once more and his hand dropped around to the front of her pants. He fumbled with the button on her jeans and folded the edges back, ready to explore a place he would never get to go otherwise.

Perhaps it was her vulnerability, her lifeless lack of response that made him stop. More likely it was simply his conscience. Maybe he wasn't on their level, at least not yet. But even an undiscovered secret, harmless or not, was still a sin, he knew that, and his hand backed away from her open jeans before they could enter. He stepped back, afraid to look around. In a guilty panic he didn't bother fastening her button and he scurried down the sidewalk back to his car. The Sun-Herald's subscription department would likely get a few disgruntled calls but he'd come up with an apology and a good excuse once he had a chance to calm down.

* * * * *

Randy reached for the vibrating phone on his nightstand. He didn't have to look to know the caller. After a few words the call ended and he glanced as the digital clock: 6:12. He fell back on the pillow, then turned over and threw an arm around Karen and borrowed some warmth from her body. At least he'd get eighteen more restful minutes of half-sleep before the alarm decided it was time. It'd be another hour and a half before he'd place the call to Jack Damron about the special package that would be waiting for one of his teams out on Flat Creek Road.

* * * * *

Winston Marshall closed the heavy oak front door behind him. With his briefcase in one hand he used the other to pick up the morning paper and he shook it open to the headlines. More of the same: another bombing in Syria; a flap last night between their planning commission and a group of high-flying developers; and of course the gaggle of syndicated stories concerning the national election and its never-ending stream of political spin and made-up scandals. Anymore it wasn't worth his time. They were all vultures who'd lost their way. He dropped the open paper on the wicker chair—his wife would get it when she woke up—and weighed it down with a pillow before he headed down the brick walkway to his car.

It startled him, the white Ford pickup truck parked on the other side of his BMW Z4 Roadster. His wife had been rattling on for a week about her plans for landscaping but had she gone ahead and made arrangements without telling him? Even so, it was way too early in the day to start a project. With no one in the front yard he walked around to check the side and back. No one there either.

He dropped his briefcase into the passenger seat of the roadster and tentatively opened the truck's door. No estimate book, no business cards, no tools behind the seat. With one hand on the steering wheel he found a set of keys dangling in the ignition. Odd, he thought. Maybe they had gone for coffee and were waiting for them to wake up.

At the very least the truck's dingy white paint job made the Valencia orange metallic paint of his roadster look that much snazzier. He beamed as he lowered his overweight body into the leather driver's seat. His Monday morning planning meeting at Sunspring Foods would take at least an hour, maybe more. After that he'd call his wife, give her a little grief for what she had done without consulting him. All in all it was probably better this way. His interest in landscaping was near the bottom of the list.

Chapter 53

AXLE TURNED HIS TRUCK AROUND in the weed-choked driveway next to the birthing shed and shut off the motor. His eyes swept across the grounds.

"It's got its charm," he scoffed.

"I guess the old places like this couldn't keep up when the big farms moved in," Pat said, lamenting a history he knew little about. "Don't get me wrong, I like bacon and all, but the things that went on here—I'm not sure I want to know."

He got out with Axle behind and both men stalked through the knee-high grass toward the metal shed. It took some muscle to slide the door back on rusted rollers. His Harley Davidson was there under the tarp where he left it.

"I wasn't sure it'd still be here. Guess nobody comes around anymore."

He straddled the seat and backed it out and squared it up with the door opening. Once he inserted the key and hit the ignition button the motor roared to life. In time-honored biker tradition he revved it more times than necessary and the deep guttural roar of the muffler reverberated off the corrugated walls of the building. He dropped the kickstand and dismounted and let it idle as he walked out into an open driveway littered with abandoned equipment and scrap metal and the detritus of trash that had blown in off the road over months and years.

"These farms, they feed us, but after everything I've seen, there's got to be a better way," he said.

"That bad?"

Pat glanced back through the open door where his motorcycle was idling. He stared into the depths of the dilapidated shed. Buried in the shadows were the blood-stained cages lined up side by side and the feed buckets and torn sacks of rotten feed spilled on the floor, and he could almost hear the squeals of helplessness, short-term lives calling for help.

"Worse," he said.

They stood in silence for a minute.

"You gonna follow me back?" Axle said.

Pat had been thinking about that very thing on the ride back from Durham. He'd considered a quick stop at Fox Hill but decided no purpose would be served there. It was probably still overrun with officials in one form or another, if not law enforcement then likely some regulatory agencies that had jurisdiction over the industry. But there was another location that interested him.

"You know, I think I'll hang around for a bit," he said. "A little unfinished business."

He offered his hand to Axle.

"I appreciate your help, bud, following me back. That's a long haul."

"No problem. Semper Fi and all that crap."

Pat gave him a long appreciative look.

"We did a good thing here, you know that, don't you?"

"I do. We all do. When you get back, we'll gather for a proper celebration. Granny said the first round was on you."

Axle's fire-engine red pickup tearing down the Carolina county road almost seemed fitting for a commercial, Pat thought.

He walked to his bike and mounted. A few more well-timed revs and his Harley traded the gravel drive for pavement. It was time for breakfast.

* * * * *

A dozen girls huddled around her while the housemother dabbed her forehead with a cold rag. She was starting to stir. The whispers had already started. It wasn't like her, taking off like she did, no explanation to anybody, but this . . . this was definitely out of character. They had already removed the nearly empty half-pint from her hand and set it off to the side. Why she hadn't simply let herself in was the big question, but maybe in her condition, who knows.

The housemother had buttoned her jeans but the word was already out. A few sisters expressed shock, others simply shrugged. Deep down they all knew it was no one's place to judge, but that wouldn't stop the whispers from roaming the halls over the next few months.

When she finally rose in the recliner and gathered her bearings she recognized the crowd gawking and filled with questions. She started to offer a few words of explanation, then thought better of it. Perhaps a call to the police first? But as her brain kicked in she slowly began to recall her frustrating conversation with Patrick Grainger on the long ride back and decided some personal reflection was in order.

They helped her up and into the house. Within minutes she was in her bed sipping a cool drink on the bedside. Her roommates were huddled around her, the questions coming in short cautious bursts, no one quite sure what to say or how much to pry. Finally she gave up and turned toward the wall. A little rest before she decided her next move.

* * * * *

The bell tinkling over the door drew a few bored looks. His favorite counter stool next to the cash register was already taken by a heavy-set man in grease-stained coveralls. Pat's eyes explored the diner. No familiar face behind the counter, only an assortment of stragglers at the tables and booths scattered around the room, stabbing at eggs and sides.

He saw her, four booths down along the front window, engaged in lively banter with two gray-hairs while she jotted down their order. No surprise there. He stood quietly for a moment, second-guessing the wisdom of his visit. Finally he gathered his confidence and eased across the floor and leaned on an empty stool. He watched as she shifted in place, a few animated gyrations while she described some event or local character. The diners laughed at the shared moment. When she turned to log in the order she saw him, a startled look, a brief hitch in her stride, then the confident smile he had expected as she continued over to him.

"You're running a little late for breakfast, aren't you?" she said, glancing at the clock on the wall.

The mischievous glint was still there. *Maybe this wasn't such a bad idea after all.*

"To tell the truth, I'm a little too tired for breakfast. It's been a long night."

"I'll bet," she said, her eyebrows arching in sarcastic accusation.

"It's not what you think," he said, as he flashed back to Teresa Sandoval on the recliner. "I've been on the road for ten or twelve hours."

"Well, if you're not here for breakfast, then what . . . blueberry muffin and coffee to go?"

"No, I need to crash for few hours, but . . . I was kinda wondering . . . if you might be interested in . . . grabbing dinner, like . . . a little later on, if you're not busy."

Her arms dropped dramatically to her side, her sarcasm on full display. "Did you drive *all night* just to ask me out?"

Despite his near exhaustion he couldn't hold back a wide grin. Her irreverent manner just kept coming and he wasn't sure he could keep up, at least not until he got some rest.

"Look, I haven't done this in a long time. I'm struggling here, Doris."

She studied him. Handsome, rugged, a hint of shyness beneath the banter, and probably a heart-breaker, but maybe it couldn't hurt. She tilted her head to the side, then wrote her number on the back of a guest check.

"Why not," she said. "I had a slow weekend. Call me when you wake up and we'll talk."

He grinned a sigh of relief. It had been a long time. Maybe it would do them both good.

"You pick the place," he said. He glanced down at his jeans. "Some place casual where I can order anything besides pork."

He backed away and slipped out the door. She watched him through the window as he mounted his Harley Davidson and roared out of the parking lot on the way to the nearest cheap motel. After a brief second of reflection she wheeled back toward the kitchen with the gray-hairs' order and the hint of a smile. As she passed the corner of the counter, Hank Lyvers, all three-hundred pounds of him in his grease-stained coveralls, was finishing his coffee. He was a regular and he'd managed to eavesdrop on the entire conversation.

"So, you going out with him?" he asked.

She slipped the guest check in the order strip in the window and grabbed a coffee pot. On the way down the counter she answered Hank over her shoulder.

"A girl's got to eat."

Chapter 54

PAT HELD THE DOOR OPEN for the elderly couple behind him and followed them in. Randy's car parked three spaces down from Two Sisters Cafe was a reassuring sign that he may not have to wait for a table. Over the full house he spotted Randy and Doc in the corner. He threw a flirty nod to Sheila behind the cash register and dodged past tables of chatty customers and pulled out a chair.

They were nearly through their good-mornings and end-of-the-week complaints when Sheila showed up with a clean cup for Pat and a half-full pot of coffee.

"You boys ready to order?" she asked as she poured, even though she already knew the answer. "No hurry," she said finally as she turned back to the room and hunted for empty cups.

"Aimee had another good night," Randy opened. "Eight hours of sound sleep. She's not letting this thing get to her."

Pat nodded. "Tell Julie I *really* appreciate her hanging tight 'till things get back to normal."

"They've been like sisters since last year anyway," Randy said. "This just brought 'em closer."

They chatted awhile about the fallout and the way Aimee's classmates were dealing with it while the multiple versions of the truth circulated through the halls of school. Randy's sanitized article in the State Journal made for quite a story, but how different it might be, Pat thought, if any of her peers really understood what she had gone through: the rifle shot that nearly took her life, her forced abduction, days chained to a post in a dank basement, a loaded pistol aimed at her head. It had been a made-for-Hollywood tale that unfolded in a quiet Kentucky town where the biggest stories involved utility rates or stolen cases of Pappy Van Winkle. But it was over now.

He thought back how his actions out of the gate had brought things to a critical mass and he wondered if maybe it was time to dial down the tempo. As he stared into his coffee he paid no attention to Doc tearing open another packet of Splenda.

"You catching flak from the cops?" Doc asked.

Pat blew across the top of his cup and ventured a careful sip before he answered.

"They've grilled me pretty good," he said. "First the State Police, then the FBI. Can't blame 'em, all that trouble I stirred up at Fox Hill after Aimee got shot. But other than a possible breaking-and-entering at the farm, what can they get me for? I'm just another out-of-control father who wanted to get even."

"Well there's that minor issue of kidnapping and transporting a minor across state lines," Doc said.

Pat spent a couple minutes reconstructing the same solid trail of alibi's he'd laid out for a disappointed Teresa Sandoval on the way back to Duke. "I figured she'd file charges. The FBI's investigating, asking all the right questions. Obviously I had the means, motive, and opportunity, but that's not enough to arrest me. There's this pesky little thing called evidence, and they don't have any."

"How about that run-in at Fox Hill?" Doc asked, with a glint in his eye. "You know, the one that made you go looking for a good chiropractor."

"What about it?"

"This is hearsay, of course," he said glancing at Randy, "but is it possible some fatalities might have come out of that? Bodies tend to leave a trail."

"Once I escaped, the farm couldn't take a chance in case the cops showed up. My guess is, with nine warehouses full of hungry hogs, any bodies lying around would be nothing but pig shit by now."

Randy shuddered.

Sheila was making her rounds, back at the table, and rested a hand on Pat's shoulder. "Still deciding?" Menus flipped opened, orders were placed. When she left, Pat had a few questions of his own.

"Has Damron given you an update? Did Enrique ever call in?" Pat thought back to his last conversation with a desperate, obsessed grandfather on the road to New York in a foolish, overmatched, quixotic attempt to rescue his granddaughter. Pat had tried to reach him the day after Costilla's capture, a follow up on his promise, but his calls had all gone to voice mail.

"Phil said the FBI did get a call. One of their New York field offices got a tip on a hot house on Roosevelt Avenue in Queens. Caller left no name. But it led to a raid on an old three-story hotel filled with young girls, most of them Hispanic. Every one a trafficking victim." He took another sip of coffee. "I asked Phil if they were able to get a list of names."

"And?"

" There was one 'Clio' on the list."

Pat closed his eyes and offered a silent thank you.

"How about Enrique?"

"Still no word."

Pat smiled inwardly. The text yesterday from Enrique's cell phone had been cryptic. Something about God and absolution. And another one an hour later, text mutterings about going home. It made no sense at the time, but now . . . maybe now it did. If the gods of retribution had compassion, maybe this was their way to end it. Enrique was the last known contact with a man found butchered and hanging on an assembly line. It was clearly the FBI's prerogative to initiate paperwork and go hunting for the killer. But in the grand scheme of winners and losers in the boundless cartel wars would they spend time and money hunting for one man who 'might' have been involved in the death of another man who bought and sold thousands of innocent girls. Priorities. Always priorities. Maybe this time, he hoped, the pendulum that marked the settling of scores would swing in the right direction.

Plates with eggs and sides finally made the table along with another round of coffee refills. Between bites, Pat finally let it out, the question that had been bothering him for too long.

"Doc, are you ever going to let us in on who the hell you are?"

"Another time," he said. "Sometimes power and money and the need to win can get lost in what really matters."

Pat simply nodded. He reflected on the killing fields from another life, the rush of unfettered power where conquest often trumped morals. Maybe he'd have that conversation with Doc when the time was right.

Randy was spooning more gravy onto his biscuit when he jumped in.

"Back to Teresa Sandoval," Randy said. "Phil Damron said she identified the truck you supposedly used to kidnap her. A 2012 white Ford F-150."

"Identified how?" Doc interrupted.

"License plate," Randy said, his eyes on Pat. "Says she got it from the registration in the glove compartment when you weren't looking."

"I'd have to be pretty careless to let that happen, wouldn't I?"

Randy continued. "That vehicle turned up at a private residence in Raleigh on Monday. Anonymous tip. One Winston Marshall, Vice President of Marketing at Sunspring Foods." He glared at Pat. "The same name you asked me to look up for you."

"That *is* a coincidence," Pat said, his eyes on his food.

"He claims he never saw the truck in his life, but his prints are on the door handle and the steering wheel." His eyebrows raised. "So they did a little more digging. Seems that every single contract for hogs supplied to Sunspring over the last few years have been negotiated at the sole discretion of Mr. Marshall."

"So?" Doc asked.

"The Feds found recurring transfers of money into Marshall's bank account. Always a day or two after each contract season, and all in six-figure amounts. Turns out the man's got a fat bank account in Panama, all non-taxed of course, and he's having a little trouble explaining it. Considering that one of his hog suppliers is actually a cover for a human trafficking ring, and considering the truck used to transport the daughter of that trafficking ring's kingpin was found in his driveway, it's not such a coincidence anymore."

"They ought to check again with Teresa," Pat said. "Maybe she got the license plate wrong."

"They tried. She terminated her enrollment at Duke University yesterday."

Chapter 55

THE TABLE WAS A DARK, RICH MAHOGANY harvested in Honduras and crafted by a local artisan from the mountains of Magdalena. An elegant but simple piece, and other than the fluted designs carved into the legs, the only detail was a single strip of inlaid silver that trimmed the perimeter. It had been custom built for the room to accommodate large gatherings, typically oversized family feasts or social events that too often sparked rumors of wild excess. Today its ambitious length would come in handy.

Six men sat in tall-backed wooden chairs on one side of the table, five on the other. All of them were aware of Joaquin Costilla's arrest in the United States. What they didn't know was why they had been called to *Los Pelecanos* on such short notice.

Footsteps echoed on hardwood as they marched the length of the hallway and a man in a tailored suit entered the room, followed by a young lady and a second woman a generation older. Horatio Villarreal took the chair at the head of the table while the two women slid silently into empty chairs on both sides. He heard the nervous coughs from men at the table as he poured a short glass of water. After a sip he cast a calculated glare around the table at each man before opening the leather notebook.

"*El Araña* is in custody. A team of lawyers from our offices and our American counterparts are making every effort to secure his release. Until that occurs, we have business matters to attend to."

Luis Fernando Fuentes was always the most outspoken of the lieutenants. It came as no surprise that he raised the first objection.

"What business, Villarreal? We have no business. *Araña* is out of commission. Suarez is dead. Carolina is closed down. Our US accounts have been seized. The cartel is a vacuum waiting to be filled. Every other group in Mexico sees this and the vultures are flying."

Villarreal dismissed the man's outburst. "I count eleven lieutenants," he continued.

Fuentes nodded.

"That does not change." He pulled out a sheet from the notebook. With reading glasses perched on the bridge of his nose he read the list. "Tenancingo, Xalapa, Costa de Oro, Puebla, Matamoros, Cuernavaca, and five cells in Mexico City. This is still correct?" he said to the room.

Heads nodded and muttered agreement.

"Each man's territory stays the same. Obviously there will be a number of weeks of down time while we build up our infrastructure. You are to maintain your sources and be ready."

"Ready for what? We have no business. We are dead."

"You will wait. When you get my instructions you will go back to what you have always done, recruiting new women and girls."

"And then what, Horatio? Where do we send our shipments now that North Carolina is gone?"

"We are working on a new location."

"We?" he said. "If *Araña* is in prison, he cannot lead us. By tomorrow we will be looking over our shoulders to see which cartel wants to step into his shoes. Look around this room. There is not one man who does not want to hold onto his territory but how are we to do this?"

"*Araña* built this organization. Are you challenging him?" Villarreal said.

"You have known me for years. I have always been loyal. But who is going to run the business?"

"I am," the girl said, her voice confident and in charge.

Teresa Sandoval Costilla pushed back from the table and stood. She strolled down the right side of the table and back up the left, all eyes glued to her, her hand grazing the back of each chair. She stopped beside the older woman. "My father will teach me."

The room fell quiet. A volatile thread of tension hung there, waiting for the next move. Eduardo Morales was another who often spoke his piece and he had been holding back until now.

"Villarreal, are we to believe this is *Arana's* wish, to have his daughter, not even old enough to drink, running our business? Fuentes is right," he said. "This is a gang war ready to explode in our faces. We will be targets for every other cartel in Mexico."

"Do not forget whose business it is. Our instructions come from *Araña* himself. I have personally spoken with him."

"Teresa, I have known you since you were a child," said Fuentes. "I mean no disrespect but we are not selling souvenirs at the market. We buy and sell people, girls, many no older than you. How can you do this?"

"It is a business, Luis Fernando, one that has made you rich. It will remain so." She looked around the table. "Unless there is one here who chooses to challenge my father . . .?"

Other than the creak of chairs, a silence filled the room.

"Until we gather our arms around the details," Villarreal finally said, "you will receive your instructions from me. Rest assured I have no plans to do anything but practice law and facilitate an orderly transfer of power. Until then, prepare."

The clamor of eleven confused men grumbling on the way out was something Teresa had expected. These were hard men with a passion for violence and a lot at stake. She had no doubt their conversations and questions would not end here. As the days and weeks passed there would likely be one or two whose ambition would drive them toward making a fatal decision. She was prepared for that as well.

She gave Horatio Villarreal a hug and escorted him to the door. When she returned she sat down beside the woman still sitting quietly at the table.

"I will need your counsel, Marcela," she said.

"I have always been here, child. How can I not now, with all this trouble?"

Teresa gave her a hug.

"It has been hard for you, this thing between you and my father."

"Not so much any more," she said. "Maybe more for your mother, knowing that he continued to take care of me and Rosa. But he chose to remain with your mother, and for that I respect him."

She laid a hand on Teresa's arm.

"Are you prepared for what is to come?"

"Only business."

el final

Reader Reviews for
One Tenth of the Law
(the first in the Patrick Grainger series)

(Read Chapter One - immediately following)

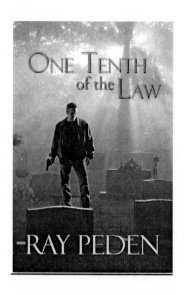

"*In his debut novel Ray Peden crafts a powerful, page-turning, thriller that will grab you from the first page and not let you go until you breathlessly reach the end.... I highly recommend (it).*" – BILL NOEL, *author of 10 mysteries in the wildly-popular* Folly Beach *series.*

"*A thriller is expected to have lots of action and in* One Tenth of the Law, *Ray Peden doesn't disappoint. But there's more here. Care in heart and care in craft shine through and deliver a much bigger experience than just an adrenaline-soaked spree.*" – JAMIE MASON, *author of NYT acclaimed thrillers* Three Graves Full *and* Monday's Lie.

"*This is what you hope for in a first novel by a new author...a flawed and empathetic hero, fully fleshed out on the page, the narrative nicely woven, the dialogue tight, the action compelling, and the characters multi-dimensional. Readers will be coming back for more.*" – BARON R. BIRTCHER, *best-selling author of* Rain Dogs *and the acclaimed Mike Travis mystery series*

"*...an edge-of-your-seat story that...skillfully pulls you deeper and deeper into an intricate plot that blazes with action and grips your emotions...nonstop momentum all the way to a satisfying ending.* – VIRGINIA SMITH, *author of 28 novels.*

"This is a great book. The writing is well constructed, the plot is exciting and well crafted...I seriously couldn't put it down. I love mystery books and action books. This one belongs with some of the best!"

"I have read many authors of this genre. This book ranks right up there with Patterson, King, Connolly, Blake and others."

"The intense writing style with vivid attention to detail, short chapters and interesting characters sets a pace that creates a clear entertaining and dynamic story...murder, revenge and military intrigue cemented in places you can relate to. I highly recommend this debut novel. You won't want to put down this engaging thriller!"

"...completely captivated by the story and the way in which it was crafted. It kept my interest from the first page...couldn't put it down."

"... hooked from the first chapter...detailed, intense, believable...flaws in the book's heroes and tender moments to the villains...an author after my own heart and mind: not every detail is explained and not every subplot is wrapped up with paper and ribbon...the first in a series...bring 'em on."

"Ray Peden has burst out of the starting gate in the lead with his freshman novel. His attention to detail is superb. His methods of introducing plot twists are perfectly timed. He uses life experiences to infuse his tale with the panorama of Southeastern states so well that you can just taste the waffles and sausage links at the roadside diner or smell the aroma of hay and liniment rolling out of the horse barn or feel the fear of a kidnap victim that doesn't foresee a good outcome. You will be glad you started reading this guy's work from the beginning of what is sure to be a thrilling series of novels."

"...wonderfully written! ...makes me want to start my fiction addiction again, but I'm afraid I won't find one I like as well as this one!"

"I could hardly put it down...plot twists and turns and kept me turning page after page..."

"Just WOW! From the opening page to the final act, it delivers enough action, conflict, and complex emotions to fill two novels. Never a slow moment. I kept waiting for a good stopping point so I could go to bed, or eat, but every chapter's last page lured me in with another hook...and twists and surprises I never saw coming. Every time I had something figured out, the author took me in another direction. He got me involved in every character's inter struggle, made it personal and intense. The attention to detail was absorbing, shoving me into every scene where I could eaves-drop on the characters, feel their fears, watch weapons do their work. The inventive way the author delivers justice to the bad guys, let's just say you'll pump your arm and go...YES!!! I can't remember the last time a novel has been this entertaining. An ABSOLUTE experience!!"

"...like watching an action packed movie that you cannot take your eyes off of the screen. I could not put the book down as the pages and chapters seemed to fly thru my fingers. Kept picking the book up and reading chapter after chapter. A really well written action thriller."

"...an effective writer paints a picture with his/her words. Ray did just that. As I read, I was immediately drawn into the story line...a book that was not to be put down. The writing style so vividly described each of the scenes, from the sights to the sounds to the smells of the story. And just when I thought that I had it all figured out, another twist and turn took me to another place. A combination of suspense, action, and endearing love was an unusual mixture that couldn't help but engage the reader. I cannot wait to see what Patrick Grainger is up to next."

"...enjoyed the characters as well as the pace of this book. Grainger started into action mode almost immediately... reminiscent of the young Jack Reacher in Lee Child's series. As a reader of this genre, I absolutely loved this first book from Ray Peden."

"Absolutely loved this book! It kept me in suspense from cover to cover. One of those reads that one doesn't want to put it down...it would make a great movie."

CHAPTER 1 – ONE TENTH OF THE LAW

THE ASSAULT on Patrick Grainger lasted less than three seconds. A deafening explosion; the Humvee rising into the air; a rush of flames through the floorboard; the powerful blast wave that slung him like a piece of overhead luggage through the driver's side door.

As his body went airborne he cursed fate that his number had finally been called, an instant before he slammed back-first onto the gravel shoulder, plowing through limestone aggregate, shredding uniform and skin. The brutal impact emptied his lungs, and key life functions ceased for a moment in a desperate, convulsive struggle for air. Only after he managed to gulp a first new breath did he feel the searing pain, compliments of the roofing nails, ball-bearings, and scalding shards of undercarriage buried in his butchered right leg.

In the fog of chaos he watched a pair of hands, apparently his own, slapping silently at the patches of flame that swarmed the right side of his desert fatigues. A quick roll onto his stomach, scorched hands pressing into the coarse desert scrub, and he pushed himself up with a tortured scream, but he heard nothing. The roar from the roadside bomb had also disappeared, replaced by a hollowed-out silence and a faint high-pitched tone droning from somewhere deep in his skull.

Within seconds blisters sprouted on his face and neck from the inferno twenty feet away. In a desperate scramble to drag his body away from agonizing heat his leading hand fell against something soft, spongy, covered in coarse cloth. Even in his daze he recognized the 100th Division patch on the sleeve of an arm no longer attached to a person.

Frantically his eyes scoured his own body and he cringed at the bloody canvas of shredded and charred flesh, but no major parts missing. Then the only explanation came to him and he twisted toward the Humvee, a mangled carcass of metal and glass canted on its side in an asphalt crater, engulfed in a silent movie of flames.

No one heard his howl of anguish at the sight of two half-formed silhouettes, Harrelson and Willis, enlisted men like him who had not been thrown free by the blast. They'd stopped thrashing, their bodies swallowed in a raging coffin of yellow and orange while an angry plume of smoke billowed out of control, carrying their ashes and private dreams away into a desert air already thick with the flavor of burning diesel fuel.

As he fought the pain, his world shifted into slow motion and for a brief moment he pictured two mothers, distraught in front of closed caskets somewhere back in Kentucky, desperate to believe their sons had not suffered.

He never heard the other soldiers' approach from the convoy, only a mute rush of shadows and boots. He barely felt the rough tug under his arms while they dragged him away from the burn. When his head flopped backward his face took the full brunt of the sun, blinding even during a Kuwaiti winter, and he tried to turn away. Then a powerful shudder—a second blast wave from an exploding fuel tank. Arms that had been dragging him lost their grip.

Minutes or seconds, he had no idea, and out of desperation a second sense forced his hand down to his belt. The satellite phone had survived the ordeal, battered but still secure in its leather holster. The veil of blood streaming down his face made it impossible to see, but it didn't stop his fingers as they fumbled to release the leather strap. His index finger guided itself to the keypad, painstaking jabs as he entered a familiar number.

With his head packed in virtual silence he knew he would hear no ring tone so he forced himself to be still, feel the vibrations. *Middle of the night. Asleep.* After four rings the vibrations stopped. He willed his arm to raise the phone to his ear and began stammering a stream-of-consciousness ramble to a wife he prayed was on the other end.

The false swagger he carried into every firefight, that followed them around every suspicious corner, was swept away now, and he broke down, words pouring out unguarded while the crackle of flames flooded the background.

When shock finally took him over, his eyes rolled back in his head and the SAT phone fell to the sand, the connection still alive, while the scratchy sound of Allison Grainger's panicked cries streamed through the static and stifling desert air.

* * * * *

From a low-rise rocky hillside two hundred meters away a pair of high-powered binoculars observed the carnage playing out below. The truck's passenger noted the time on a titanium watch. He dropped the remote device onto the seat and hit his cell phone's speed dial. On the other end of the call a pair of hands laid a manifest for field rations on his desk blotter and retrieved the vibrating phone from his breast pocket.

"It's done," said the caller. He issued an order to the driver, and the battered Toyota pickup truck disappeared into the barren mountain landscape.

ACKNOWLEDGEMENTS

Professionals in the business of writing usually say the second novel is easier. They were wrong.

For sure this story took less time to write, and with a well-stocked toolbox of learned rules by my side the mistakes were fewer and easier to spot. But the degree of difficulty swelled in my efforts to improve on the past. Thank goodness for supportive folks who made the job go easier.

Gene Burch once again did a masterful job on the cover. Armed with an antique meat cleaver, Jaap and Kim van der Oort's antique butcher block, and my pint of homemade blood courtesy of Google, he pulled off the shot and then did his Photoshop magic. He had no idea he would wind up a character in the pivotal final scene, but that's another story.

Mike Barnes, the public face of Patrick Grainger, is a big cheerleader. He's not only a gifted businessman but a model/actor represented by Images Model and Talent Agency. Mike met Gene and I at Bill Rodgers studio and the four of us created the grisly image on the cover.

Thanks once again to special Beta Readers MaryAnne Burch and Pat Huddleston who provided invaluable insight in manuscript evaluation and made the story better. Sis Sleadd was merely a fan of book one, but when she offered to proofread book two, not only did she become a vacuum cleaner for all of my grammar and punctuation misses, I gained a close friend and cheerleader for the entire program.

One unexpected contributor was Michael Hillyer, my long-time chiropractor. Over dozens of spinal adjustments we became friends, but it was his near daily suggestions and wacky ideas and encouragement that made it almost impossible not to include him in this novel. The character of Dr. Jonathan Hall is part Hillyer, part another professional I met years ago (who was in fact heavily invested in developing surveillance equipment for the CIA). Needless to say, fiction can turn ordinary men into heroes.

My scene about the cartel aircraft and local airports would have been grounded without the help of David Freed, fellow author of several acclaimed mysteries and a pilot himself. I texted 6 quick and dirty questions and he responded with two pages of detailed information. Our fraternity of supportive writers is a pretty neat thing.

Heidi Maynard, Nurse Technician at the Central Baptist emergency room, gave me enough detail to make my ER scene realistic and believable, so I had to make her a character too. And the day I got stuck on UPS protocol and equipment, who should drive up but a UPS truck. The driver, who shall remain unnamed, gave me a quick lowdown on their equipment and protocol.

Finally, Two-Sisters Cafe once again had to be the scene of the final denouement.

I do offer a mild apology to Chi Omega Sorority at Duke University. I meant no offense to their organization or members. I simply had to pick one. I've never been to Duke but with Google Maps I kinda was. However I do not apologize to Christian Laettner for using his name. I still don't forgive him for that shot.

It's been said: Give someone a book, they'll read for a day. Teach someone to write a book . . . and they'll spend a lifetime mired in paralyzing self doubt. There's a little truth in that, but it's worth it. In the words of a well-respected poet, one of my favorites:

> *Listen to the mustn'ts, child. Listen to the don'ts.*
> *Listen to the shouldn'ts, the impossibles, the won'ts.*
> *Listen to the never haves, then listen close to me...*
> *Anything can happen, child. Anything can be.*
> *– Shel Silverstein*

Ray Peden's professional career spans 43 years as a Civil Engineer, General Contractor, Home Builder and Designer, Land Developer, Project Manager, and Public Relations Copywriter. Along the way he found time for other pursuits: magazine editor, R&B guitar, painter of fine art and some not so fine, drill sergeant, carpenter, stone mason. Throw in three ex-wives, three amazing daughters, four grandchildren and counting, and it was time to retire to a new career, the thrill-a-minute life as a novelist, counting bodies, conspiracies, and emotional upheaval while he sips bourbon and watches the Kentucky River roll by.

Website – www.writerontheriver.com
Email – raypeden101@gmail.com
Available @ Amazon and select independent bookstores.